PRAISE FOR CONNIE BROCKWAY
AND HER PREVIOUS ROMANCES

PROMISE ME HEAVEN

"[Connie Brockway's] beautiful and touching novel is so enthralling that the audience will not be able to put it down for even a nanosecond. *Promise Me Heaven* is so polished and complex that readers will disbelieve that this is the author's first work."
—*Affaire de Coeur*

"Graced with a marvelous, tortured hero and a spirited heroine, *Promise Me Heaven* is a book that delivers on all its promises." —*Romantic Times*

ANYTHING FOR LOVE

"Connie Brockway has written a fun-filled romp. The lovers will find a way into your heart."
—*Romantic Times*

"*Anything for Love* is a book to savor . . . Connie Brockway is definitely an author who belongs on your 'must have' list." —*A Little Romance*

"With her second novel, Connie Brockway has shown that she's definitely one of the up-and-coming superstars of the romance genre." —*Affaire de Coeur*

"Vivid characters, wild romantic trysts, and the comical antics of the mountain men will glue you to the pages until the end. A truly unique historical romance." —*Rendezvous*

W9-AMX-161

HE TOOK ADVANTAGE

Slowly, he lifted his hands and bracketed the sides of her face, his thumbs resting near her parted lips, his forefingers grazing the downy hair at her temples.

Stop. Now, before you scare her. But he could not.

Her eyes widened. The gold-ash irises glinted in the firelight. Her lashes fluttered, sweeping feathered silkiness against his fingertips. He moved closer, oblique and cautious, his breath shallow, trying not to alarm her, thief that he was.

It was so easy.

She tilted her head and he stooped over her and kissed her. His lips touched a silken brow, each lid, the corner of her soft, trembling mouth. She sighed— sweet, sweet sound, delicious and erotic. He found her mouth, aware in some appalled recess of his consciousness that his restraint had vanished but unable to call himself back from the edge of the passion engulfing him.

She was here and while he could hold her, devour her with hand and mouth and breath, she held back the night, her sweet body offered a sanctuary. His heart raced and his thoughts spun blackly.

She started to speak and he closed her mouth with his. He would not let her say no. He dipped and caught her behind the knees, swinging her up into his arms. . . . She whimpered and lust careened through him. She clung to him, overpowered by his insistence, her ardor, his passion.

He strode with her to the great, dark-curtained bed and laid her upon the dark, shimmering counterpane and followed her down. . . .

Connie Brockway

Brockway

A Dangerous Man

A Dell Book

Published by
Dell Publishing
a division of
Bantam Doubleday Dell Publishing Group, Inc.
1540 Broadway
New York, New York 10036

ISBN: 0-440-22198-6

Printed in the United States of America

Published simultaneously in Canada

July 1996

10 9 8 7 6 5 4 3 2 1

OPM

To Don and Betina.
If even a shadow of their real life love affair is
reflected in one of my books, I'll know I've
succeeded in writing a Romance.

A DANGEROUS MAN is a very special book to me and I owe a huge debt to those who inspired (and sometimes bullied) me into giving this manuscript the best I have to offer. I would like to thank my agent, Damaris Rowland, for her ardent and skillful championship of my work, Laura Cifelli at Dell for putting me on her "wish list," my editor Marjorie Braman for her enthusiasm and insightful suggestions, and Sally Mitchell at Temple University for always so graciously making herself available to answer questions about Victoriana. Finally I would like to thank Susan Kay Law for critiquing at any hour of any given day, Susan Sizemore for plotting on the spur of the moment, and Christina Dodd for saying, "This is going to be great!"—and repeating it anytime I asked her to.

Prologue

Texas Panhandle, 1872

"Real tough, huh?" the outlaw sneered.

"Yeah. Sure." The "Duke" tried to keep his gun aimed at the man's head, but it was hard. The kid kept thrashing around in the outlaw's obscene parody of an embrace. He gritted his teeth, the palm cupping the butt of his pistol making fractional adjustments as the outlaw's head appeared and disappeared behind the kid's.

"You don't look so damn tough now, Duke," the man snarled.

"Whatever you say," he answered in a soft, distracted voice.

Behind the dirty forearm covering her mouth, the kid's green eyes stared at him. Tears ran freely from them. But unless he missed his guess, they were tears of frustration and anger, not panic.

The kid had guts. He'd give her that.

"Yeah!" the outlaw crowed. "You just remember that, Duke. Whatever *I* say! Me! I got the upper hand here and you better not forget it."

With a huge sense of inner relief that he never allowed his face to mirror, the Duke saw that the kid was wearing out. Just a few seconds without her twisting around, that's all he needed.

"I won't. Just let her go."

"What the hell do you think I am? Stupid?" the outlaw asked, punctuating his anger by savagely jerking the kid's head next to his. She moaned.

"No. Course not."

"That's right. That's right, you limey piece of shit! You're the stupid one! You! Gonna be hard gettin' your boss to fork over all that blood money he owes you when you have to tell him that his little girl got snatched, ain't it?" he said, staggering back toward the door. He hauled the kid's meager weight up on his hip, using her as a shield. She felt the movement, knew what it meant, and started twisting in his arms with renewed fervor.

"Fuck." Duke spat the word dispassionately. A few steps more and they were gone and the kid could just kiss good-bye to life—if she'd even want to live it after what this man would do to her.

"Yeah." An ugly smile creased the man's filthy face. "My plan exactly."

"You aren't going to get away," Duke said softly, trying to fake the man into making a mistake. That was the thing with these tough guys, they always wanted to talk. Right now, talk was the only thing Duke had going for him.

"The hell I'm not. I got me a nice little insurance policy here. Your employer's only baby girl. Found her choking on one of Daddy's imported cee-gars. Ain't she sweet?" He laughed as the kid squirmed again, kicking back with her feet. He nuzzled his head into the crook of her neck, keeping his eyes fixed on Duke's gun. "Well, maybe she ain't so sweet. But she's gonna keep you from following me, now, ain't she?"

He pulled her with him, working his way back toward the door. "Drop the iron, Duke." A few steps and they'd be gone.

Drop the gun and they were both dead. He knew it and this man knew it. "No."

The ugly humor fled from the outlaw's face. "I said drop it."

"And I said, *no*."

There was only one thing to do. Get rid of the shield. It was a risk, but one he'd have to take.

Without a flicker of emotion crossing his face, Duke fired.

The impact sent the kid careening back into the outlaw, knocking them both into the closed door. With a groan the kid fainted, her sudden deadweight dragging her out of the outlaw's hold and onto the floor. Incredulous, the outlaw stared at the blood blossoming from the kid's shoulder.

"You shot her!" he said wonderingly. "You really are one evil son of a bit—"

"Yeah," Duke said, and took the head shot.

Chapter 1

"*B*egad, it's good to see you again, Perth!" A tall, lanky young man hailed Hart Moreland, Earl of Perth, and bounded down the steps of the Actons' magnificent country house. A bit breathless, he gained Perth's side.

Hart nodded in response to the greeting of his brother-in-law, Richard Whitcombe, Viscount Claredon. He pulled off his soft kid gloves and looked over the commotion in the yard. Though the Actons' country house lay just west of London by a short hour's ride, the luggage that was piling up on the drive suggested it lay at the ends of the earth.

The other houseguests were arriving. Landaus and hansoms deposited their elegantly bejeweled, beribboned, and beruffled occupants on the magnificent sweeping steps leading to the house's imposing pink granite facade. He recognized none of the guests. Not that he would. In spite of his titled position he'd had little experience with English society.

"Fanny will be beyond pleased when she sees you've arrived," Richard continued. "We haven't seen you since our wedding nearly a year ago. And I know Beryl and Henley will be delighted, when they get here. As will Annabelle. All three of your sisters believe the sun rises and falls on you."

"Good of them," Hart cut in. "Where *is* Beryl?"

"Apparently Henley had to remain in town for some sort of political meeting."

"Annabelle is with them?" Hart asked severely.

"Of course," Richard assured him. "Beryl keeps the baby of the family well guarded, you may rest assured. Too well guarded, if you ask me. The child is as timid as a barn cat."

"Richard," Hart said coolly, "I am sure your colloquialisms mean no disrespect, but I would just as soon you refrain from comparing Annabelle to a cat, barn or otherwise."

The friendliness faltered on Richard's homely mien. Perhaps, Hart thought, he was being too hard on the young viscount. Certainly his rebuke would not make Richard—who'd always seemed nervous in his company—any more at ease. But if the next few weeks were to go as he'd planned, it was imperative that Annabelle be seen in only the most gracious and laudatory light: a light designed specifically so that the Duke of Acton would see in her a young woman magnificently tailored to bear the title Duchess.

"Of course, Perth. Didn't mean to offend," Richard said, chewing his lip and unhappily casting about for another topic of conversation. It wasn't necessary. Perth was quite comfortable with silence.

"Heard you'd arrived back in London but, must say, didn't expect to find you here. Must say, didn't expect to find myself here, truth be told. Rather exalted company for a country gent like myself. Can't think why Fan and I have been included. And you! Didn't think you went in for these country-house-party affairs."

"I don't," Hart said shortly. "Beryl wrote me in Paris, asking me to come. Apparently Acton is pressing his suit for Annabelle. Beryl expects this house party has been arranged to announce their engagement."

"Really?" Richard said, beaming happily. "Well, jolly good for old Annabelle."

Hart ignored Richard's enthusiasm. "I find it hard to believe that His Grace would act without first speaking to me as head of the family." The narrowing of Hart's eyes made clear how he viewed this oversight.

Richard shifted uncomfortably on his feet. "Well, Perth, it is common knowledge that you had a rather extensive investigation of Acton done before you even allowed him through the door to see Annabelle. You did the same to me. 'Spect you did it to old Henley too. Your approval has been assumed. And Acton is quite one of society's most eligible bachelors—with the notable exception of yourself."

"Does Annabelle like Acton?" he asked, ignoring Richard's arch comment.

"Why—why yes, I think so," Richard said, considering the question. "I believe she likes him very well. Didn't see much of society myself this season, but when Fan and I were in town, Annabelle seemed quite happy in Acton's company."

Hart nodded, somewhat mollified, and began mounting the stairs. His brother-in-law fell in step beside him.

"Where is your wife?" Hart asked suddenly.

"Oh, Fanny will be down directly she hears you're arrived. She is not feeling all she might. She's taking a rest before dinner."

"Not feeling well?" Hart stopped and turned a chill, inquiring look on Richard. The viscount hitched his shoulders uncomfortably, like a puppy that has been scolded and isn't sure why. Richard's awe inspired a feeling of exasperation in Hart. It turned to surprise when the younger man blushed.

"I might as well tell you," Richard said. "Though Fanny wanted to do so herself. Fanny is increasing."

"Increasing."

"She . . . This Easter she will present me with an heir." Richard lifted his chin high, his pride apparent.

A flicker of deep pleasure pierced Hart. *A child. His own sister's baby.* Envy cloaked in anguish suddenly welled up within him. He extinguished it, rid himself of the unworthy emotion as he extinguished everything he did not want to feel. "Congratulations," he said sincerely.

"Thank you. We are—we are so damned pleased!"

Hart nearly smiled at Richard's excitement. But Hart was not given to smiles, so instead he offered Richard his hand, which the younger man grasped in his huge paws and pumped enthusiastically. Once more they climbed the flight of stairs.

Thus far Hart was pleased with both of his sisters' spouses. Richard was not only heir to a considerable estate, but more importantly, he was an earnest young man, committed to his family home, his farms, and his poultry business. He might not be sophisticated, but he had a kind nature and wished above all things for a household filled with children. Qualities that made him the perfect partner for hearth-loving Fanny.

Henley Wrexhall, Beryl's husband, had no title behind his name, but he was an up-and-coming young member of Parliament, having taken his seat for the second time in the House of Commons. Clever and astute, his zeal tempered by a practical nature, he was a highly commendable mate for Hart's eldest sister, Beryl, whose ambition and social graces would best find expression as a politician's spouse.

That left only Annabelle, his youngest sister. Finding Annabelle a mate had taken a bit more judicious scrutiny. Annabelle had no obvious requirements in a husband.

She was modest and sweet and charming but her enthusiasms were a mystery to Hart, as were her aspirations. She was ten years his junior, and except for infrequent visits, he'd missed most of her growing up. He did not know Annabelle as well as he did his other two sisters. It was well that she liked Acton. If she fancied herself in love with him, all the better. Better still, he thought sternly, if Acton fancied himself in love with her.

Passing through the massive double doors at the top of the steps, Hart entered the house. The hall was crowded with guests; ladies clutching jewelry cases were frowning at their maidservants; gentleman milled about as they gave instructions to the army of valets regarding various heaps of luggage.

"How large a party is it?" Hart asked Richard.

"Quite a gathering. Upwards of thirty, I believe. Baron Coffey is here with his sons. A few relatives of Acton's. Some old ex-major, the Dowager's brother. Name of Sotbey, I believe. The Marchants are due to arrive. A few others." Richard shrugged.

"I see."

"I brought one of my lads, er, footmen, along to offer you his services as valet during your stay here, Perth," Richard said shyly.

Hart forced back a surge of annoyance. Richard could not know how the kindly gesture taunted Hart as a reminder of his own weaknesses. *A valet to witness his lapses of control?* NEVER. "Thank you, but I'll do quite well on my own. As I always have."

"Oh. Of course," Richard said uncomfortably. "I'm afraid it will be some time before they have the room arrangements straightened out. The Dowager Duchess is in the reception hall. She's had a buffet set out for those arriving. If you would care to join me?" Richard indicated the direction.

Hart nodded but took a moment to casually study the various adornments in the entry, from the gleaming—though now dirt flecked—black-and-white marble parquet flooring to the Beauvais tapestries suspended above the landing of the massive double staircase. A well-tended house. No telltale stains on the clean white walls betrayed the sale of some pricey picture. Ornate silver candelabras and Sèvres bowls brimming with chrysanthemums crowded gleaming ebony tables.

Very good, he thought, allowing Richard to proceed him into the drawing room, *Acton knows how to keep his wealth.*

"Is Acton here?" he asked. "I wish to meet him."

"You've not met him?" Richard asked, surprised.

"It isn't necessary to see a man to judge his worth. Indeed, sometimes assumptions based on physical appearances can unduly influence one. I assume he is unexceptional?"

"Ah, yes. Quite unexceptional."

Hart nodded, scanning the gathered guests

quickly. "You must point him out to me. The elderly woman in the burgundy dress, she is the Dowager Duchess?"

"Yes."

"If you'd be so kind as to introduce me?"

Richard, who'd just been reaching for a cake on the silver tray a footman was presenting him, quickly withdrew his hand. "Of course."

Richard led Hart through the throng of irritable- and weary-looking travelers. They stood in little queues engaged in desultory conversation, sipping lemonade and nibbling on toast and cakes, one and all impatient to be appointed their rooms so that they could cleanse themselves and rest before the evening festivities.

The stout old fellow with the grizzled muttonchops and the rigid bearing must be the ex-major. The tall, emaciated-looking gentleman with a luxuriant shock of silver hair who was flanked by two equally thin young men had to be Baron Coffey.

A loud peremptory voice suddenly called out. The footman in front of them started, turning too quickly. The tray he was carrying collided with Hart's elbow and the champagne flutes slipped across the smooth silver surface. Reflexively, Hart grabbed the tray with one hand and caught the unbalanced footman's elbow with the other.

"Have a care, man," he snapped at the flustered servant, steadying him. He brushed at the wine droplets dotting his sleeve and tensed. Someone was watching him. He looked up.

A woman in a dun-colored riding outfit on the far side of the room was regarding him. She was openly amused. Her face—a winsome arrangement of large, dark eyes; slender, straight nose; and full, soft lips—was alive with mirth. He could not tell the color of her hair, hidden as it was by a short black veil fluttering from the brim of the fashionable hat she wore at a jaunty angle. And he was too far away to be able to discern the color of those heavy-lidded eyes. He suddenly realized that if he was staring at her, she was doing the same to him.

Brazen creature. She did not even pretend that she was not looking. She met his gaze boldly. Apparently no pretty sense of modesty went along with that pretty face.

For a second more their gazes locked, and then she broke off her study of him and turned back to the young man at her side—one of the Baron's heirs, by the reedy look of him. From the dust that powdered the black pleats hemming her sweeping skirts, it was clear that she had traveled as hard and long as any of the other guests. How, then, did she contrive to look so fresh?

The man beside her bent closer. She turned her head, listening attentively, and then she laughed. Her lips parted, her eyes crinkled at the corners. Hart watched, telling himself he did so indifferently. His sisters had been trained to laugh decorously; a musical, closed-mouthed trill. This woman's mouth opened, revealing a glimpse of even white teeth, a dimple—

"Hart?"

Startled out of his preoccupation, Hart looked at Richard.

"Shall we?" Richard motioned toward the Dowager Duchess.

"Lead on," Hart said, glancing back at the unknown woman.

She was watching him again, and when she saw that he was looking at her, she feigned a start of shock, as though she'd read his mind about her lack of decorum and it amused her. With what could only be called a playful toss of her head, she pursed her lips and silently mouthed a *tch tch* of reproach in his direction.

How dare she mock him? Without giving her the satisfaction of a response, Hart turned, following the direction Richard had taken through the crowd.

Richard was waiting for him beside the Dowager Duchess. She was a tiny, ancient woman; wizened, white haired, with deep-set, opaque eyes beneath tissue-thin lids. There were faint circles of rouge on her sallow cheeks and the age-narrowed line of her lips could not be hidden beneath a coat of pink salve.

Richard cleared his throat. "Your Grace, may I present Hart Moreland, Earl of Perth?"

"Perth, how pleasant of you to come," the Dowager Duchess said in a raspy soprano. "We feel quite honored to have secured your presence. Apparently, from what my son tells me, few do."

There was an edge of irony in the polite words and instantly Hart reassessed the Dowager Duchess. She might look like a superannuated porcelain doll, but there was intelligence here. She would make a worthy opponent—and a worthier advocate.

"The honor is all mine, madam."

She allowed him to carry one heavily veined, beringed hand to his lips. "We have grown quite fond of your young sister, Perth."

"I am pleased to hear it. I trust she has made herself pleasant?" he asked, confident of the answer.

"Very pleasant. But how could one fail to appreciate so agreeable a young lady?"

"Indeed. I am gratified."

She was about to add another comment when a small commotion near the entry caught her attention.

"Fie!" Her thin lips pressed into a tighter line, smearing her lip salve. "The Countess Marchant, no doubt. Demanding immediate attention. I expect I'd best go do what I can about soothing her offended dignity. Gentlemen." Both Hart and Richard snapped sharply forward at the waist as she left.

Hart straightened slowly, his thoughts on the Dowager Duchess's veiled remark about his exclusivity. He had been careful, always circumspect, always proper. In the past five years he had lived his life so that not one aspect of his behavior would reflect poorly on his sisters—or their futures.

Richard fidgeted, craning his neck this way

and that as he looked around and then leaning close. "Who is she?" he asked.

"Who?"

"The woman you were staring at."

Hart tensed, his gaze following Richard's to where the elegantly garbed woman appeared and disappeared among the ever-shifting, ever-increasing throng. She moved too swiftly, he thought.

Her pale hands sketched fleeting stories in the air, her head dipped and tilted—quick, bright movements—as she listened and replied to those about her. Yet, he allowed, there was nothing awkward in her haste. She was as graceful as a dancer. No, nothing so choreographed as a dance. Perhaps some agile forest creature. Some forest prey, he amended harshly, too feckless to realize its danger and thus happy to gambol about the forest.

It concerned him he had been so gauche as to have been caught staring. If even Richard had noted his interest, he must have been near goggle eyed.

"Well?" Richard prompted.

"I don't know who she is," he answered in a tight voice.

"You don't?" Richard asked.

"No," Hart clipped out. "I know it was mannerless of me to . . . watch her so intently"—he refused to say *stare*—"but I do not claim the acquaintance of every woman I chance to spend a few seconds regarding."

Richard waved away his words. "No. No. It's not because you were staring that I thought you knew her. She's as pretty as a newborn filly. Lord, I'd stare at her myself if I weren't so devoted to Fanny."

Somehow, Hart thought, he must convince Fanny to break Richard of his bucolic cant.

"—It's because she's been asking after you ever since she arrived this morning."

"What?"

Richard nodded vigorously. "It's true. Heard her asking the Dowager Duchess myself. 'Has Lord Perth arrived?' she asked, clear as spring water. Fanny said she'd heard her ask another lady, too, and a gentleman."

"Who is she?"

Richard did not trouble masking his exasperation. "I don't know. That's why *I* asked *you.*"

Hart frowned. "Well, since the lady is so eager to make my acquaintance, I mustn't keep her waiting."

"Too late, old boy." Richard clapped him on the shoulder. "She's just left. Ah, well, you'll see her soon enough. She's probably some nabob's daughter or the wife of one of your old calvary chappies."

Wife. She didn't look like a wife. For some reason that thought was even more disagreeable than the notion of having a woman he had never met asking about him.

"Might as well enjoy the mystery while it lasts," Richard continued, blithely disregarding Hart's scowl.

"*I,*" said Hart tightly, "do not like mysteries."

Chapter 2

"She's an American," Richard said triumphantly, returning to Hart's side after a short trip around the room.

The evening festivities had begun. Hart had come down from his guest room a quarter of an hour earlier, the thought of the unknown woman having driven him here earlier than he would have normally arrived.

He did not pretend to misunderstand Richard. "Well, that explains her demeanor," he said.

"How so?"

Hart shrugged. "American women: undisciplined, impulsive, intractable."

Richard's homely mien took on a pensive, troubled expression. "I don't think she has given any cause to support such an estimation—"

"What is her name?" Hart broke in. He'd had experience with American women. Richard, kindhearted as he undoubtedly was, had not.

"I don't know. The few people I know well enough to ask are as in the dark as we. Can't ask a stranger about a stranger, now, can I? Would seem forward. If Annabelle's to be a duchess I'd best start behaving properly."

"What did you find out?"

"She was apparently added to the guest list at the last minute at the Dowager Duchess's behest. It's all the thing, you know. Adopting American gels and chaperoning them about society. Quite the rage."

"I didn't know."

"Anyway, the thing is that none of the chappies I know have been presented to her yet. They're all anticipating that privilege. Fetching little piece."

"I see," Hart said, forcing the American girl from his thoughts. "Is Fanny not coming down?"

Richard colored. "She can't. This heir-producing thing has her most indisposed. Most. Poor little thing."

Hart studied Richard carefully to see if he was attempting a jest at his sister's expense. Fanny, though handsome and dear, was in no way "little." She was tall and buxom and round. "I'm sure she'll survive," Hart said.

"Oh, doubtless, doubtless. Just wish she needn't be so wretched doing so. Poor old Fan," Richard answered miserably. "I say, here's your mystery woman now."

Hart looked up. A few feet away "his" woman paused at the threshold of the room.

Dark red. Her hair was deep, dark red. The

color of an autumn deer's coat, rich and vibrant and sleek. The sumptuous pine-green dress she wore acted as a foil for it. Her locks spilled over the soft velvet like rare strands of gleaming garnet laid out for display.

She turned and her gaze found his. They might as well have been alone. Leaf-green and gold, he thought, her eyes sparkled like a sun-dappled woodland pond. Shifting pale amber lights bedded between dark, mahogany-colored lashes; curling lashes, long lashes. So thick that from a distance they had made her eyes look dark.

She paused and lifted her chin above the glistening silk net shawl draped around her shoulders. It was a trifling movement, but it made the slender column of her throat look longer. It made a man want to measure its length with his hands.

"As the Dowager Duchess is acting as her chaperone, and she has yet to arrive," Richard whispered, "I'm afraid we'll simply have to wait before an introduction can be made."

Hart would have thought he'd be adept at waiting by now. For years he had schooled himself in patience, never jumping the gun, always awaiting the most opportune moments to act. But now he didn't want to wait for the Dowager Duchess. The woman was flirting with him, her gaze drifting deliberately over him, a languid perusal followed by a question in the form of a dark, arched brow.

"Damnation," he muttered. "Someone *must* know the chit's name."

"True. But I've never seen her before. Acton

and I hardly travel in the same set, you know. Maybe Beryl knows."

"And where the deuce *are* Beryl and Annabelle?"

"Delayed," Richard said. "Meant to tell you. Had a note waiting for me in the room. They'll be arriving tomorrow."

No Fanny, no Beryl, no Annabelle. He might as well go back upstairs himself and save himself the interminable evening of scrutiny and speculation his brief appearances in English society always provoked.

But then, he wouldn't be able to solve the enigma of the American woman.

With that odd, liquid swiftness, she moved past him, walking toward the library. There she stopped, turning and looking him directly in the eye. She lifted a hand, brushing it forward along the edge of her shawl in a open invitation for him to join her. Alone.

She glanced about, a circumspect and rapid survey of the room. Satisfied that no one was watching, she pinned him with one more compelling glance and slipped into the darkened library, closing the door behind her.

Hart's eyes narrowed. Occasionally women, challenged by their fool notion of him as some sort of cold-blooded eunuch, tested his purported impassiveness. He appreciated the irony. Right now, his body was reacting as aggressively as that of a buck in rut. He was amazed by the force of his longing. It had been years since the talons of sexual

desire had pierced his control over his thoughts and body.

"Think I'll go get a plate of something to take to Fan," Richard was saying. His tone was innocent. "A custard or some toast and tea. You'll excuse me?" He didn't wait for an answer, leaving Hart studying the library door.

He lasted less than a minute before he went to her.

He told himself he was going to discover how she knew him. But it was more than that. There was something about her boldness that quickened his pulse. Some elemental attraction, an imbalance of humors or blood, that must be accountable for the sudden awakening of his benumbed body. If he found her eager for a tryst, maybe this time he would let down his guard and oblige.

After all, she was obviously an American adventuress. She could do no real harm to his reputation or, more important, his sisters' expectations. A quick tumble—which she was highly unlikely to report—and back she went to New York, or Boston, or San Francisco, or wherever the hell she came from, and he would have assuaged this unaccustomed urgency in his loins.

He opened the door and, once inside, closed it behind him. He didn't want any distractions. He was distracted enough.

She was standing beside the window. The gaslight from the wall sconces picked out sepia highlights in her hair, burnishing the satiny smooth curve of her cheek. She straightened as he ap-

proached, pulling her shawl closer about her as
though cold. Her green-gold eyes held his.

"You know me?" he asked.

"Yes." Definitely American. A husky, low-
pitched voice. Her lips, plum-stained and plush,
trembled. Was she trembling with eagerness—or
was she afraid? Abruptly, he stopped, disappointed and suddenly weary. It was just another
game. This was no true desire, no honest attraction.
He was just a challenge she'd set herself.

"You want something from me."

"Yes."

"What?" He would make her say it.

She swallowed, took a deep breath. Her hands,
clutched in the netting at her throat, looked white.
"Your . . . cooperation."

He closed his eyes. She sounded anxious, not
passionate.

"Why?"

"Your reputation, I want—"

Well, there was honesty. "No," he said in a low
voice. *"You* do not *want.* You do not know the first
thing about want."

Her creamy complexion paled even further.
Despair touched him with pity. She had not done
anything a dozen other women in a half dozen past
years hadn't. It was not her fault she had aroused
him where those others hadn't.

"Leave," he said softly. He didn't want to hear
her, didn't want to see her trying to wrap herself
against his legendary coldness with her pitiable
shawl. "Leave now. Tell yourself it wasn't worth

the price. Tell yourself I was as coldblooded as a serpent. Tell yourself anything you like. Mark it all down to experience."

"I don't understand."

She frowned. The scowl did not cause the faintest line to traverse her smooth forehead. Perfection.

"Just leave," he said, his frustration growing in measure with each moment of unslaked desire. "Please."

"I won't go. Not yet. Not until—"

He was on her in a second, moving so swiftly and silently that she gasped. She raised her hands to ward him off and he took hold of her wrists, jerking her face within inches of his.

He cursed, revolted by his impulsive brutality. He'd never used physical force to dominate someone as weak as she. It sickened and angered him. And it made him angrier still that she didn't seem to realize how trifling her strength was, how effortlessly he could snap one of the delicate wrists his hands encircled, could *take* what she'd so carelessly offered.

"Until what?" he asked in a purposely deadened voice. "Until you get a little thrill?"

"No!" she said, twisting. He couldn't let her go. Not yet. This close, he could see a pale white scar high on a silk-textured cheek, feel each agitated breath fan his mouth. He stood, impaled by want, denying himself for no other reason than some misspent notion of honesty.

He'd thought—God help him—he'd thought

she wanted *him*. For some damnable reason it hurt that she hadn't.

"Until what, then?" he demanded, giving her a little shake.

Anger flashed in her eyes. She bared her teeth and with a feral little growl wrenched around, twisting free of his grasp. Her shawl caught in his signet ring and was jerked off her shoulders. In the sudden silence the shimmering net drifted down between them, the lost plumage of an arrow-struck bird. He stared at her.

A few inches above her low décolletage, beneath the jointure of arm and shoulder, a circular pucker of old scar tissue the size of a pence marked her pale skin.

He heard her voice, as if from a long distance. "Not *until* you have heard what I have to say— *Duke*."

Chapter 3

"Mercy Coltrane."

"You remember my name," Mercy said, surprised. His mouth, a sensualist's mouth that had been refused its natural expression, nearly curved. Nearly. But then the curve flattened and his remote, impassive expression returned.

"Well, I haven't shot all that many young girls," he said. His voice was the same as she remembered: a deep, even tenor crafted with an elegant aristocratic accent.

"Oh. Of course not," she said, dropping to her knees to retrieve her shawl. She looked up at him from her kneeling position. His lean, spare figure loomed motionlessly over her, backlit by the low-burning wall sconces. *A dark man, shadow made,* she thought.

It was impossible to tell how he felt about being recognized. Nothing was betrayed on that imperturbable countenance. When she made to rise,

he bent and took her by her elbows, effortlessly
lifting her to her feet. Without asking her permission he turned her hand over and studied her
wrist.

"Did I hurt you?"

"Good heavens, no," Mercy said. His grip had
been unbreakable, but it had never been painful.
His strength was well controlled. But everything
about the man seemed inhumanly well controlled.

Satisfied by her answer, he retired once more
into watchful silence, waiting for her to speak, pre-
ternaturally patient.

"I didn't believe it was you," she murmured,
studying him. As "Duke" he'd worn his hair long,
in the western style. He'd also had a full beard to
protect his skin from the prairie winds. Now his
hair was clipped short, grazing the collar of his impeccable white shirt. Thick hair, mink-brown. And
his chin was bare, revealing a sharp angled jaw, a
square chin with a slight cleft in it.

"Believe it was me?" he prompted, breaking
her contemplation.

"In London. I saw you get off the train at Victo-
ria Station. I thought it was you but when I asked
the porter who you were, he said the Earl of
Perth."

"So I am."

"You're also Duke, my father's hired gun."

"So I was."

She smiled, and he stepped back as though her
amusement confounded him. "Well," she ex-

plained, "you can understand my confusion. In fact, at first, I was sure I was deluded."

"I see. And may I ask what inspired you to reassess?"

"Your eyes."

"My eyes," he said. "Come now, Miss—it is Miss?—Coltrane. You saw me only a few times when I . . . worked for your father. You expect me to believe you recognized me from my *eyes*?"

His tone was insolent and his relentlessly cool manner was beginning to provoke her. "I find," she said haughtily, "that one tends to remember the last thing one expects to see in this life. When that *thing* is the eyes of the man she is certain has killed her, it creates a rather lasting impression."

His face remained impassive, untouched by her heated sarcasm. Irrelevantly, she found herself wondering what he would look like smiling. He was much younger than she'd remembered; certainly less than a decade separated them. And though tallish, he was not the gigantic figure cloaked in a dusty trail coat and denim jeans, a Stetson pulled low over his brow, that she remembered. But his eyes, pale greenish-blue, too light to be called turquoise, were the same. As was the lack of emotion in them.

A chill raised gooseflesh on her bare arms and she wrapped her shawl tighter around her.

"Excuse me for doubting the reliability of your memory." His tone had more disdain than apology in it.

"You're forgiven," she answered shortly, reminding herself not to let her temper get the better of her. She had to make him understand how important it had been for her to find and follow him. "Anyway, I asked after you. I had met the Dowager Duchess Acton in London some weeks earlier. We had already grown friendly and I was at loose ends. My chaperone, Lady Timmons, had an accident on the crossing and was—is—convalescing. When I discovered that Lady Acton was giving a house party during the off-season—a party *you* were expected to attend—I was quite shameless about securing an invitation."

"Why?"

"I need your help."

The slight tension that held him immobile grew. "Help."

"Yes. I cannot tell you how thankful I was to see you. I didn't know where to turn, who to ask for help," she said. "When I recognized you, it was like an answer to my prayers."

His mouth may have twitched toward a grim smile. "I doubt heaven has much to do with anything concerning me. What, may I ask, do you require help with?"

She took a deep breath. "My brother."

One of his dark, slanted eyebrows lifted.

"William. Will. You never met him, he was in Boston at school when you were working at the Circle Bar."

"I never worked at the Circle Bar," he reminded her, growing even more remote. "I worked the range, tracking down your father's enemies."

There was a flavor of self-recrimination in his tone that she did not understand.

"They were shooting our ranch hands," she said.

He shrugged. "Go on. You were talking about your brother. He was supposed to have come back to the ranch, the same as you. Wasn't that why you were there—your father had to take you and your brother from your boarding schools in order to pay my fee?"

"Yes," Mercy said. She didn't want to explain her brother to this indifferent aristocrat. But she knew no other way to secure his aid. "He didn't come home. He stayed with some of mother's relatives back East. Texas, the ranch . . . he never liked our life there."

"Really. Fancy that," Hart said.

"I never could understand his aversion to it," she admitted.

"Maybe it has something to do with lice . . . or fleas . . . or ambushing dust storms that blind you as they scour the skin from your face and choke your throat with sand. Or nights so cold, it hurts your eyes to hold them open. Or a land populated by men who would blast the back of your head open for the price of a lame mule."

She stared at him. There was real emotion, raw and fervent, in his voice.

"You didn't like it much."

He laughed; an abbreviated, rusty sound. "You, Miss Coltrane, are a mistress of understatement. No. I didn't like it much."

"But surely you must have seen how magnificent, how—"

"You were telling me about your brother."

Mercy started. "Yes," she said softly. "Excuse me, but when someone maligns my home I want—"

"That is the trouble with you Americans. You want something and you must have it, regardless of how you get it. You want something from me, so you flout convention and society, risk not only your name but the name of your hostess, and invite me here for a tryst."

"It is not a tryst!"

"Explain that to the people who watched you enter," he countered. "No. You must have your way. After all, you 'want.' So damned be the consequences. You are blind to modesty. If you are so determined to get your own way, can you not do so with feminine gentleness and soft words?"

"Feminine guile, you mean?" she asked hotly, and immediately regretted her temper. By sheer will she stifled the urge to give him a proper setdown.

She wouldn't fail. And whatever this harsh, disapproving man thought of her, she needed his help.

"I'm sorry," he was saying brusquely. "Forgive me. My lamentable lack of manners merely betrays my own brief residency in your land."

"Oh!"

"Now, once and finally, what have I to do with your brother?"

She took a deep breath. "Will . . . he always loved society, culture, what he called 'civilization.' At least, I think he did. We"—her gaze fell for the first time during the interview—"we were never close. My fault. I never understood him and I made no attempt to do so. He hated the ranch." She shrugged. "I loved it."

She glanced up. Why was she telling him this? Perhaps because of his indifference. There would be no sympathy here. False or real. But there would be no judgment either.

"A year ago my mother died. Will and she were very close. She adored Will and the feeling was returned. He begged Father to send him to England then. He said he couldn't bear to be in the house, with constant reminders of our mother. My father agreed. Will was to stay three months, but three turned into six and six into nine."

"He's been here nine months?"

"Ten," Mercy said. "His letters home grew more and more sporadic and . . . changed. The last ones were little more than scribbled requests for money. What he wrote early on suggested that he was running with bad company. We haven't had a letter in three months now."

"Oh?" Hart prompted.

"My father refused to send him any more money. I believe that is why he ceased writing, as a way of punishing Father. They've never gotten along."

"And now your father has allowed you, little

more than a girl yourself, to come looking for him?'' Hart asked.

''No.'' She hurried to defend her father. ''No, Father thinks I am here to find a husband.''

His blue eyes flashed with the merest hint of surprise. ''Excuse me?''

''A husband.'' She felt herself blushing. She would not have been so blunt had not everything about her situation required straightforwardness. She was not nearly the coarse creature that he believed—and made no effort to hide that he did so.

''My mother, God rest her soul, always wanted for us, above all things, a genteel life. To be quite frank—you needn't look like that, you have made it abundantly clear what you think of my candor— she wished us to marry into the aristocracy. Whether it was Mrs. Ascot's New York aristocracy or your own English variety made no difference.''

He didn't say a word and she plunged on. ''My father worshiped Mother. That is why he agreed to have us schooled in Boston. That is why he let me come here to be squired about by Lady Timmons after we met her last winter in New York and she kindly offered me her sponsorship. Father agreed but only because Mother would have wished it.''

''Ah, yes. The conveniently convalescing chaperone,'' he said.

She had to bite the inside of her cheeks to keep from telling him to go to hell. *At least*, she told herself with faint hope, *he is listening*. ''The Dowager and Lady Timmons are great friends.''

"I see. So your father thinks you are here to fulfill your mother's aspirations."

"Yes."

"But in actuality you are here to find your brother."

"Yes. I have to find him. Father has been threatening to disinherit Will. I need to heal this breach." Her voice dropped to a whisper. "I promised our mother. Before she died, I promised her I would see that Will and Father were reconciled. But to do that I have to find Will. I want you to find him."

He turned from her, an odd impatient gesture, and she watched as he shook his head as if in disbelief. In profile his straight nose was large and aggressive. His jaw, tensed as it was, looked cut from rock.

"There's one more thing," she said.

"Yes?" he muttered.

"Will knows I'm here. I don't know how, but a week after I arrived I received a note from him. He asked for some money and intimated he was in some sort of financial straits. I sent money according to his directions. Since then there have been two other notes, each more terse than the last, each asking for a greater sum. And in each he has refused to see me."

"Jesus," Hart swore. She crept closer to him, hating the role of petitioner but unable to keep the beggarly tone from her voice. She needed him. She'd tried every other avenue she could think of.

"I've kept the notes and I have letters that

mention the names of some establishments. You
can—"

"Miss Coltrane." He turned. His eyes pierced
her from his greater height. A lock of hair had
fallen across his forehead. It cast a dark stripe of
shadow across his lean face. His expression was
unreadable. "Whatever I was in the past, I am now
the Earl of Perth."

"I know that. I also know you were once in
need of money. My father has prospered, Mr.
Perth—"

"Hart Moreland, Lord Perth," he corrected au-
tomatically. "Perth. Or Hart. Not Mr. Perth."

"Yes, yes," she said. "At any rate, my father is
an exceedingly wealthy man and very generous
with my allowance. I have no real need for the
money he gives me and have consequently
amassed a very tidy sum."

"Oh, God," he muttered.

"I do not know what your current financial situation is, but after having spent some time in the
dilapidated castles and mansions you aristocrats
feel compelled to maintain, I can only assume it
could be better. I am willing to offer you a substan-
tial sum for your trouble."

"Oh, God," he repeated.

She gulped. "You don't have to kill anyone."

He closed his eyes for a second, and when he
opened them the blue-green irises gleamed in the
gaslight. "I don't have to kill anyone." Dead, cold
voice.

"No," she hurried to assure him. "Nothing of

the sort. You don't have to do anything but find Will. I shall do the rest. I don't know London. I haven't a clue where to begin. I've asked where I could, but each time I have been stonewalled, politely but absolutely."

"I see." His tone should have numbed her, but her need to find her brother was too important to be sidetracked by a chill voice and hot, passionate eyes.

"Will you help me?"

"No," he said flatly. "Go home, Miss Coltrane. Go back to America. I am sure your brother is just having himself a little fling before he returns to his family's loving arms and begins in earnest the business of producing cattle and babies."

She stepped back in confusion. Had she not made clear how important this was? What could she say to make him understand that she couldn't lose Will . . . she couldn't *fail*?

"You don't understand. Will is risking his future. My father is an incredibly obstinate man. He does not forgive easily. Will has been more than defiant. He's been . . . Perhaps I haven't made clear how he's changed since he—"

"You have made *everything* painfully clear," he broke in. "Go home, Miss Coltrane. And I strongly advise you to forget you ever recognized me. My position in society must not be threatened. It is imperative that my past stay *past*. People's futures, as well as their happiness—people I care a great deal about—depend on it. I will protect them, Miss Coltrane. At all costs."

She drew herself up, salvaging pride from her disappointment. He cared a great deal about some person or persons. The thought touched her with jealousy. What would it be like to have someone so strong, so capable, care for her? Well, he wasn't the only one with people to protect. "I would never betray a confidence."

"I haven't given you my confidence," he said. "You have stolen it."

"I will not tell a soul who you really are. Your *secret* is safe with me, Lord Perth," she said with haughty dignity. "You see? I do know the proper form of address. Our eastern schools are quite thorough in drumming English hero-worship into their students' heads. I shall have to remind myself of the error of misplaced veneration."

"Quite. Now, forget me and, if I may make so bold, forget your brother."

She would not answer him, neither his ill-concealed warning nor his presumptuous advice. She whirled around, her stiff taffeta petticoats hissing as they passed over the tops of his boots.

"And when you leave, for God's sake try to be discreet. I would not like to have us discovered closeted alone in here."

His words brought her skidding to a halt by the door.

She reached for the door handle and jerked it wide open. Conversation and light flooded into the room. She caught a glimpse of anger hardening his features just before he stepped back into the shadows.

Good, she thought. *Let the Earl jump!*

Those near the door turned curious faces to see who was exiting the library.

"I will not forget him," she declared loudly. "I will find him."

Chapter 4

*D*amnation! Hart thought. He wanted to follow the chit out into the drawing room, catch her by the arm, and spin her around and then . . . He ground his teeth. Instead, he stood shrinking in the shadows, trying to figure out how to exit the library unseen.

Though he was furious he'd allowed himself to be put in such a position, a flash of misplaced amusement underscored his anger. The little wretch. Offering him cash to find her cursed brother and soothingly assuring him he needn't "kill anyone." There was only one person who was in danger of that and she had just swept out of range.

Thank God, years of self-discipline had stood him in good stead during that horrendous interview. She hadn't realized with what shock he'd recognized the young girl he'd shot in that Texas shack nearly six years ago.

Shock. A novel experience. He'd thought himself well beyond feeling even remotely surprised by whatever malicious games life threw his way.

But he hadn't been prepared for her.

That she should reappear now, a green-eyed specter from his past, just when he was finishing the task he'd set himself over a decade ago, really was diabolically amusing.

Here he was about to settle the last of his sisters into the life he'd worked and sweated and— and *killed* to achieve for them and *she* appeared; gold-leaf-flecked eyes and laughing mouth, a tumble of burnished red hair . . . and a hole in her shoulder.

Her presence threatened it all. His hand curled into a fist. He forced himself to relax it. He'd have to make certain she didn't destroy what he'd worked so hard to achieve. He would do whatever it took to assure her silence. Perhaps it would be as simple as having said no. Surely she realized his threat was serious.

He looked around the library. Any moment now some bright-eyed inquisitive would peek in to see who Mercy Coltrane had been with. Even if she didn't give a damn for her own reputation, he couldn't afford to be casual with his. A few whispered words to Acton and Annabelle's engagement to him could be forgotten. The Actons were notorious sticklers.

Hart stalked to the window and jerked it open. A quick glance showed that the library stood a story above the groomed lawns on the east side of the mansion. Without a second's hesitation he gripped the sill and lowered himself down, out of the window, along the exterior wall. He hung easily for a second before looking straight below.

Rosebuses. An entire battalion of rosebushes crowded the ancient walls beneath him. Adding another curse to the litany he'd already produced since meeting Mercy Coltrane, Hart let go of the sill.

———————————◆◆◆———————————

"Hart!" Fanny called as Hart entered the morning room the next day.

It was early afternoon and the room was filled with guests awaiting the musical entertainment Acton had arranged. With a little grunt Fanny heaved herself up from the settee as Richard hastened to her, catching her under the arm and pulling. Hart eyed his sister in mute surprise.

Always a softly rounded woman, Fanny had grown substantially rounder. Her cheeks were pink dumplings, her throat necklaced by puffy little rolls of flesh. She held her hands out in fond greeting. One look at his face, however, and she dropped them. "Whatever happened?"

"Happened?" he echoed, still amazed by Fanny's increased girth. He touched his face. "Oh. This. I was riding this morning and didn't attend where I was going. When my head was turned the horse ran me through some branches."

"Nasty, that," Richard said, peering at the raw scratches crisscrossing the side of Hart's face.

"That doesn't sound like you," Fanny said.

"Well, it was me," Hart said in a tone that suggested she forget the incident.

"Ah, yes. As it's your face, it would have to be, wouldn't it?"

Dear Fanny. Lovely, loving, but not particularly bright. Her gleaming honey-gold curls bounced as she nodded sagely. Her bosom, a mountain of tightly constrained flesh, bounced in counterpoint.

"And you, I trust, are doing well this morning?" Hart asked. She lowered her eyes and smiled shyly. Every exposed part of her person turned some variation on the shade pink.

"Yes. So far, at least." She glanced up. "Richard has told you?"

"Yes, Fan. Congratulations. I cannot tell you how very pleased I am for you both. Whatever child you have will be most fortunate in his parents . . . particularly his mother."

"Oh, Hart!" Tears shimmered in her large cornflower-blue eyes.

"Don't cry, Francesca." Hart shifted uneasily on his feet.

"I'm sorry, Hart. I know how such displays distress you, but this motherhood thing has me so . . . emotional!"

"So I see."

"I promise I won't cry anymore." She sniffed and took three deep breaths. The seams of her bodice creaked. "There. I'm better now." She smiled a brave, watery smile. "See? I shall contrive to be a

perfectly composed mother"—she gulped—"to
. . . to . . . be!" She buried her face in the large
linen handkerchief Richard produced.

"Do something," Hart said to him.

Richard, aside from gazing sympathetically at
his wife, didn't move.

"Oh! A mother! Me!" Fanny said, hiccuping
uncontrollably.

"Do something, man!" Hart repeated more
forcefully.

"What?" Richard asked. "She's been crying off
and on for weeks now. I've purchased two score
handkerchiefs since Fan's been breeding. Not much
else to do, 'cept keep myself well stocked with the
tear towels, don't you know."

"Is she all right?" Hart asked. "She's not sick,
is she?"

"No." Fanny shook her head. "She's not sick.
She's expecting . . . a . . . a . . . *baby!*"

"Poor Fan." Richard patted her shoulder.

"Get her some Devonshire cream," Hart said
on a sudden inspiration. "She always liked Devonshire cream when she was a lass. Would you like
some Devonshire cream, Fan?"

She nodded, still sniffing. "Devonshire cream
would be nice."

"Get it," Hart ordered Richard.

"Perhaps we can have Acton's cook find something," Richard cooed. "Come along, Fan, dearest.
We'll search out a nice little cubbyhole and have
ourselves a cream tea, shall we?"

Hart let out the breath he'd been holding as

Richard escorted his sister from the room. *Good Lord*, he thought. *If pregnancy affects steady, even-tempered Fan this way, just think what it would do to someone like Mercy Coltrane.* His brows snapped together. *Where the bloody hell did that thought come from?*

As if in response to some internal—and infernal—call he'd made, the woman who was responsible for his scratched face, whose actions—or rather the contemplation of whose potential actions—had driven off what little rest he found in slumber, appeared. Beside her was the Dowager Duchess and a man he assumed was James Trent, Duke of Acton.

Try as he might, Hart was unable to concentrate on Acton with Mercy standing so close. He contented himself with giving his potential brother-in-law a cursory study. A bit beneath average height, barrel chested, curling ginger-colored hair receding from a pleasant, blocky face. Hart's gaze passed over him to Mercy.

She did not give any indication they had met before. She looked at him with no more than polite interest, her mouth trembling on the cusp of a smile. She was rigged out in some impossible pink plaid outfit, the heavy skirts draped behind her knees, a waterfall of pale lace and ruffles tumbling behind her as she advanced with that too-long stride of hers. It was, he noted, a high-collared gown, unlike the décolletage of the other ladies in the room. Did she always take pains to hide the scar he had given her? His jaw tightened.

The Dowager Duchess snapped a huge white ostrich feather fan open as they approached. She raised her thin silver eyebrows.

"Perth," she said. He bowed from the neck. She turned and rapped her son sharply on the arm. "James, may I present Hart Moreland, Earl of Perth. Perth, my son, James Trent, Duke of Acton."

Acton stepped forward and offered his hand. Hart took it and they shook. Then Acton turned.

"Miss Coltrane, may I present—"

"The Earl of Perth? So I heard." She dimpled saucily. "Yes. You may present him. And *I* will present myself. Mercy Coltrane, Mr. Perth. Late of Texas. That's a territory in the United States of America," she said. "And where do you hang your hat, sir?"

"Here and there." He was aware his voice was not as smooth as he'd have liked. Impudent little baggage.

"Perth is an inveterate tourist. Spends all his time roaming about the world," the Dowager said. "We are most fortunate he has postponed his latest sojourn in order attend our little party."

"Not at all, madam. It is my pleasure."

"Well, I'm pleased to make the acquaintance of someone as well traveled as yourself, sir," Mercy said. "You must have some interesting tales to tell."

She stuck out her bare hand.

He had no choice but to take it. Her fingers were warm and delicate and utterly feminine. She *knew* it wasn't decent to extend an ungloved hand.

She was mocking him. It was there in the challenging glint of her eye, the defiant angle of her chin.

He did not resist the temptation to hold her hand a bit tighter than necessary or, when it was clear she actually expected him to shake it, carry it to his lips, pressing a kiss on the back of her long fingers. *Velvet softness*— He was gratified to hear a tiny gasp. She pulled her hand free.

Mannerless little American heathen. She'd be lucky if society put up with her brazenness for a fortnight. He lifted his gaze to find both the Duchess and Acton had turned indulgent smiles on the redheaded chit, as if charmed by her bold behavior.

"Miss Coltrane," he muttered.

"Dear heavens, sir!" Mercy exclaimed, a riotous flush high on her cheeks. "Whatever happened to your face?" She covered her lips with the tips of her fingers in a theatrical display of concern. Hart was certain she was covering a smile. Brat.

"A horse," he said evenly, "ran with me through some low-hanging branches across the riding trail."

"And you couldn't control him?" Mercy asked, her gold-spackled eyes opening even wider. She turned to Acton. "Your Grace, you will have to speak to your grooms about fitting a rider's talent to his mount. Otherwise nasty accidents like that which has befallen Mr. Perth will be bound to happen."

"Lord Perth," Hart corrected. "And the horse was not beyond my abilities." Damn it all, she'd provoked him into defending his equestrian skill.

She ceased fluttering her eyelashes at Acton, who was nodding sententiously. The Duke looked as though he were plotting a riding program for him. She turned back. Her eyes gleamed with triumph. "Did you say something, sir?" she asked sweetly.

"He wants you to call him by his proper title, Miss Coltrane," the Duchess said.

"And that is?"

"Lord Perth."

"I see," Mercy said, looking from Acton to the Duchess in a pretty study of consternation. "Well, I must admit I feel quite inordinately pleased with myself for managing as much as I have in keeping your hierarchy straight. Wouldn't you just accept my competence in remembering the *important* titles and forgive me my ineptitude with the *little* ones?" She fluttered again.

He felt a constriction in his throat but managed to hold off laughing. The impossible hoyden. It would never do to encourage her.

Acton, however, showed no such restraint. He laughed heartily. Mercy, looking as though having someone laugh at her was the most delightful experience in the world, smiled at Acton, sharing his humor. Even the Duchess gave an unladylike snort. "You are a naughty gel to tease Perth so. He doesn't understand your American sense of the absurd," she chided.

"I hope Miss Coltrane will allow me to remedy that oversight," Hart said, shooting Mercy a telling glance.

"Acton," the Dowager Duchess said, her gaze fixed beyond her son's shoulder, "Mr. and Mrs. Wrexhall have arrived. With Miss Moreland." She directed their attention to the doorway.

Sure enough, his eldest sister, Beryl, and her husband, Henley Wrexhall, had arrived. They looked enough alike to be mistaken for siblings. Both were of medium height with slender, spare builds. Both of them had brunette hair and dark eyes and their similarly sharp features revealed quick intelligence. Though Henley, Hart noted, looked distracted and his gaze slipped from side to side as he nodded a greeting to those he passed.

Behind them, a vision of petite femininity, Annabelle appeared, the hem of her lacy gown barely moving as she approached. Hart felt a familiar swell of pride. She was like a tiny, pretty little rosebud. Her hair was a shade popularly referred to as strawberry-blond. When she was a toddler, he'd teased her by telling her it was pink.

Perfect, ladylike Annabelle. She played the piano with something near talent, she was fluent in three languages, and she was—if the written reports from her governesses and instructors were to be believed—exceptional at mathematics. She would make a fine duchess.

True to her inherently decorous nature, Annabelle did not rush forward in unseemly haste. She moved slowly, with measured steps, an expression of cordial recognition on her serene countenance.

"Hart," she said. "It is wonderful to see you

again." Trust Annabelle not to make any untoward comment about his scratched face.

"Hart, whatever has happened to your cheek?" Beryl demanded as soon as she was within speaking range.

Henley, stopping behind his wife, puckered his brow and cleared his throat. "That looks painful. What happened?"

"Riding accident," Mercy Coltrane offered from his side.

No manners. None at all.

Beryl and Annabelle turned inquiring gazes on the American interloper and Hart found himself once more studying her. She looked stridently exotic in her bright pink dress, bold and vivacious. The contrast between her and his sweet-faced, pastel-clad sisters was acute. He hoped Acton noted it.

The Duke stepped forward, bowing in his most formal manner. "Miss Henley, Mrs. Wrexhall, Mr. Wrexhall, how very delighted we are that you have arrived. I trust your trip was uneventful?"

"Yes, it was fine," Beryl said. Annabelle smiled shyly.

"May I present Miss Mercy Coltrane?" Acton asked. "She is doing us the honor of being our guest while her friend and chaperone, Lady Timmons, recuperates from an unfortunate accident."

The women murmured "Pleased to make your acquaintance" at each other and Henley claimed his "charm" at having been introduced.

"We haven't seen you in far too long, Hart,"

Beryl said, turning back to him. "When will you come home?"

"Bentwood is your home now, Beryl. Yours and Henley's. I am only a guest there."

"Nonsense," Henley said staunchly, a moody shadow crossing his narrow features. "Bentwood has belonged to the earls of Perth for generations. We only hold it in trust for the day you bring your own bride there, Hart. Beryl and I would do quite well in town. Quite well."

"Bentwood needs an overseer. I travel far too much to see it properly managed," he said. It was an old conversation and he was disconcerted that Henley's words still had the power to awake a small, hopeless longing.

He dare not live in England again, no matter how he longed for Bentwood. There were too many opportunities for his past to be discovered here. Too many people came and went between England and America these days. Witness Mercy Coltrane.

He still did not know exactly what to do about her. If she was very good, and very wise, and kept up her pretense of not knowing him, perhaps he wouldn't have to do anything at all.

Polite conversation sprang up about him and he bent his head dutifully so that he would appear to be attending Annabelle's soft dialogue. He couldn't concentrate. He was too aware of Mercy.

He would not turn. He didn't need to. He could smell her, a fragrance he'd learned in one brief conversation and that he intuitively knew he would never forget. A sharp woodsy scent. No pleasant florals for Mercy Coltrane.

A footman approached and whispered something to the Duchess. She nodded and dismissed the servant before saying, "Acton, you must inform our guest that the orchestra is ready to play. I will not be attending. I have the beginning of the headache."

Annabelle and Beryl expressed immediate concern and asked if they might do something to relieve their hostess. Mercy silently regarded the Duchess.

The Dowager waved down the sisters' solicitude. "Thank you, but you can best serve me by not calling attention to my absence. Take our guests into the conservatory, Acton."

"Of course, Mother," Acton said, holding his arm out for Annabelle. With a glance at Hart for approval—which he gave with a slight nod—Annabelle laid the tips of her fingers on Acton's arm and was led off. Henley cleared his throat again—a nervous habit Hart did not remember from past acquaintance—and after darting a quick glance at him made a lavish court bow to his wife. She linked her hand through his arm and they, too, departed.

That left him standing with Mercy among the flux of people heading for the conservatory.

He turned toward her, giving her a predatory smile. "It would appear, Miss Coltrane, that you have been left in my care."

Chapter 5

❦

"*Y*ou'd best stick to the unapproachable guise," Mercy said, gratified by the bemusement her words surprised on Hart's face.

"Miss Coltrane?"

"The threatening mien is not nearly so effective as that Olympian detachment." It wasn't much of an indication of his thoughts, but there was a definite tightening of his features. With a bit of patience, Mercy thought, she would have him shouting at her within the week. And she wanted to make him shout.

She wanted to break down that icy facade and make him feel something: anger, worry, amusement. If she could touch the well-hidden humanity in the man, perhaps then he might help her find Will.

But not, she thought, *yet*. This indifferent man would know nothing of desperation. He would know nothing of how it felt to lose one's family. He would know nothing of promises made to dying mothers or healing a breach that one was responsible for.

He was regarding her dispassionately, and it was obvious only his impeccable manners kept him from abandoning her while the last of the party departed the room. *Wouldn't want to raise comment by leaving a lady standing alone and unattended, would we?* she thought.

"I'm not going to the musicale, Mr. Perth. So you needn't stand here wondering who you can foist me on."

"If you cannot find the wherewithal to call me *Lord* Perth, perhaps a simple Perth might not be beyond your abilities."

She shrugged. "Perhaps . . . Perth."

Not a shred of emotion. "If you are not attending the entertainment that your host has gone through the trouble to arrange, where are you going? To practice your lariat skills on Acton's tame deer?"

She laughed, startling him into a fleeting glance of bafflement. *What? No one ever laughed at his quips?* "Now, how did you know I was an absolute magician with a lariat? But, no. I am going to the kitchen."

"If you require some refreshment, all you have to do is ask your maid to fetch it."

"I don't have a maid. I make use of one of the Dowager's tweenies when necessary. Never could understand why someone would want another person hovering about for the sole purpose of picking up the odd thread trailed in. Seems demeaning. And I wouldn't want to demean Brenna. She's a darling girl. Loads of hair. She's promised to help me arrange my own. Isn't that sweet? I mean, this woman has hair"—she paused, trying to find some way to describe the magnificence of Brenna's tresses—"*abundant* hair. She wears rats atop her head."

He was silent a minute. "Rats?" he asked, curiosity apparently overcoming his aversion to talking with her.

"Yes," she answered. "They are these structures you perch like a hat on your head and then cover with your hair. Quite wondrous. She's promised that she will help me with my own—"

"I don't really care to hear about the tweenie's coiffure," he said. "The point I was attempting to make is, if you want something, ask one of the servants."

"Oh, that would never do. I need to make a special tea."

"How special can tea be?" he asked. "I'm sure Acton's cook can produce an acceptable cup."

She refused to be drawn in to an argument with him. "I'm going to the kitchen."

"You know where the kitchen is?"

She didn't deign to answer this question. Of course she knew where the kitchen was. She started past him, surprised when he followed.

"It's not that large a house," she said over her shoulder. "I won't get lost."

"I feel a certain obligation to my host to see

that none of his guests provokes undue comment. You shouldn't be seen wandering about the house alone, peeking through doors."

She shot him an indignant look. Satisfaction awoke in his blue eyes.

"Suit yourself," she said, marching down the hallway toward the green baize door at the end. She pushed through the smoothly swinging door and immediately found herself in the kitchen.

Two young girls perched on stools were peeling vegetables. A stalwart aproned cook was hefting an enormous pan filled with plump chicken breasts into a cavernous oven while another cook stirred a copper pot. The third cook, a rotund woman cloaked in flour dust, was pounding a huge slab of dough on a scarred and pitted table, her plump upper arms jiggling with her effort.

As soon as they entered, the servants stopped their activity and stared at them in amazed silence.

"How are you, Minnie?" Mercy asked the pastry chef.

"Ah, fine. Fine, miss," mumbled Minnie.

Behind her, Hart stopped. "Miss Coltrane requires the use of the kitchen," he announced. "Please leave."

"No, no. They needn't—"

"Now," Hart said.

The members of the kitchen staff dispersed like quail from a covey, fleeing through the various doors in the kitchen as Mercy made unheeded sounds of protest. In a matter of seconds she and Hart were alone.

"You didn't have to disrupt their work!" She swung around angrily.

"You will not give grist to the gossip mill with your uncivilized behavior. The less people know about this bizarre insistence on brewing your own tea, the better. Do you think someone is going to try to poison you? I can assure you that I am the only one likely, or for that matter with the incentive, to do so."

"You *really* mean you don't want any witnesses to *your* almighty presence among those who must earn their livelihoods."

"Miss Coltrane," he said slowly, "you know better than anybody else in this house, the unthinkable things I've done to earn money—things nobody here would ever consider doing."

Confused, she dropped her gaze. He was an enigma. It made no sense that he should be so autocratic that he resented being seen here, and at the same time remind her of his past. Each moment with him made that past seem more implausible. The lank, sun-scarred range rider was gone. He was the complete aristocrat now: remote, imperious, sophisticated.

"Besides, you aren't really concerned about keeping them from their work, are you?" he asked.

"Of course I am. Now I will have put them off their schedule and they will be playing catch-up for the rest of the day."

"Consider that I have given them an unexpected holiday."

"I suppose I'll have to," she answered tartly,

crossing to the pantry door and swinging it open to study the contents.

Barrels lined the far end of the cramped room. Above her swung cheeses cloaked in wax, garlic braids, and colorful bundles of dried herbs. Tins of spices, jars of jewel-colored jellies, and muslin bags of dried legumes marched along the various shelves. Mercy peered at the neatly labeled ceramic jars and selected two. She plucked a wreath of dried flowers from a hook overhead, adding it to her armful of ingredients.

Returning to the table, she deposited them. After rolling up her sleeves she began snapping the flower heads from their stalks.

"A complicated brew you drink," Hart said from where he stood in rigid disapproval, watching her.

"Oh, do sit down," she chided him. "You might as well be comfortable. All that glowering must be wearing."

"I am not glowering," he said, but, she noted with an inward smile, he'd ironed his voice of any inflection. He pulled over one of the stools the kitchen girls had used and took a seat.

"Those two women are really your sisters?" she asked casually, filling a kettle of water and setting it on the stove.

"Yes."

"Who would have believed it?" she murmured, returning to the table and measuring herbs into a silver tea ball. "The scourge of the Texas Panhandle has two doting sisters."

He made a disparaging sound. "Three. And they hardly dote."

"Three?" she echoed, shaking her head. "Here. If you insist on standing around, you might as well make yourself useful. Grind these flower heads." She handed him the mortar and pestle. He stared at them as though she'd just handed him some complicated Oriental puzzle box. "You pound them with the pestle," she said encouragingly.

He flashed her a look of disdain but complied, crushing the dried buds with unprecedented enthusiasm.

"Why is that so hard to believe?" he asked suddenly, sounding as though he hadn't wanted to ask and was having a hard time figuring out why he had.

"Well," she said, "given your reputation—or rather your *former* reputation—as a sort of soulless demon of destruction, I'd rather assumed you'd sprung from a dragon's tooth . . . like one of the soldiers in Cadmus' army."

He stared at her a second and then, suddenly, impossibly, he threw back his head and laughed. He had a wonderful laugh: deep throated, rich, and infectious. And his smile transformed his face. He looked young, very young, and handsome, *very* handsome.

"So you think I'm some mythical monster, eh?" he asked, his bluish-green eyes glowing with sardonic amusement.

Mythical. Yes.

"Like a minotaur or a gryphon?" he asked, finishing the task she'd set him.

"Or a centaur." As soon as she'd said the word, she blushed. The centaur was more a libidinous creature than a bellicose one.

Disconcerted, she reached to take the bowl from him. Her fingers brushed against his. Sudden, potent recognition shivered through her with the brief contact. Her breath caught in her throat and she pulled her hand back.

She was attracted to Hart Moreland. As a man.

He had played a role in every nightmare she'd had for the past six years. Every terror that chased her from sleep had featured his cold, inimical eyes stonily regarding her just before agony ripped through her shoulder.

She had never thought of "Duke" as a man. He was all at once more and less than human. Pitiless, ruthless, and, above all, infallible. That is why she had followed him. That is why she had approached him. That is why she needed him. Duke did not "fail."

But she had never thought of him as a man. And had never realized that he was a young, virile man whose rare smiles and rarer laughter were incredibly appealing, undermining her intention by making her too acutely aware of him; his scent; the breadth of his shoulders; the flat, hard silhouette she'd seen last night. She scowled as she fetched the whistling teakettle and filled a hefty mug with water. Her breathing was staggered, her pulse thrummed erratically. She wanted to touch his hand again.

How that would amuse him. The graceless, gauche American girl agitated into a state of feminine vapors over the Earl of Perth. Her back to him, she took a deep, steadying breath. She refused to set herself up as an object of derision, or worse, pity. Even if it was a private derision. She doubted Hart ever confided any of his concerns or feelings to another person, let alone his amusements.

"I suppose you'll want to drink it here," he was saying.

"Drink it? Oh," she murmured. "This isn't for me. It's for the Dowager Duchess."

"You have once more confounded me. I applaud you. Why are you making tea for the Dowager? Since you are so concerned with servants' feelings, might I point out that Her Grace's maid will doubtless take exception to your performing her duties?"

"It's for her headache. A tisane. I learned it from our ranch cook."

He hesitated a second before replying. "That was thoughtful of you. Here, allow me," he said, rising from his seat. "That kettle looks heavy."

His fingers—long, elegant, fashioned for an artist's hands—closed over hers. Even though she anticipated it this time, her response still shook her. Sensual awareness rippled through her, making her hand tremble, sloshing burning tea on her fingers.

"Damn!" She hissed with pain.

He strode to the sink and grabbed the bucket of peeled carrots that stood in ice water. He returned with it and swung it up onto the table. Catching hold of her wrist, he plunged her hand into the cool water, holding it there.

"Damn, damn, damn my clumsiness," she said.

"Your language," he said.

"What of it?" she asked crossly, angry she'd been so clumsy, angry his masculinity had caused her to be clumsy, angry his tone was so coldly disapproving. "It hurts, *damn it.*"

"You are no lady, Miss Coltrane."

"And you are no *gentleman*, Perth!"

"I guess that makes us both imposters," he said, releasing her hand and indifferently offering her a dry towel.

"Not both of us," she said, plucking the towel from his extended hand. "*I* am not pretending to be a lady."

His eyes narrowed between the thick fringe of bronze lashes. "And I"—he leaned closer to her. She could see the slight flare of his diamond shaped nostrils, like a panther scenting for fear in its prey—"I do not pretend to be a *gentle* man. You'd be wise to remember that."

She stared at him, knowing she should be frightened. There was a gleam deep in the glacial eyes and his words were delivered in a low, even tone, all the more frightening for its lack of inflection.

"Don't play games with me, Mercy," he said.

"Don't whisper a word about our past association. The ramifications would be . . . unpleasant. For everyone. But most especially for you. That is why I followed you here. To remind you of your promise. You are no lady, but you needn't be a lady to be wise."

Before she could frame a response, he disappeared through the green baize door.

Shaken, she dabbed at the wet edge of her sleeve, undraping a carrot peel that had coiled around her wrist.

He was right. She was no lady.

Oh, she had manufactured a nice veneer. But deep inside, as soon as she was alone, restlessness pricked her, frustration nipped at her.

As hard as she'd tried, as much as she'd wanted to, she'd never succeeded in becoming the lady her mother had yearned for her to be. The knowledge that she'd disappointed her sweet mother ached like an unhealed bruise, always there, touching every unfeminine pleasure she indulged in with the taint of guilt.

She had tried. She had tried to find pleasure in trotting a horse along a prescribed halter path; she wanted to gallop across an untracked field of waist-high grass. She had tried to be an undemanding font of tranquillity; she liked laughter too well. She had tried to develop her hand at watercolor artistry but she was too impatient; the bright colors she used always ended up running together.

It was an appropriate metaphor for her. All her bright colors collided with one another. And when she tried to blend them together, they dulled and disappointed. Neither delicate nor vibrant, just muddled.

She stood up. She could not change what she was—the years had taught her that—but she could keep her promise and, after finding Will, heal the breach between her father and brother. Particularly since she was responsible for that breach.

She bit down on her lip. Mother had been so proud of Will; his polish, his sophistication. But Father . . . their father had no use for his bright, witty, urbane son. Except for their devotion to the same woman, they had nothing in common. So, Father had turned an all-too-willing tomboy daughter into a surrogate son. Herself.

Thoughtfully, Mercy placed the teacup and pot on a serving platter. Her father was so proud of her; her riding ability, her shooting prowess, her skill with a fishing pole. He'd held her up as an example for Will, goading him with her achievements.

And, God help her, she'd liked it. She'd liked being the apple of someone's eye. She'd liked the attention, the approval. She'd deliberately set herself between them, widening the rift, afraid that someday their father would realize Will's worth and her own feminine deficiency.

She had to make up for it. Now all she had left were Will, their father, and a promise she was going to keep.

If Hart Moreland would not help her, she would help herself. He could keep his damned secrets! She had time. Will had been living here for months; a few more weeks would hardly matter.

The sound of a door swishing open drew her attention. One of the kitchen maids peeped in. The girl's eyes grew wide when she saw the tray Mercy was holding. She mumbled an apology and disappeared again.

Mercy smiled, but her amusement was bittersweet. Not a lady, no longer a Texas tomboy. A fraud in either world.

But for a moment, with Hart Moreland, she'd felt . . . real. All the colors had been there, but for once they hadn't battled for ascendancy.

Picking up the tray, Mercy headed for the servants' stairs to the Duchess's private quarters. She seemed destined to insult, offend, and outrage Hart Moreland.

But, she could not help remembering, she'd also made him laugh.

Chapter 6

"Thank you," the Dowager Duchess said, placing the emptied teacup on the table beside the fainting couch. "But, naughty as it is, I must confess I believe much of my headache was a result of anticipating two hours of Mozart."

She was a handsome enough child, thought the Dowager as Mercy dimpled. A bit bold featured and too many shades of brown to be truly pretty, but she had a clear complexion and fine teeth.

"If you do not like Mozart, why on earth did you instruct the chamber orchestra to play him?"

The Dowager sniffed. Handsome though she undoubtedly was, Mercy Coltrane was in many ways still deplorably naive. "Because it is fashionable and expected. You must learn to be anticipated if you are to make your way in English society, Miss Coltrane."

The Dowager gave a mental sigh. Some long-dormant mischievousness must have been responsible for her having undertaken Mercy's cause. She was still surprised to find herself acting as duenna to this potentially embarrassing American. Potentially embarrassing, but perceptive. She could make use of the gel.

"What do you think of Annabelle Moreland?" she asked. She would never have dared be so open with one of her peers. But in Mercy she had the unique advantage of a listener who would simply not be given credence should she relate any private conversation. She was, after all, only an American. If Mercy Coltrane was to repeat any of her words, she'd find herself immediately ostracized.

"Miss Moreland?" Mercy asked. "She seems a very nice, agreeable, lovely young lady."

"Yes," the Duchess said, "she does."

"Why do you ask?"

"I fully expected Acton to be up here singing her praises to me—certainly the boy did little else last season—and urging me to allow him to make an announcement of his engagement at Friday's ball."

"And he has not?"

"No." The Duchess sighed.

"And this disappoints you?"

Again the Dowager sighed, her thin, powdered cheeks dishing slightly as if she tasted lemon. "I simply don't know my mind on the subject of Miss Moreland. All season I have endeavored to acquaint myself with her, but she remains an enigma."

Mercy inclined her head.

"She is utterly unlike you, Mercy," the Dowager said, allowing the faintest shading of reproof to color her words. "You wear your every emotion for all to see and energetically express opinions on any given subject."

Mercy squirmed. "Lord Acton *asked* me what I thought of animal husbandry."

"Quite. It is perhaps best not to answer every question posed us."

Mercy lowered her hazel eyes. She did, noted the Dowager, have extravagantly luxuriant eyelashes.

"But I am not here to chide you. Forgive me. I was asking your opinion."

"At least on the subject of Miss Moreland, I haven't any," Mercy returned.

"That's the problem; neither have I. One ought to have an opinion regarding one's potential daughter-in-law and a future duchess, do you not think?"

"Is there anything about her you take exception to?" Mercy asked in the tone of one who is trying to be helpful and hasn't a notion of how to go about it.

"No. Her family is well connected. The Morelands are a revered and ancient country family. As is the one they've aligned themselves with, the Whitcombes. And Wrexhall is a promising young politician from an unexceptional family."

"And Lord Perth?"

"Perth is, like his sister, an enigma. I have asked wherever seemly and possible after him. His father was something of a wastrel but the mother was a Quinton. Soon after his father's ship was lost off the coast of New Guinea, Perth enlisted in the army. He saw action in North Africa as a regular." The Dowager frowned. "It would have been better had Perth been an officer, but he joined the army when he was a lad. Romantic notions boys have. Too bad the mother wasn't able to persuade him to wait until he could have had a commission."

Mercy was regarding her intently.

"Perth inherited the earldom from a cousin. Quite unexpected and, I should think, fortuitous. The girls would not have married so well had Perth been simply Mr. Moreland."

"It must have brought him a certain amount of wealth too," Mercy said.

"No," the Dowager clipped out, embarrassed by this discussion of money. Finances were a man's province. Not that she hadn't looked into Perth's financial situation. She had. But she disliked admitting it, even tacitly. "The estate had fallen into extreme disrepair. Perth restored it to its past glory, but he could not have done so from inherited wealth. Apparently he filled the family coffers with coin netted from various investments in your own country."

"I see."

"But I did not ask you to discuss finances, and at any rate that is all I have learned about them."

"I'm sorry I am not of more help," Mercy said.

"No matter. I have time to form an opinion of

the girl. Acton does not seem quite as eager for an announcement as I'd thought him to be."

The girl nodded, but her expression was distracted.

"What is it, my dear?"

Mercy hesitated. Her dark brows dipped together in a worried frown. "Your Grace, you said as how you looked into Perth's history."

The Dowager slowly nodded.

"There must have been people you talked to—acquaintances who were able to provide you with information. . . ."

"Yes," the Dowager said, a touch of frost in her words. "But I assure you I was most discreet. I only asked where and when opportune and never did so in such a manner as would excite undue comment or reflect poorly on the object of my inquiries."

"I am sure," Mercy said hurriedly. "The thing is, Your Grace, I know so very few people in England. No more than a handful."

"Do you espy a potential candidate for husband, Mercy?" The Dowager's thin brows rose and she smiled with imperial graciousness. "I can certainly find out what a young man's prospects are, if that is what you—"

"No. Oh, dear, no. I am doing this so badly." Mercy shook her head. "Your Grace, I have to find my brother."

"Of course you do, my dear," the Dowager said calmly. "I remember you asked if I knew him when we first met. Simply tell me where he has taken lodgings and I will have your letter delivered tomorrow before noon. Quite proper of you not to hie yourself off unchaperoned to an unknown address. For all you know, it might be a gentlemen's club!"

"I do not know his current address," Mercy said. "He seems to change them quite often."

"I see. Well, that presents something of a problem. What was his last known address?"

"I'm not certain. Some of his letters did mention clubs," Mercy said dubiously.

"Ah." The Dowager sat back and steepled her index fingers. "Now we are getting somewhere. What clubs, my dear?"

"A place called the Peacock's Tail. And another named Harmony. I think there was an establishment he frequented called the Hound Master— Whatever is wrong?"

The Dowager sank back, indignation and shock on her face. "My heavens, gel," she said. "At least one of those places is notorious. Quite beyond the pale."

Mercy swallowed. Her eyes held the Dowager's, pleading with her.

"You must understand," the Dowager said. "I cannot possibly make inquiries about a young man whose proclivities are so suspect."

"You can't."

"No." The Dowager shook her head. "Ascertaining a few facts about Perth, for all that he is something of a cold character, was a simple matter of asking a few old family friends. It is not the same as asking about an American with such low tendencies."

She could not bring herself to meet the disappointment and reproach in Mercy's eyes. To her great shame her own gaze slid away. "I am sure you would not ask it of me."

"Of course not," Mercy murmured.

The heat that warmed the Dowager's face crept farther down her throat and centered in her chest. She had worked her entire lifetime to be a perfect duchess, a perfect lady. A lady simply did not go asking after people who visited gaming hells and houses of ill repute. A lady did not even acknowledge the existence of such. And she was far too old to start risking social censure now, when she had spent her life abiding by its rules. Especially not for a social foundling. She would not. She could not.

"We'll forget I ever mentioned it," Mercy said.

"Yes, we shall," the Dowager readily agreed, eager to put their relationship back on its previous footing. She was unused to feeling that she had acted the coward. She did not like it. And she disliked it that Mercy Coltrane had inspired such feelings.

"Yes, that will be for the best," she repeated more forcefully. "Now tell me what you are going to wear to the ball."

Annabelle sank back in her seat with a small gratified smile. The violinists had been superb and the rest of the orchestra more than competent.

She glanced over at Acton. He was not the most handsome of men or the most witty. But he was easy, undemanding company, intelligent without being intellectual, and most important, he was a duke in need of a duchess. And she had every intention of wearing that coronet.

From her eighth year Annabelle had been groomed for just such a match. It had become more than a goal, it had been the focus of her life. But now, so close to achieving it, she found herself floundering. And, she thought with an uncontrollable pursing of her mouth, she suspected the reason why.

"That was wonderful," she said.

"Yes," Acton replied distractedly. "I shall have to congratulate the conductor." He looked around at the guests gathering shawls and mantles and gloves. "I do not see Miss Coltrane."

"Miss Coltrane?" Annabelle repeated. Her hands tightened in her lap.

"Our American guest," Acton said, frowning. "I introduced her to you just before we entered."

"Ah, yes. The woman in the . . . extravagantly colored gown."

Acton smiled at her approvingly, and Annabelle released an inward sigh. If Acton did not take exception to her subtle criticism, perhaps she had misread a personal interest in Mercy Coltrane where there was nothing more than a polite host's concern for his mother's guest.

"Extravagant plumage for a rara avis, eh?" he asked.

"Quite exotic," Annabelle murmured, pulling on her gloves and snapping the leather forcefully down over her fingers.

"Oh, more than exotic. She's marvelous. She is a truly charming creature. So energetic and spontaneous and such . . . well, *fun*," Acton enthused.

Annabelle contrived to keep her expression pleasant. "I'm sure she's delightful. And, as you have pointed out, quite unique."

"Oh, dear me, yes," Acton said, rising and offering her his arm. She touched her fingertips to his sleeve and flowed to her feet.

Nathan Hillard strolled by, offering his distracted smile. Annabelle did not know the man well, but still, she was surprised to find him here, at so tame an entertainment. Rumor had it Hillard was one step ahead of his creditors. Perhaps he'd sought respite here, in his usual guise of professional houseguest.

Too bad, he had excellent deportment and good breeding, Annabelle thought before turning back to more pressing concerns.

"The unique is so often entrancing. Exciting, one might say," Annabelle remarked as Acton escorted her forward.

"Exciting? I must say, that seems an odd choice of words," Acton replied, his brow furrowed beneath his ginger curls.

"Stimulating, then," Annabelle said. "You know"—she paused as if a thought had just occurred to her—"I find it quite interesting that while the stimulating activities we indulge in ultimately become wearing, that isn't necessarily the case with stimulating personalities. Is it?" She glanced sideways at him. His brow had smoothed. He was paying her scant attention now, his gaze roving restlessly among the guests. She slowed her step, determinedly silent. She was not some negligible creature who needed to parrot her own questions for the simple courtesy of a reply.

Noting her sudden silence, he looked down at her. Having been caught openly inattentive, his square face colored a dull brick red. "Please excuse me, Miss Moreland. I was concerned that something untoward had happened to my mother's protégée, keeping her from our company. May I beg you to repeat yourself?"

"Oh," she said lightly, "'twas nothing of consequence."

He patted her gloved hand gratefully and led her into the Great Hall, where he waved one of Baron Coffey's acne-scarred sons over. The lad scuttled forward like an overeager puppy, all legs and feet. "Carlton here has expressed a great interest in—in your opinon on Mozart. I, alas, cannot neglect my duties as host. I must inquire after Miss Coltrane. Rest assured, I shall inform you if anything is amiss. If you'll excuse me?" He bowed quickly before turning and trotting up the stairs.

"Ah, Miss Moreland," Carlton Coffey said,

beaming with delight. "Now, let me see. Mozart. Mote-zart. Hungarian writer chappie, is he not?"

Only years of strict schoolroom discipline allowed Annabelle to form a polite expression of interest.

Something would have to be done about Mercy Coltrane.

Chapter 7

"*Y*ou know that American girl, Mercy Coltrane?" Beryl asked the next day. Hart reined his horse in next to where she stood. She looked up at him, her eyes bright. "She has a bullet hole in her shoulder."

Anger and astonishment froze Hart in the act of dismounting. Had Mercy already broken her promises—or was she taunting him by hinting at their past? He swung down out of the saddle and tossed the reins to a waiting attendant. He'd damn well throttle her himself if she'd revealed where she'd received that scar.

"How do you know this?" he asked.

"I saw it myself last night, and then this morning, after breakfast Lady Jane Carr actually had the audacity to express an interest."

"Jane Carr sounds a mannerless chit." He cast an angry eye over the men and women sauntering beneath the autumn-flushed boughs of aspens bordering Acton's parkland, searching for the object of his ire. All he saw were elaborately bundled women milling about men who were comparing rifles with ceremonial conspicuousness.

The afternoon's entertainment was to include a shooting match for the male guests. The women, he assumed, were there to murmur appreciative sounds. Not that he had any intention of joining. He'd had enough shooting to last him a dozen lifetimes over . . . unless the target was a woman with auburn hair.

"Oh, forget Jane Carr. She didn't even bring her doddering old husband with her. The point is she asked and Miss Coltrane told us, calm as you please," Beryl said with some exasperation. "Did you hear what I said?"

"Yes."

"Isn't it the most deliciously exciting thing you've ever heard?" she asked. He ignored her, striding toward the assembly of houseguests.

"Well?" Beryl demanded from behind him. With a sense of frustration Hart adjusted his speed to his sister's more decorous pace.

"Fascinating."

"She's so nonchalant about it," Beryl continued. "She says she received it at the hands of a— oh, this is too, too rich—*gunslinger*!"

So, she *did* think to taunt him. Obviously, Miss Coltrane and he needed to have another conversation. "Beryl—" He stopped just out of hearing of the other guests.

"I am quite in awe of her," Beryl babbled on.

"I wonder if she's ever met any red Indians. I will have to ask her. I expect she's had any number of harrowing escapades. That wound! As big as a shilling and dreadful-looking. How painful it must have been! What a thrilling life she's lived and yet she's really the sweetest, most dear—"

"Beryl, is this *gossip*?"

Abruptly, Beryl left off enthusing over Mercy Coltrane. She blinked at him in consternation, as though he'd asked, Beryl, are you speaking English?

"Well, yes, Hart," she said patiently, "I expect it is."

"Beryl, you do *not* gossip."

"Yes, I do," she replied. "I always have. I love gossip. Oh, not the tittle-tattle of the chambermaids—unless they're chambermaids to *really* interesting people. But I do so love to be in on all the news, the first to know when a scandal is about to break. Who's doing what, where, and"—her eyes twinkled with relish—"with whom."

"Good Lord."

"Oh, come, Hart. You can't tell me you don't like discovering things about people."

"Have you ever considered that the things people conceal are often hidden for very good reasons?" A random memory flickered through his mind: a shadow in a doorway, a gun barrel catching a ray of sunlight, the revolver jerking in his palm, a corpse tumbling through a swinging door. Blood. The smell of gunpowder.

He waited, biting back on his fear. Sometimes a

random memory triggered it. It might start with the tightening of his joints, the feel of his flesh shrinking on his muscles, his heart hammering as if he were racing from the devil. Panic. Fear. Rising up to overwhelm every other sensation.

If it happened here, now, he'd have to get away. He'd have to master it, privately, without drawing attention to himself.

"Hart?"

He waited the space of two more heartbeats. Nothing. "There are very probably excellent reasons people keep certain matters private," he continued as if nothing had happened.

"Rubbish," Beryl stated. "Secrets are best exposed. They're robbed of their power to harm that way. And if they are, indeed, heinous, then 'tis best that people know about them. Forewarned is forearmed."

There would be no convincing her. Things were so simple and clear cut for Beryl. *And that is the way it should be,* he reminded himself. He'd done everything in his power to ensure it would be so, for her and his other sisters. No night horrors, no soul-damning choices that dogged them through the years, no shadows from the past obscuring every pleasure. Still, this base preoccupation with scandal needed to be addressed.

"Does Henley know about your—interest, shall we say?—in other people's lives?"

For an instant unhappiness clouded Beryl's bright eyes, but then she shook her head and smiled with renewed vivacity. "Of course. He likes his information just as much as I like mine. And, let me tell you"—she tapped him playfully on the cheek—"my . . . fact-gathering capabilities, shall we say?—have been quite useful to Henley's career." She preened. There was no other word for it. "It's quite an asset for a politician's wife."

"No," Hart said. "Your deportment, your diplomacy, these are the qualities that make you—"

"Dear Hart." She smiled at him. "Such a lamb. Yes, yes. It's all very useful, knowing how deep a curtsy each member of the House warrants. But it's only stage dressing. A well-trained poodle could manage as much. I have more to offer Henley's career than a wrist strong enough to pour out tea for fifty. It's what happens *after* the tea is poured that is significant." She nodded, her eyes flickering over the assembly. "Look. There's Miss Coltrane now. Come along, Hart. I am determined to befriend her."

"For God's sake, why?"

"It will add considerably to my cachet," she answered, claiming his arm and tugging him forward. "She's becoming quite sought after."

In the center of the small group Beryl towed him toward stood Mercy Coltrane. She was dressed in a plain tan skirt and white shirtwaist, an old battered Stetson shading her eyes and hiding her glorious red hair. The cool air had kissed color to her full lips. A few rare strands of gleaming auburn hair rippled against the open collar of her shirt. She was smiling again.

Always smiles and animation. Even for him

there had been smiles. He'd never met anyone like her before. And she was, whatever her shortcomings, so very pretty.

Her head was angled attentively toward Acton and another man, a sleek blond gentleman with a rifle perched casually on his shoulder. Beside her, the picture of modest repose in a minty-colored dress tiered with lace, was Annabelle.

"Ah, Mrs. Wrexhall, Perth," Acton hailed upon spying them. "Delightful of you to join our little shooting exhibition. Do you know Nathan Hillard?" He stepped back, indicating the man at Mercy's side.

"I don't believe I've had the pleasure," Hillard murmured, bowing over Beryl's hand and nodding to Hart. Hart assessed him as Acton made the necessary introductions.

Expensively attired in a tweed shooting jacket, middling height, closer to forty than thirty, fair. Interesting face. As a whole he was handsome, but taken apart his features belied each other. His chin was blunt, yet his nose was aesthetically pinched. His lips were full and gentle; his eyes, unusually bright. His high forehead beneath the thick blond hair was unlined, yet deep furrows were etched on either side of a wide mouth.

"Will your husband be joining us, Mrs. Wrexhall?" Acton asked.

"No," she said softly. "Henley is not particularly fond of shooting and such. He's gone to London for the afternoon. A political appointment."

"I see," Acton said. "Well, then, we will simply

wait for your brother-in-law to arrive before we commence."

"Richard?" Beryl asked. "Richard doesn't shoot."

"Oh." The single utterance, coupled with Acton's befuddled expression, held a gentle reproof. Annabelle darted a quick beseeching glance in their direction.

"But Hart here is simply rabid on firearms," Beryl hurriedly said as though visualizing Acton checking off a demerit against Annabelle's name. "Aren't you, Hart?"

"No." If Annabelle's qualifications as a duchess rested solely on whether the males in her family shot things, Acton could go to blazes and good riddance.

Acton flushed at his curtness. "Well, then," he said, turning to Mercy, "shall we start?"

Hart's gaze jumped to Mercy. *Start what? Good Lord, the woman isn't going to make a spectacle of herself by competing with the men?* If she did, she could kiss good-bye to any hopes she'd ever have of landing herself a titled husband, whether or not she claimed that as her main objective. Men might find her brass entertaining but their mamas most definitely would not. And most coronets came with dowagers' fingers attached.

"If you would do me the honor of using my rifle, Miss Coltrane?" Hillard unshouldered his gun and offered it to her. She smiled, accepting the rifle.

"Miss Coltrane is shooting?" Beryl asked, admiration and pleasurable shock mingling in her voice.

"Yes," Nathan Hillard said, his bright eyes glowing with open admiration. "In Texas many women are accomplished shootists."

"Ah," said Mercy, "you didn't tell me you'd been to Texas, Mr. Hillard."

"Oh! I haven't," he said, his smile self-deprecating. "No, I'm afraid I've never been off English soil. But I'm most fortunate in my friends. They've regaled me with tales of their own travels in your country, Miss Coltrane. I hope I have the opportunity to hear accounts of your brave young land from yourself."

"I'd be delighted, sir." She moved closer to Hillard, her face alive with delight. "Texas is—"

"And you say Miss Coltrane will be shooting?" Hart still couldn't believe she would be so bold.

The abrupt interruption gained him a startled glance from his sister. Mercy's gaze swung back to meet his.

"Yes," Acton said. "Miss Coltrane has succumbed to my entreaties and agreed to show us her prowess with a rifle."

Hart relaxed. A simple display of shooting ability. Though why he should give a bloody damn if Mercy Coltrane made her name a byword for vulgar exhibitionism was beyond him.

"Oh, how utterly splendid!" Beryl said. "Is that not delightful, Hart?"

"Wondrous."

Acton clapped, drawing his other guests' attention. Annabelle stepped back, properly unwilling to place herself in a significant position by Acton's side. There was a hard, assessing set to her dainty features that Hart had never noticed before.

"As you know, this afternoon's enjoyment is a shooting match among the gentlemen," Acton said. "But first, I have a very special surprise for you. Miss Mercy Coltrane, late of Texas, has honored us by agreeing to demonstrate shooting in the western style. If you would all please stand well away from the avenue?"

The guests dutifully moved back against the length of pennant-hung rope stretched between the tall poplars lining either side of the bridle path. Some forty yards away the lane had been blocked off. Hart glanced down the avenue, looking for the target. Immediately, disbelievingly, his gaze swung back.

Square in the middle of the path, its head lowered menacingly, monstrously exaggerated horns gleaming atop its yarn-covered head, stood a life-sized papier-mâché buffalo. It would have been a fine facsimile except for the pink ribbon tied about its string tail.

Hart glanced at Mercy. She was staring in horrified bemusement at the thing. She swallowed and looked up, catching his eye. Her lush lips flattened and she notched her chin higher in the air.

"Very pretty buffalo, Acton," Hart said, watching Mercy with amusement. She looked indignant, apparently suspicious that her precious Texas was being ridiculed. "I particularly like the tail adornment. Was it your idea, perchance?"

"Why, yes," Acton said, flushing with pleasure.

Hart nodded. "It renders the beast less frightening for the women. How thoughtful of you to take under consideration the delicate sensibilities of your feminine guests. Well, most of them, at any rate."

"What am I to shoot at, sir?" Mercy asked, eyeing the pink ribbon with obvious plans.

"Why, the bison, Miss Coltrane."

"Yes. But what part of the bison?"

Acton and Hillard exchanged knowing smiles. "Any part you care to hit, dear lady," Acton said.

The man had the makings of a prime ass, Hart decided in disgust. A child of eight would be hard pressed *not* to hit the damned thing at this range. Acton's implication that he had orchestrated the event so that Mercy could not possibly fail was insufferably patronizing.

"The horns," Hart clipped out. "See if you can shoot one of the horns, Miss Coltrane."

Mercy's gaze swerved toward him. "Which horn, *Mr.* Perth?"

Little egotist. "The far one. I have a guinea that says you cannot hit the far one cleanly." Now, there was a target to test one's skill. From here less than a foot of the appendage was showing.

"Oh, come now, Perth," Hillard protested. "A gentleman wouldn't make a wager of that sort with a lady. She hasn't any chance—"

"Done!" Mercy said, and without a moment's hesitation shouldered the rifle and fired. The sudden report silenced all conversation. Heads swung up, sentences hung unfinished in the air, eyes widened. They stared at the paper sculpture. Both horns still stood atop its massive head.

"I'm sorry, m'dear," Acton said kindly. "Perhaps you'd like to try again? Not that you have to. You can pick whatever target you like. The head? The sides?"

Mercy laughed. "Oh, I hit the horn. About four inches from the tip, I should say."

"Of course you did, Miss Coltrane," Acton agreed. "Now, would you care to try for another—"

"Begad, she *did* hit the bloody thing!" a male voice called in disbelief. Down the alley Lady Acton's military brother, Major Sotbey, was peering at the horn. He stuck a finger through the papier-mâché and wriggled it. "Dead center!"

Acton and Hillard turned amazed stares at Mercy. She, however, was not looking at them. There was a mocking quirk to one dark brow and her saucy smile was all for Hart. "My guinea, Your High-handedness—or is it Lordliness? Unless you'd care to make another wager?"

"As you wish, Miss Coltrane," he replied. "Do you think that you could hit the same target again?"

"Certainly," she returned, and called down to the group of men studying the horn. "Sirs, would you please stand back?" They scurried to the safety of the trees. Once more, she shot. All three of Baron Coffey's sons broke from the crowd and ran toward the target.

"Dead center!" one of them called. "A few inches higher, this time!"

Mercy smiled at him, wickedly triumphant, before lowering her lashes and murmuring modestly, "I must be lucky today."

"Yes," he responded, his word rife with meaning. "You must."

He reached into his pocket and was in the act of withdrawing a gold coin when he heard her say, "You wouldn't care to make a contest of it, would you?"

Of all the conceited, self-satisfied—! "No."

She sighed, contriving to look contrite. "Oh, I'm so sorry. I just assumed . . . That is, I thought you might know something about . . . But how foolish of me. You aren't a sportsman, are you? I mean, what with your horse running away with you I should have realized . . ." She grinned apologetically and shrugged.

He handed her the guinea, aware he was doing so with ill grace, but she was the most provoking female he'd ever encountered. *And provocative*, a part of him added.

She received the coin and bounced it up in down in her palm, regarding him with an intimacy born of shared history . . . *teasing* him, by God!

"Oh, Hart. Do!" Beryl said. "You are so very adept with firearms."

"Is he?" Mercy asked, managing to invest a world of disbelief in the query.

"Yes. He fought in North Africa, you know. He was little more than a boy and still the best shot in his regiment." Damn it, Beryl needn't announce his past to the entire world. "He was medaled any number of times for bravery. His fellow soldiers thought his prowess with a gun quite supernatural."

"Ah." Mercy nodded. "That explains his reluctance to compete."

He was in the act of turning away from the group when her words arrested him.

"How so?" he heard Annabelle ask.

"Well," she explained, "one wouldn't want to tarnish past glories with current defeats."

He froze. Impossible that she was baiting him. Impossible, but true.

"Oh, I'm sure Hart could still manage some very nice shots, were he of a mind to," Beryl insisted.

"Yes. Of course he could," Mercy said in a soothing, not entirely convincing manner.

"Really, Miss Coltrane," Beryl said. "He never misses."

"In his salad days he was undoubtedly peerless. I'm only sorry I've placed him in an untenable situation."

"What situation is that?" Beryl asked.

"If he loses, well . . . it might be uncomfortable for him to be bested by a woman. If he wins"—her voice dripped with incredulity over such a likelihood—"why then he may appear to be less than a *gentleman*—"

"Yes," he bit out, rounding and glaring at her. If she had set her mind on making herself and him the subject of conversation, so be it. If he was an accomplice in her social downfall, it was because she'd insisted.

"Yes?" How could lashes that long and thick flutter that fast? "Yes what, Lord Mr. Perth?"

"Yes. I'll compete. How could I refuse so gracious an invitation?"

"Here, now, Perth. Miss Coltrane had the right of it. A gentleman competing against a lady? 'Tisn't done," Acton protested.

"Oh, surely an exception can be made?" Annabelle asked sweetly. "I mean, if both participants are willing and it is a friendly sort of competition . . . ?" Several of their audience raised concurring votes.

"Allow me to act as your loader, Miss Coltrane," Nathan Hillard offered. The man was unctuous, his presence at Mercy's side ubiquitous, and his smile too warm by half. He'd invite comment if he continued to hound Mercy with his attention like this. Mercy, however, did not look hounded. She looked pleased.

She dimpled at Hillard before blinking innocently at the rest of them. Her gold-flecked eyes grew large. "Oh, of course it's friendly!"

"I think I'll just go talk to some of the other ladies," Beryl said nervously, finally awakening to the vulgar situation her words had embroiled them in. She hurried away, disappearing into the throng.

"Well, if you really want to, Miss Coltrane . . ." Acton said dubiously.

"Oh, I do!" she assured him. She held out her rifle. "Here, Mr. Perth. See if you can hit the horn too."

His eyes narrowing on Mercy's innocent face, Hart shrugged out of his jacket and tossed it to one of the men. He rolled his sleeves back over his forearms and took the rifle from her.

For just a second his fingers brushed the back of her smooth, pale hand. He felt her skin too acutely—soft and velvety, chill with autumn's breath. It was just like when he had touched her in that damn kitchen. Too intense. Too much . . . attraction.

"I will try not to disappoint, Miss Coltrane," he said.

Chapter 8

⁕⬥⬥⬥⬥⬥⬥⬥⬥⬥⬥⬥⬥⬥⬥⬥⬥⬥⬥⬥⬥⬥⬥⬥⬥⬥⬥⬥⬥⬥

*M*ercy rubbed the back of her hand as she watched Hart check the action on the Winchester. The place his fingers had brushed still felt traced with electricity, a harmless fire of sensation. *Harmless?* There was nothing in the least harmless about Hart Moreland.

He was scowling, sighting down the barrel. The hard sinews in his forearm, exposed by his turned shirtsleeves, flexed beneath tanned skin as he lifted the rifle. His wrists looked strong. His hands were beautiful, elegant . . . a blind sculptor should have such hands. Not a gunslinger.

He glanced over at her and his sapphire-shot eyes glinted with rueful enjoyment. The light from overhead, rendered by a capricious wind dancing in the leaves, touched his soft brown hair with golden highlights and patterned his lean face with flickering shadows. She glanced at the other guests: well-tended, dutiful, safe gentlemen and women.

They didn't even realize there was a shape-shifter in their midst. Dark and light, illumination and obscurity . . .

"The horn?" he asked.

"Ah, yes," she mumbled, forcing her gaze away. "If you think you can—"

He shot.

It was casual, the way he had brought the rifle up. He didn't even shoulder it. Just raised it and fired. There was nothing vainglorious or showy in the act, just smooth, economical grace.

Mercy had the notion that he only raised it as far as he did so as *not* to appear ostentatious. She bet he could have fired from the hip and still shot the papier-mâché horn off.

"Good show! Bang on!" shouted several male voices.

"Next target?" Hart asked.

Mercy laughed with pleasure. There was just a hint of self-congratulation in his voice, a touch of smugness that made him seem so much more human and thus more appealing. "Shall we put a bit more distance between the target and the rifle?"

"Pace off another thirty yards," he called down the field.

Acton's liveried attendants didn't stand a chance. The gentlemen of the audience, now thoroughly involved in the impromptu competition, rushed to accommodate.

"*Ladies* first," Hart said.

"The ribbon?" Carefully sighting down the barrel, she released her breath in a long, steady exhalation, her weight on her forward foot, her back straight as her father had taught her. She squeezed the trigger. The ribbon jumped and landed on the ground.

"Brava, Miss Coltrane," Hart said. "But you've robbed me of my target."

"Set it up again!" called Hillard as he offered her a flute filled with champagne. "To the victor goes the spoils."

Mercy laughed, accepting the glass and taking a sip, eyeing Hillard over the brim. He looked delighted by her skill.

"You are as talented as you are lovely," Hillard announced, his gaze as warm as Hart's was cool.

"Is she not?" Acton agreed.

The ribbon was retied and Hart stepped forward. With no more haste or preparation than he'd evinced on his first shot, he fired. Once more, the ribbon fluttered to the ground. More cheers went up and, interspersed with the cheers, wagers.

Acton called a servant over. "Set up a table," he told the attendant. "Hillard, be a good chap and take the bets, will you? We'll make it a charity event." He touched her briefly on the arm. "Would you be so kind as to delay a few minutes, Miss Coltrane? Some of the guests would like to wager on the outcome of your contest."

"Of course."

"I will, of course, wager on you, m'dear." Hillard's voice was soft, but from the sudden tensing of Hart's long body it was apparent Hart had heard him all too clearly.

"Oh, please don't," Mercy returned, for the first time a note of fret coloring her round American accents. She didn't want to be responsible for anyone's money, and from the little bits and pieces she'd overheard, she could only assume that Nathan Hillard did not have money to wager on frivolous bets.

Hillard shrugged. "It's for charity. And besides, you can't possibly lose. You've already won the hearts . . . of us all."

His words were, again, spoken quietly, but something in the set cast of Hart's face told her he'd heard, and while Nathan's approval warmed her, it was perhaps more because of embarrassment than pleasure.

"Thank you, sir."

Acton motioned to Hillard, who cast her one last regretful glance before following their host. She was suddenly alone with Hart. Annabelle was some few yards away, her eyes narrowed on Acton's back.

"What next, Miss Coltrane?" Hart asked in a low voice. "Another thirty yards? Or do we simply flay chunks off that contraption's paper hide until there's nothing left but wire? How long do you insist we make spectacles of ourselves? People are *betting* on us, as if we were some Cheapside entertainment."

His disapproval touched a raw nerve. Her cheeks warmed once more, but not with pleasure. She was mortified by his condemnation—once more a guilty girl-child caught wearing her brother's trousers and boots. And with mortification, anger rose.

She had been chided by the Dowager for asking for aid. She had been stymied and stonewalled by every person whom she'd approached seeking information about her brother. Every query she'd made had elicited the same appalled response. "A lady does not ask such things. A lady does not know of such places. A lady does not possibly make such inquiries."

Damn them all! she thought furiously. She had committed no crime by demonstrating her skills and she would not let this glacial-eyed stranger rob her of her simple pleasure in her accomplishments.

"You can bow out at any time," she said.

"I wouldn't dream of disappointing a *lady's* whim."

"Miss Moreland," she called to Annabelle, still standing statue-still nearby. "If you would please throw your champagne glass in the air."

"Excuse me?"

"On my mark, throw it as high into the air as you can," Mercy said tightly. "You *do* know how to throw? Your brother did allow you to toss things on occasion, did he not?"

Annabelle flushed, nodding, and Mercy felt like a cad. It wasn't the child's fault Hart was her brother. "Excuse my manners. If you would, please?"

"Certainly."

Mercy raised the rifle. "Now."

The crystal flute spun twenty feet into the air.

Just as it hit the top of its arc, Mercy fired. Splinters of glass sparkled for an instant against the pure blue sky.

"Here, now," a man called reproachfully. "The wagers hadn't been set yet!"

Hart ignored him. "Throw this, Annabelle," he said, scooping up an abandoned champagne flute and tossing it to his sister. He held out his hand for the rifle and Mercy slapped the butt into his waiting palm.

Before he'd said a word or even shouldered the gun, Annabelle hurled the glass high overhead. The rifle snapped into place. The glass shattered.

Still angry, Mercy cast about for another target, dimly aware of gasps of astonishment rippling through the crowd.

"You there, sir!" she hailed a befuddled-looking youngster standing on the edge of the alley two dozen yards away. Undoubtedly one of Baron Coffey's boys. "You in the deerstalker. Yes, you, sir. Kindly throw your hat."

Roars erupted as the guest scurried to place bets.

Mercy settled the rifle against her shoulder. The young man looked fondly at his hat, sighed, and heaved it into the air.

------◆◆◆------

The dinner had been excellent and filling. For three hours courses were presented in rapid-fire succession: consommé, salmon croquettes, *petits pois* napped with mint, *salade russe*, galantine of pigeon, tournedos of beef, *crème de framboise* and meringues, and finally cheeses served alongside pears and apricots fresh from Acton's quarter-mile-long glasshouse.

As each course had been brought to the table, and each wine decanted and consumed, the conversation had grown more and more laudatory. It all revolved around the afternoon's shooting match.

The women, taking their cue from the gentlemen's approval and the Duchess's indulgent if forced-looking smile, had reservedly adopted Mercy into their sphere. They plied her with questions about her life in Texas and congratulated her on her skill. Mercy could not refrain from spearing Hart with an occasional triumphant glance. He surprised her by accepting her superior smiles with a gleam of amusement.

Now, dinner ended, the women chatted as they waited for the men to reappear, pungent with smoke and after-dinner brandy.

Annabelle drifted toward her, apparently worried that her approach would not be welcome. Mercy silently chided herself for her earlier rudeness to the girl.

"Please, sit by me, Miss Moreland," she asked, rearranging her plum- and turquoise-striped skirt to make room on the chintz-covered settee. With a murmured thank-you Annabelle sank to the edge of the cushion, hands folded gracefully in her lap.

It took Mercy a minute to realize that Annabelle was covertly studying her. For the life of her Mercy could not think of a single topic of conversation to broach with such a paragon. And she could not help returning those sidelong glances. Annabelle was so completely a lady. Her mother would have been transported had she raised so angelic a creature as this.

The other women were sharing intimacies, renewing friendships, while she and Annabelle sat here like roosting chickens waiting for each other to cluck. There had to be something they could say to each other.

"Does your brother ever miss?" Mercy finally asked.

"Miss?" Annabelle echoed.

"His target. He did not miss one shot this afternoon. Not one. No matter what the distance, or the target, or the angle."

"Oh, that. By all accounts he is a rather exceptional shot."

Rather exceptional. Tepid praise from a loving sister. But tepidness was prized in this society. No unbecoming excitement, no disturbing emotions . . . no passion. She turned her attention to Fanny Whitcombe, who, ensconced in the corner of the opposite divan, was staring moonily at a painting of a Madonna and Child hanging on the wall.

"Mrs. Whitcombe," she asked, "does your brother ever miss?"

Fanny loosened her gaze from the picture. Her cornflower-blue eyes swam with tears. "Isn't she lovely?" she whispered.

Lovely? thought Mercy incredulously. The fat Madonna looked as if she wanted to drop the decidedly lascivious-looking child pinching her breast. No, it was not lovely. The thought crossed her mind that Fanny might not be too tightly knit.

"I was wondering about your brother's skill with a rifle," she said. "He's very good."

"Guns are dangerous. No child of mine will ever, ever play with a gun," Fanny said, her lower lip quivering.

Mercy gaped at her, startled by her vehemence. "Indeed not. I wasn't suggesting such, Lady Whitcombe. I was simply wondering if your brother had ever missed his chosen target."

"I wouldn't know, Miss Coltrane." Fanny said, her gaze—and interest—returning to the painting.

Mercy frowned. *Didn't know? He was her brother, wasn't he?* But then, Will was her brother, she thought. And what did she know of him?

"I can answer that, Miss Coltrane." It was Hart's eldest sister, Beryl. She was the most animated of the three sisters. There was also compassion and a hint of sorrow about the wide mouth so like her brother's. "The answer is no."

"No?" Mercy laughed, delighted with such frank pride.

"No." She returned her smile. "He never misses. Never. But then again," she added, "in my memory he has never put himself to the test. He certainly did so this afternoon. You and he were quite the center of attention."

Mercy looked away, unsure whether the comment was meant as a criticism.

"Oh, do excuse me, Miss Coltrane." Beryl hastened forward and sat down, squeezing Annabelle aside as she covered Mercy's hand and gave it a friendly pat. "I in no way meant to imply your behavior was outré. It was most charming. Particularly as you left Hart the field after he'd hit those three guineas you tossed. Quite decent of you."

"I don't think your brother thought so," Mercy replied dubiously. "He seemed quite displeased."

"I know. Wonderful, wasn't it?" Beryl said, her dark eyes aglow. "Hart loathes being patronized."

"I wasn't patronizing him," protested Mercy. "I couldn't possibly have hit those guineas. I publicly admitted that hitting one of them was more luck than skill on my part."

"Hart will never believe it. He suspects you bowed out to salvage his masculine pride. Are you sure you didn't? You're quite an extraordinary marksman." Beryl cocked her head.

"No," Mercy said, scowling. "Believe me, had I been able to prick your brother's conceit, I would have."

Beryl laughed.

"You seem rather pleased at the prospect of your brother's discomfort," Mercy said. What kind of family was this? One sister little more than an automaton, another a teary-eyed daydreamer, and this one . . . ?

"Oh, I am," Beryl agreed, nodding emphatically.

"Beryl," Annabelle interjected in soft, anxious tones. "Should you—"

"Annabelle," Beryl broke in, "Fanny is looking a mite peaked."

Mercy stared. She'd rarely seen a more . . . robust-looking woman than Fanny Whitcombe. "I believe you should escort her to her room."

Annabelle's honey-gold curls bobbed as she swung an alarmed glance in her middle sister's direction. The watery-eyed Fanny blinked at them.

"Fanny, you need to rest. Go to your room," Beryl said in the autocratic tones of an elder sibling. Docilely, Fanny rose to her feet and, aided by a frustrated-looking Annabelle, toddled away.

"Now," Beryl said, smoothing her skirts, "where were we? Oh, yes. Hart. And why I purely enjoy seeing him discomfited. It's quite simple. I haven't seen him display that much emotion in over a decade. And I think it's good for him."

Mercy frowned.

"Hart always used to love a challenge. He enjoyed the game as much as the outcome. And he was an incautious player," Beryl said, her expression reflecting fond memories, "fierce, eager, always demanding more of himself and his opponent. At the risk of sounding forward, a decade or so ago you would have liked Hart. I caught a glimpse of him as he used to be, today. Even if that glimpse was of his willful, autocratic side, I still delighted in seeing it."

She had no right to ask, but she couldn't help herself. "What happened to change him?" She flushed, aware she was being unconscionably forward. "That is . . . he seems a very reserved gentleman."

"He wasn't always so. My father . . . My father left us in conscribed circumstances when Hart was fifteen. He immediately joined the army. He swore it was what he wanted, but I suspect he didn't want to burden our mother with an additional soul to provide for. And then, while Hart was in North Africa, Mother died."

"I'm so sorry," Mercy said.

Beryl studied her a moment before smiling. "I believe you are, my dear," she murmured. "Well, at any rate, Hart was left with three young sisters, a pocketful of debts, and not a sou to our names. He took it all very seriously—and don't imagine for one minute I'm not thankful he did. If it hadn't been for Hart, we'd all still be in that moldering pile of bricks up Nottingham way. But Hart had changed when he came back from North Africa . . . and I don't think it was simply because of his added responsibilities."

"He managed to provide for you at such a young age?" Mercy could not keep from asking.

"Not at once, but soon thereafter," Beryl said. "He went to America shortly after his return. He said he planned to look into some investment opportunities. While there, he inherited his title. He returned after a few years.

"The first thing he did upon returning was repair the Perth estate, Bentwood." She once again gave that odd, crooked smile. "There is nothing so enticing to would-be suitors as a title that has a well-maintained estate attached to it. And Hart loves Bentwood. Yet he has Henley manage it. He rarely even visits. Odd."

"He was in America?" Mercy asked, falling on this bit of information. How much did Beryl know of Hart's activities there?

"Yes." Beryl nodded. "He entered into some partnerships with ranchers in the some of the western territories."

That was certainly one way to put it.

"Your own father is a rancher, is he not?"

"Yes. In Texas," Mercy said.

"Texas is near where Hart was." Beryl's keen gaze rested on Mercy.

"It's a big country, Mrs. Wrexhall."

"Call me Beryl. I insist. And, yes it is big, so Hart says. Not that he talks much about it. Or anything else. Of course, he's never in England much anymore. He developed quite a wanderlust during the last decade. I miss him. But I have been told that you, too, have a brother you miss." She threaded her fingers together in her lap.

"Yes," Mercy said quietly. She did miss Will, she realized. She wanted to find him not only because of her promise and her guilt, she wanted to find him because she missed him. She'd almost forgotten.

Her mother had aspirations for her, but it had been her brother who tried to help her achieve them. And he had done so affectionately. Will had never been jealous of her. He'd been her rival, but she'd never been his.

Instead, he had been the person who'd introduced her to those odd and breathtaking things called arias, who'd sharpened her sense of the absurd with his own discerning and dry wit, who'd gifted her with an appreciation of art and literature. Her eyes felt hot and scratchy.

Yes, she wanted her brother back.

"You know," Beryl said into the ensuing silence, "I miss how Hart used to be. I miss the big brother who teased me and shamelessly embarrassed me in front of his friends. Don't look too surprised, m'dear," Beryl said. "At one time Hart had quite a number of friends. And quite an enjoyable sense of humor." She shook off the melancholy mood. "So now you know why I applaud your ability to touch a spark to what I had given up on as a bed of cold ashes."

"I'm not sure Lord Perth would agree."

"I think *Lord Perth* has had entirely too many people agree with him, and obey him, and tiptoe around him," Beryl said. "Ah, the gentlemen have arrived. We mustn't sit about looking melancholy. Gentlemen do so dislike sentimental moods. I have enjoyed our conversation, Miss Coltrane. We must have another. Soon."

Chapter 9

"How did I get this bullet scar on my shoulder?" Mercy repeated.

The men, having rejoined the women after spending what was, in Hart's opinion, far too long making masculine noises at each other over imported brandy, stopped dead in their conversations. A few actually sidled closer to Mercy. Her pale shoulders and bosom were bathed in the golden glow of gaslight, the puckered scar a pearlescent circle on otherwise flawless flesh.

Was that skin as soft and warm as her hand had been? Could it be softer?

"I wouldn't want to bore you," she said.

"Oh, I'm sure it's a fascinating story. Please tell us," Beryl said.

His own sister, a gossip. Thank God, Annabelle and Fanny had retired. Henley, Hart noticed darkly, was nodding in concurrence from behind his bird-witted wife.

Mercy's amused gaze passed over him. He felt himself tense. Absurd. She wasn't going to expose him. At no time during their shooting match had she even hinted at a previous acquaintance with him. *Acquaintance.* Such a civil word for such brutal knowledge. Ah, well. A hoyden she might be, she was an honest hoyden. She took her promises seriously.

"Yes, oh, do tell us, Miss Coltrane!" Nathan Hillard said. "We lead such tame lives here."

"Now, that's doing it a bit dun, Hillard," Henley objected. "You cannot go about claiming your own existence is 'tame,' Nate. I know you too well."

Hillard smiled at Henley. "Compared to what Miss Coltrane's life has been, I'm sure it is. I have never lived a hundred miles from the nearest town."

"Now, how did you know our ranch was a hundred miles from the nearest town?" Mercy laughed.

Hillard waved away the coy question. "Aren't all Texas ranches a hundred miles from the nearest town?" he asked in mock innocence, drawing laughter from the assembled guests. "Come, now, tell us."

Making a great show of modesty, Mercy smoothed her skirts and demurred, shaking her head, a little smile of apology on her lips. "Well, I don't really think—"

"I'm sure Miss Coltrane would like to forget

whatever unfortunate choices led to her getting herself shot," Hart broke in.

Mercy's bowed head snapped upright. For just an instant her gaze locked with his. Little pinpricks of challenge flashed at him.

"Oh, I don't mind," she said. "I'd be pleased to share the story and 'unfortunate choice.' That is, if you are all certain it's worth your time?"

Assurances poured forth. Hart drummed his fingertips on his chair's arm. The group surrounded Mercy, the gentlemen pulling up chairs for their ladies and taking positions behind them. From the rapt expressions of Baron Coffey's sons Hart expected them to flop like hounds at Mercy's feet. Somehow they managed to restrain themselves.

"Well, then," Mercy began, "I had returned at my father's behest from my Boston school to our ranch, the Circle Bar. It is in one of the most uncivilized sections of the Texas territory, a place known as the Panhandle."

"Uncivilized? There are red Indians?" breathed Beryl.

"Oh, my, yes." Mercy nodded. "But the native population was not nearly so deadly nor so dangerous as our fellow Texans. Greed, I am afraid, will cause men to do any number of despicable things."

He waited for her to spear him with a telling glance, but she continued on, ignoring him. She was, he realized in surprise, not referring to him. He frowned, puzzled.

"What was to become my father's land had been used for years by other ranchers. Instead of purchasing the land themselves they made free use of it to graze their herds. With my father's acquisition of the Circle Bar, the free range was no longer available. They thus determined to drive my father off his ranch."

"How?" a pretty, dark-haired woman asked. Doubtless it was the inquisitive Carr woman.

Mercy lowered her voice dramatically. "By hiring a gang of unscrupulous and murderous blackguards to rustle our cattle and terrorize our wranglers. Indeed, a full eight of our men were wounded at the hands of these scoundrels." Sorrow lowered her voice. "Two died."

A gasp arose from the listeners. Baron Coffey's sons looked as if they were about to dash off in search of dueling pistols.

For a moment it seemed Mercy was not going to continue her story. She sat silently, her knuckles white in her lap, her face stark with remembered tragedy. Hart took a step forward. This had gone on long enough.

"And one of these blackguards shot you, Miss Coltrane?" Nathan Hillard's indignant voice rose above the flurry of consternation. He placed his hand briefly on Mercy's shoulder, a small comforting gesture, and Mercy looked up at him. Hart quelled the desire to strike Hillard's hand from her shoulder. What matter to him if she encouraged the advances of a man nearly old enough to be her father?

"Did they?" Acton repeated Hillard's question.

Mercy had best close her mouth, thought Hart, watching her gaze rest on Hillard's damnably handsome face. There were flies in the room.

"No," she said, returning her attention to her listeners. "The 'bodyguard' my father hired to protect our family shot me."

"What?"

Mercy nodded complacently.

"And *why* would he have done that?" Hart asked dryly.

"Was the bastard—excuse me, Miss Coltrane—was this creature bribed into switching his allegiance?" demanded Hillard.

Hart's fingers ceased drumming. His hands rolled into fists on the arms of the chair. "Well?"

Mercy glanced at him as if just realizing his presence. "Oh, I'm so sorry, Your Near Grace. I didn't mean to hold you breathless."

He held back a retort. The rest of the party were looking at him curiously. A few of the women—including the wretched Beryl—tittered.

"As for your kind concern, Mr. Hillard, having given your suggestion its due consideration I must say I do not believe a switch in loyalties can account for this person's actions."

"Well, why on earth would he have shot you?" asked Acton. Hillard scowled.

"I cannot say, or ever suggest I could *begin* to understand the mind of such a man."

"I should hope not," averred Acton. Hart narrowed his eyes on him. He might have to reevaluate his original approval of Acton's suit for Annabelle. Acton was apparently not nearly as discerning or intelligent as he'd thought.

"But I can tell you how it came about," Mercy said.

"Please do," chorused Baron Coffey and his sons. Even the Countess Marchant nodded encouragingly.

"Let me first say that I love Texas," said Mercy. "It is, to my mind, the most singularly beautiful place on earth. Its skies are wider, its colors richer, its face infinitely more grand and majestic, than anything I have experienced or hope to experience, elsewhere. So it was with unalloyed joy that I answered my father's summons home from my Boston school in the spring of 1872."

"You were in America then, were you not, Hart?" Beryl asked brightly.

"Yes," he said.

Mercy shot him a quick glance and hurried on. "My homecoming was not all happy. My father, in hopes of counteracting the despicable actions of the gang of murderous rogues, had hired what he euphemistically called a 'cattle detective.'" Her dramatic pause had its desired effect. Several of the women made swooning sounds and the men looked properly aghast that such drastic measures had been instituted. Hart's mouth flattened sardonically.

"Yes," she said, her green eyes wide in her winsome face. "He hired a *gunslinger*!"

"Whatever was he like?" It was Beryl again.

Lord, if she leaned any farther out of her chair she would fall out of it.

Mercy sat back. She shrugged. "Nothing special," she said in a bored voice.

"Oh, come now," prompted Beryl. "A man like that! You actually knew him! What was he like?"

"Dirty."

"Oh, do tell us more," another lady pleaded.

Again, Mercy shrugged. "He was tallish, flat flanked and hungry-looking, like a flea-bitten old mountain lion. He had long, lank, greasy hair and a dark skin, whether from the sun or from some questionable bloodline, I never knew."

"What else? What was he *like*?" the Dowager Duchess asked. Really. The entire family exhibited an immoderate interest in lurid tales.

"Harsh," Mercy said. "And cold. And merciless. And ruthless. And heartless. Without compassion or gentleness or wit or humor or—"

"Oh, for Chrissakes!" Hart muttered. Mercy stopped in midrecitation to fix him with a wounded look.

"Forgive me for going on so, but I *was* asked."

"And we appreciate your kindness in relating what must have been a painful episode," said Beryl, shooting him a look of dismay at his outburst. The Dowager Duchess sniffed in his direction.

"Excuse me, madam," Hart choked out. No matter how unfortunate *her* manners, he would not lower himself to being rude. He would not.

"Please continue, Miss Coltrane," Hillard

prompted, once more hovering near Mercy's shoulders.

"If you insist. Well, early one day I decided to go out riding. It was just before dawn. The dark sky stretched overhead, clouds unfurling like scarlet banners on the horizon."

"How lovely!" Beryl breathed.

Mercy looked at her approvingly. "Yes. I thought so too. I saddled my pony and rode toward a way station a few miles west of our ranch house. There I intended to view the sunrise."

"Was that wise?" Hart asked. "I mean, considering your father's situation and all."

Mercy contrived to look sad and lovely in her consternation. "No, Lord Hart. It was not wise. But I was no more than a child and a girl child at that and I had been so long from home. Children and women are impulsive, sentimental creatures, you know," she said modestly and apologetically—not that he believed she was either. Not for a minute.

What a pile of— Several of the men in the room glowered at him.

"We do not always act with the strength of purpose and single-mindedness you men do," she said.

"Just so," huffed Major Sotbey.

"I know now it was ill advised of me, but I went. There, while lost in a moment of divine reverie, I was set upon by a loathsome brigand!"

Reverie. Hart's jaw muscle started to work reflexively. The bold-faced little liar. She'd sneaked off to smoke a cigar she'd stolen from her daddy's office.

"The Lord alone knows what he might have done had I not been able to fight him," she said in low tones. "Several times I nearly made it to my stalwart little pony. But each time the monster managed to take hold of my person and haul me back.

"My strength was waning, but not my will. Whether I would have prevailed, I am not sure, though I venture to say that a woman's reverence for her chastity is a mighty impetus."

"Hear, hear!" bellowed Sotbey. Mercy smiled at him modestly.

"Our struggle was intense, we were locked in mortal combat, time was suspended. And then"— her voice dropped even lower—"the *gunslinger* appeared!

"The outlaw pulled me in front of him, fearful of the great multinotched revolver in the gunslinger's hand."

"Multinotched?"

Mercy gravely nodded her head. "One notch for every man he'd killed."

"And this gunslinger had many notches?" the Duchess asked.

"The handle was ready to drop off, the thing was so scored with notches."

"Jesus!" Hart muttered. She was incorrigible! To his astonishment he found himself suddenly hard pressed not to laugh. He hadn't heard such a heap of rubbish in years, and that it was being spoon-fed to this sophisticated company by a brat from Texas . . . ! His lips twitched.

Mercy's glance darted to meet his. There was an unholy amusement in her green eyes. Unholy and horrible . . . and horribly inviting.

"Exactly," she said piously. "I prayed, too, Mr. Perth. I had to, because I knew the gunslinger had no conscience. Like a dog set on a scent, he was single-minded in his course. He wanted only one thing. *Blood.* And I wasn't at all sure he cared whose blood it was."

He closed his eyes. If he listened to much more of this he would either laugh or swear.

"I know, Perth, it is horrible," she said, her eyes dancing. "It gets even worse."

His eyes snapped open. She'd called him "Perth"—without mockery or sarcasm. His name on her lips was disarming.

"Oh, no!" gasped the Dowager.

"Yes." Mercy's attention turned back to the others. "The monster who held me started backing out of the cabin, holding me in front of him, using me as a shield. I could tell he was afraid. And well he should have been. I have never seen a more frightening sight than that gunslinger's eyes as he looked at us." Abruptly, her voice lost its theatrical tone, trailing off.

She *had* been frightened, thought Hart, feeling the old familiar chill creep back into his heart. And she was reliving that fright now. No amount of playacting could bleed the color from her cheeks like that.

Had she really thought he would have killed her just to ensure he would collect a bounty? The thought ate at him. He fought the impulse to stand up and deny it.

"What was it like?"

"Like he found us . . . interesting," Mercy said in a soft, pensive monotone. "That's why it was so frightening. He did not look angry or fierce. He looked like he was trying to work out the pieces of a riddle and was not overly concerned whether he found an answer."

What a prime fool he'd been the other night, thinking she'd sought him out because of his reputed dispassion. His manner frightened her, disgusted her. And yet for her brother's sake she'd still sought an interview.

"And then?" someone asked.

"And then?" Mercy echoed. Her lips had parted a bit. She looked pensive, as though staring into the past. "He shot me."

"Dear God," someone murmured.

"Was he trying to kill you?"

"No." Her answer was prompt. The breath Hart hadn't even been aware he was holding left his lungs in a low whoosh. "No. He was saving my life. If he hadn't shot me, the man who held me would have dragged me from the cabin, still using me as a shield. Once to his horse, he would have got his own gun and shot the gunslinger and—and taken me away."

He stared at his white-knuckled fists braced on the chair's arms.

"Then the blackguard was simply saving his own life," Hillard said, once more grazing her shoulder with his gloved fingertips. A small yearning rose in Hart.

Mercy revived herself with a little shake of her head. "Perhaps," she allowed, and after a glance at him added, "Still, the Lord works through mysterious agents. Perhaps he was my guardian angel." She smiled and suddenly the chill he always lived with retreated, shrinking back, leaving him free to return her smile.

"What happened next?" Beryl asked.

Mercy laughed. "Does there need to be a next?"

Beryl blushed.

"The gunslinger shot the man who held me and then he rode off. I believe he went after the rest of the gang. I do not know if he found them or arrested them or drove them off. Whatever, we were never threatened again."

"He just left you there?" Acton asked, appalled.

"He went back to the ranch for my father, who arrived shortly thereafter with a wagon and took me away. It was a slow recovery, but luckily the shot missed any bone and vital organs. So"—she sat back—"that is my tale and how I have come to bear this scar. I pray, do not look so distressed. No permanent injury was sustained."

"No permanent injury! But, m'dear, you have been *marred*," the Duchess said.

"No, Lady Acton," Hart said under his breath. "She has been wounded, but she has certainly not been marred."

Beryl was the only one who heard him.

Chapter 10

*H*art came awake with a gasp. He heaved himself halfway up, bracing himself on his forearms. For a moment he knelt, head bowed, lungs working like bellows. He sank back on his haunches, wrapping his arms tightly around himself.

He should have expected this. He'd learned the hard lesson long ago; whatever peace he counterfeited was subject to violation. For eleven years he'd struggled to obliterate the bitter trophies he'd garnered in long-dead wars.

Someday he would, he resolved grimly. In the meantime he *would not* succumb to these nameless horrors. He would purge this rank cowardliness from his soul.

He stumbled to his feet, looking blindly around the dark room, searching for something to focus on, something he could use to regain the rudiments of self-possession.

"Control yourself, you flinching coward," he

muttered, half in self-condemnation, half in pleading. More than simple humiliation striped his soul. Someday he feared he would succumb to his panic and scream. And once he began screaming, he would never stop.

He stared at the gray patch of illumination on the far wall, forcing himself to mentally measure the window's frame, to give a name to the frost in the corner of the glass panes. He refused to acknowledge his spasming muscles or the invisible fist clenching around his bowels or the constriction in his throat.

He could, after all, still breathe. The thought offered some small assurance and he fell on it gratefully. Control. It was the only weapon he had.

After years of practice he should, he thought with a splinter of the blackest humor, be an expert at self-domination. But it was impossible to obliterate something without an image or a sound, but which was instead a maelstrom of impressions commandeered from his history, the featureless essence of every demon he'd ever known.

He pressed his head between his palms for a instant before angrily snatching them away. He was craven, giving in to such despicable weakness. Especially now, he jeered, when he could least afford it. For God's sake, these were nothing more than nameless phantasms.

He spun around and jerked his clothes from the tallboy. He hauled on his breeches, thrust his arms into the sleeves of a cambric shirt, and noosed his throat with a cravat. Grabbing his traveling coat from atop his trunk, he headed out the door, knowing from the rhythm of his bootheels on the thick Aubusson carpet that he was running.

———————◆———————

The sky was a featureless gray blanket. Fog slipped between rain-slicked tree trunks and nestled in the low places along the trail. Hart leaned over the withers of the green broke hunter, racing him forward, shredding the tranquil pools of mist. The gelding sawed at the bit, its breathing harsh and labored in the stillness, fighting Hart for control.

He fought back. He spurred the horse, pushing it until foam flecks from its open mouth splattered his jacket and sweat from its sides soaked his thighs. Only then, only when he felt its huge muscles trembling more than his own, did he relent, dropping his hands and allowing the beast to stumble into a walk. He groaned suddenly, sinking forward on the saddle and pressing his forehead against its great sodden neck.

"I'm sorry," he whispered.

The horse blew gustily, tossing its head and rolling its eyes as it skittered on its rear legs.

"Evil creature," Hart muttered. "I've half killed you and still you'd rather run yourself to death than be thought a simple pleasure mount."

Grimly, he waited, staring at the dark line of trees ahead of him, steeling himself for the anxiety to return. There was no running from demons that rode pillion.

And then, amid the silence of anticipation, as his heart thudded in a thick, stilted cadence, he heard a soft swishing sound. He peered forward.

A short distance away, just cresting the rise of the trail, a feminine figure limped toward him, slashing irritably at the grass with a naked branch. The first spangles of sunlight crept along her shoulders, backlighting her tumbled hair and turning it into a molten nimbus about her shadow-obscured features. He cocked his head, listening. A tuneless little hum wafted to him on the chill predawn breeze.

Mercy Coltrane.

She lifted her head and spied him. Humiliation drained the blood from his lean cheeks. Would that God had spared him this, at the very least. But God did not spare weaklings.

"Have you seen my horse?" she demanded, stepping forward. Immediately she stopped, wincing.

He sucked in a lungful of air, concern for her well-being harrying the gibbering phantoms that crowded his thoughts. "Why are you limping?" he asked hoarsely. "Are you hurt?"

"No, no," she assured him. "I'm fine. Mostly. But these wretched riding boots were not made for walking. I am sure I will have blisters the size of guineas. *Have* you seen my horse?"

He relaxed visibly and she grimaced, a wry, puckish contortion of her lovely mouth and dark straight brows. She looked so damned innocent, standing there with her head tilted and her hair loose on her shoulders, unaware of the demons that roiled beneath his surface calm, clamoring for voice. He ironed his face of all expression.

She tapped her foot, gazing at him in exasperation. He hadn't exasperated anyone for a long time. Frightened sometimes, intimidated on occasion, antagonized perhaps . . . but not this simple exasperation. It was novel to be treated so casually. It was soul healing.

"Well? Cat got your tongue? Or have you seen so many riderless horses this morning you are trying to determine which one was mine?" She impudently cocked a brow.

And as he stared at her, saw the negligent manner with which she accepted his appearance—though he knew his hair was rumpled and his face stained with tension—every remnant of the boy Hart had been answered the siren call of her youth and ease, even as the man he was responded to her profound and uncontrived womanliness.

Why, he asked himself, why now must he admit to a desire that had grown from the first moment he'd seen her? Perhaps, he allowed with a sad inward smile, he was simply too exhausted to deny it anymore. What did it matter if he could no longer do himself the kindness of a lie? It changed nothing.

She was studying him, a touch of concern coloring her expression. Or was it wariness? Perhaps their isolation was just now occurring to her. The thought scored him with bitter amusement. *Too late, Miss Coltrane,* he thought even as he asked, "What happened?"

Her consternation disappeared, replaced by chagrin. She sighed and tossed her branch away. "I wish I knew. I was . . ." She peeked up at him and drew a deep breath. "I lost my seat and fell off."

He laughed, amazed not only that she'd wrung laughter from him—now, of all times—but that amusement could coexist with desire, not superseding it but instead augmenting it, adding piquancy to his carnal thoughts. And carnal they were.

His hooded gaze traveled over her, noting the jacket molding the swell of her breasts, the way her riding skirt cupped her pert bottom. Thank God, she could not know the course of his thoughts, or how his body tightened in response to her low, delicious laughter.

She grinned, pleased she'd made him laugh. So easily, he mocked himself, did she shred each tether of the self-control he'd plaited to tie himself to sanity.

"I don't expect you'll keep this a secret, will you?" she asked impishly.

He smiled lazily and dismounted. Impossible not to tease her.

"I didn't think so." She tossed her head and her hair rippled across her shoulder, thick and glossy.

He wanted to take a silken fistful and roll it in

his palm. He wanted to feather a flake of mud from her cheek and then trace the sweet curve of her throat with his finger.

He wanted to taste her.

His desire confounded him. He had never used sex as an analgesic. In North Africa, in New Mexico, in Texas, he had known men who celebrated their survival in the most elemental fashion. He'd never been one of them.

Death, whether served or avoided, left him feeling overwhelmingly empty, with nothing left in him to give and, more, nothing within him capable of receiving. But now, as he looked at Mercy Coltrane, desire surged through his body, splintering the still, cold center he'd kept such vigilant guard over.

He tore his gaze from her quizzical gold-green eyes. He would touch her if he looked any longer. He would do more. He did not need to test his control. He was tested enough as it was. Though, he realized with astonishment, the gibbering panic had receded. It was no more than a low thrum of anxiety now. He looked about, anywhere but at her, and finally realized what he saw.

"What about your groom?" he asked. "Where is he?"

"What groom?" she mumbled, averting her eyes.

"What—?" He frowned. "Are you without an escort?"

"I go riding every morning." She spoke defiantly—to the ground. "Without a groom. I couldn't stand to have someone shadow my every move." She glanced up and immediately waved an ungloved hand at him, forestalling his protest. Her fingers looked raw. They would be cold. "Lady Acton knows, so you needn't look so disapproving. She's accepted it as part of my American eccentricity."

He must have made some disapproving sound, lost in contemplation of her hands, for she sniffed. "I have been discreet. I slip out a bit early so I'll be back, safely decked out in a morning gown, by the time your exalted friends awake."

"A bit early?" Hart demanded, angry that she had so little care for her person, let alone her reputation. "It's not yet six o'clock. If I hadn't chanced upon you, you would be walking for hours yet. Though this may not be Texas, there are still dangers awaiting foolish, impulsive, and unattended young women."

"This was an unfortunate accident. If you think I shall stay in my room, trembling over potential harm that might come my way as soon as I pop my nose out the door, you can think again. The only danger facing me now is the danger that these blisters may render me incapable of dancing at Acton's ball," she said. "Besides, why should one waste a perfectly nice morning lying in bed just because something unpleasant *might* happen? Apparently you haven't."

Her words struck too close to home. "Are you really interested in what would keep me in bed?"

he asked in a low voice. She flushed and looked away.

"That was unnecessary," he said, cursing himself for treating her so unfairly. "Forgive me. We need to get back. Here, I'll toss you up."

"Onto your horse?"

"That was the idea, yes."

She eyed the fidgeting gelding dubiously. "And then what?"

"I'll lead you back to the house."

"If you say so."

She hobbled toward the horse and grabbed the saddle's lip. He bent and held his hand out for her foot. As soon as she lifted her hem, the gelding shied, snorting and dancing, its ears flattening against its elegant head.

"I don't think he likes women any more than his rider does," Mercy mumbled, dropping her skirt and backing away.

"Why ever would you say that?" Hart asked in genuine surprise, snapping the reins to settle the evil-minded brute.

"Nothing. Just an impression. Forget I said it."

"I like women very well."

"If you say so."

"I *dislike* that phrase. Particularly coming from you. It reeks of insincerity."

"Sorry. Didn't mean to offend you. Perhaps it's just *me* you—and your horse—don't like."

"You haven't offended me," he said. "You are simply wrong. I admire women. I admire you. I just—"

"You do?" Her incredible eyes widened. They shone with unfeigned pleasure. Pleasure that he'd said he admired her? What an extraordinary notion. Sleep must have deprived him of his wits.

"Certainly," he said, leading the horse back to her side. "You're honest. You're intelligent. And your concern for your brother—even if misplaced—is very laudable."

"Oh." Disappointment permeated the utterance.

What did she want to hear? That he had sat at that damned party last night straining to hear what she might next say? That he had waited for her to look at him so he might drink of her regard like a moonstruck lad?

She had turned away from him, her head bowed as she fussed with the saddle. The back of her neck looked downy and vulnerable. He cleared his throat. "Shall we try once more?"

They ended trying not once but half a dozen more times, and each time the fractious gelding shied away from her. Finally she turned around, hands on her hips, chin angled purposefully. "You will have to take me up with you. I simply cannot walk and he will simply not be ridden by a woman."

"All right," Hart agreed as the gelding bared its teeth and feinted once more at Mercy. He swung into the saddle and held his hand out. She hesitated an instant before taking it. He'd been right, her skin was rough and cold. She sprang upward as he lifted. He caught her about the waist and settled her sideways to him in the cradle of his lap.

Her bottom snuggled intimately against him. The subtle scent of rain and ferns, underscored by soap, filled his nostrils. She was warm and sweetly curved.

Thus when he nudged the gelding forward, preparing himself for a very long ride, he found a very different brand of panic playing havoc with his body than the one that had chased him from his room.

"How did you lose your horse?" he asked finally, breaking the silence after several miles. They were within sight of the house now and yet he could not endure another moment of this focused intimacy.

He had to distract himself from the feel of her, each step rocking her bottom softly into the juncture of his thighs, the delicate strength of her shoulder blades pressing into his chest, the scent of her. It did not matter that she was enveloped in blameless wool worsted. He reacted as if naked flesh were on his lap.

And more important, it was obvious that she was as uncomfortable in his arms as he was in holding her—though the reasons for their distress could not be more dissimilar; hers having been born of modesty, his of lust. But still he wanted to relieve her distress and found in that desire proof of his own hypocrisy. For though he'd questioned her lack of caution in her relations with men, he himself needed to erase that caution when she exercised it against him.

"Mercy?" he prompted, a hint of desperation in his tone. "What happened?"

She glanced at him sidelong. "I think it was a poacher," she murmured.

He frowned. "What do you mean?"

"There was a shot. My horse bolted and I fell off. I"—she peeked at him from beneath the sable fringe of her lashes—"I really wasn't attending where I was going."

"No one came to see what had happened?"

She shook her head and her cool, satiny hair brushed his lips. "I called but no one answered. I expect once they realized I was all right, they ran off."

"Perhaps," he murmured, considering her words. Poachers? Except for the birds and game Acton released himself, the countryside this close to London was hunted out.

"It doesn't matter, does it? No real harm was done"—she shot him a wicked glance—"as long as I can dance, which I am determined to do even if I have to do so barefoot. I'm sure it's only what you'd expect from me."

He had no answer for that, and she was silent a moment before twisting around and solemnly meeting his eyes. The gelding, quick to take affront, danced sideways. She braced herself with a hand on his chest. He could feel each finger distinctly; her left thumb above his heart, her little finger branding his nipple through his cotton shirt. His mouth went dry.

"I . . . I want to thank you," she said. "You've been far kinder than I deserve. I cannot think why I am unable to resist the temptation to provoke you."

"Can you not?" he murmured. Her palm rode the rapidly accelerating rise and fall of his chest.

"No. And," she admitted with the grudging grace of duty, "I realize that your suggestions are made for what you consider to be my own good."

"I am all blameless benevolence," he returned, watching the play of emotions flicker across her face, suspicion quickly chased away by amusement.

"I expect I really shouldn't have invited you into the library," she confessed in a hushed voice.

"No." He bent his head to better hear her. The movement brought him very close. He could discern each faint inhalation, see the dusting of light cinnamon-colored freckles on the highest curve of her cheek.

"And I shouldn't have pressed an acquaintance you were unwilling to acknowledge." Another breathy apology.

Her lips were slightly parted and he caught a glimpse of the dark interior of her mouth. His eyelids slipped lower, masking the intensity of his attraction and the object of his interest. It was an insufficient ploy, for he could see her eyes widen as she discerned his intent.

"No," he answered.

"I have been unfair," she whispered, staring at him, her eyes inches from his, wonder and surprise commingled in their bright depths. And yet, and yet . . . she didn't draw away.

"Doubtless," he said, and touched his lips to hers. Her mouth shivered beneath his. "This," he said, drawing his head back, "is most ill advised."

"Doubtless," she whispered, still staring into his eyes. Foolish girl. It was her undoing.

He twined one arm about her waist, pulling her closer. With his other hand he cradled the back of her head, tipping her face and guiding her unresisting mouth to him.

"And most dangerous," he muttered, covering her lips again.

Chapter 11

She should say something, she thought dazedly when Hart finally lifted his head from hers. Something sophisticated and brittle and dismissive. Something that would prove to him that she could play these games as well as he. That was what this was about, was it not? she thought. A lesson for the naive American? That had been what he had meant in saying this was dangerous. . . .

But for the life of her she could not say a word. She was entirely lost in the sensations he aroused. Helplessly, she blinked up into his aquamarine eyes; cool, unplumbed. He stared down at her, his face an unreadable mask, only his flushed throat any clue that he had been affected at all by their kiss.

She opened her mouth to speak. On the small movement his gaze fell like a predator's. She heard the slight catch of his breath, saw the flare of his

bold nostrils, felt a shiver tighten the chest muscles
beneath her hand.

"God," he breathed, and then he was kissing
her again, his mouth warm and demanding, his
arms pulling her ever closer.

She *was* naive, she thought, twining her hands
around his neck and clinging there weakly. For
those few kisses stolen from shy cowboys had
never anticipated such . . . *hunger.* His ardor
frightened her, but more, it excited her, it inspired
in her an answering appetite.

With each caress of his restless hands over her
breasts and belly, she learned the power of her
own desire. She was entirely lost to the wanting he
awoke, and when his mouth opened over hers, co-
herent thought fled.

She did not refuse him, he thought in dim
amazement. And whether she clung to him because he had left her nothing else to cling to, or
because she wanted this, he was grateful. For with
each moment he pressed her closer and kissed the
sweet, plush velvet lips, she caught fire from his
heat, meeting his entreaty with her own, arching
herself into him, cupping the back of his head in
her hands and holding his mouth to hers.

Her lips parted and his own passionate response to such munificence made him dizzy. He
swung his leg over the saddle and, clamping her
tightly to him, slipped with her to the ground. And
still, he tried to bring her closer, arching posses-
sively over the sweet body straining up into his,
discovering the only way to do so was to invade

her warm, moist mouth with his tongue. So sweet, so passionate—

Tentatively, her tongue brushed his. He delved hungrily, begging more with tongue and lip and hands. She moaned softly. It was a tiny sound, but one of abandonment, and it awoke his fast-fleeing conscience as nothing else could have done. He drew his head back, staring down at her flushed face, the crescent of lashes feathering her cool pink cheeks.

She had given herself entirely to him, trusting him. No matter what surcease passion offered, he would not take more than what she should offer, regardless of what he needed. Abruptly, he set her on her feet.

She blinked, disoriented and lip-swollen, her hair streaming down her back, undone by the hands that trembled at his sides and itched to be buried once more in that cool satin. He forced himself to stand acquiescent. He would not embrace her again.

"Oh, my," she whispered.

"Indeed," he answered, amazed he'd been so carried away by what was really no more than a simple kiss, a few less-than-chaste embraces; uncertain of how she would interpret the clipped sound of that single word.

"So, you've proven your point," she said, her eyes averted, her cheeks blooming with bright crimson roses. "You were right."

"What do you mean?"

"I am as common as God can make a maid,

and a maid I am, it would seem, only because of a lack of opportunity." His demonstration of how easily he could effect her abandonment hurt, and she wanted to return the favor. Her words found their mark. He paled visibly. "Your point is well taken, sir."

"And what point is that?" he demanded in a rough voice.

"That I am unfit to be my own guardian. That I, most especially, must guard myself as I am at the mercy of unladylike impulses. Because, as you have very skillfully demonstrated, I am no lady."

"Unladylike?" He sounded genuinely confused.

"Yes. I am sure"—she bit back a sob—"I am sure that your sisters never reacted so to a man's kiss."

"I wouldn't have any idea," he answered, bewildered.

"Well, I do. They wouldn't even *feel* the things I did when kissing you. They aren't the things a *nice* woman feels."

"Are you sure your horse didn't upend you on your head?"

"Don't mock me! I have read many books on deportment and—and other feminine concerns and they all agree; a *nice* woman does not feel excited by a man's . . . physical displays." And now her eyes did fill with tears. Angrily, she dashed them away, facing him with as much dignity as she could muster, seeing how she could not ignore the shape of his mouth or forget the texture of it.

He shook his head. There was a touch of bitter sadness in his pale eyes, a hint of despair and yearning. How had she ever thought his face expressionless? Subtle emotions played constantly across his features. One merely had to attend.

He reached over, spanning the short distance between them, and she thought he meant to take her in his arms again. She would have gone; indeed, she swayed forward to meet the anticipated embrace. But he only tipped her chin up with a single finger.

"You are wholly lovely and uncontrived," he said, finally understanding. She'd thought he'd kissed her to teach her a lesson, to illustrate her vulnerability, and that she'd revealed instead a defect in herself, a baseness. He could not allow her to be so misled. "Any sane man would be ecstatic to know he was able to kindle in you more than curiosity with his kiss. Being a lady does not mean being dead to pleasure, Mercy, no matter what fantasies are being perpetuated by society's scribblers."

When she did not reply, he dropped his hand and stepped back, casting a glance in the direction of the house. He did not have time to convince her and he could see from the flush still staining her cheeks that she was unconvinced, clinging stubbornly to some mistaken notion that equated passionlessness with feminity.

Frustrated, he tugged on the bridle, forcing the gelding closer. Soon someone would look out his window and see them and he would have ruined

Mercy in truth. For whatever his assurances as to the naturalness of her response, he knew too well that society was *un*natural and it was according to society's rules that Mercy had chosen to live—for whatever time. They had to hurry.

"You have nothing to upbraid yourself for. *I* am entirely at fault here, Mercy," he said. "Whatever has happened, I have precipitated. I have taken complete advantage of a situation in which you should have been able to rely on me to act the gentleman. I beg your forgiveness."

She looked at him in surprise. "You're accepting all the responsibility for our . . . for my—"

"My kissing you, yes," he said tersely as a light blinked on in one of the upper windows of the Actons' house.

"Very noble," she said, scowling. "And what of my part in our kiss? I was the"—she searched for a word and found one and it did not appear to make her very happy—"the unwitting victim?"

His chest tightened. "If that is how you perceive it," he answered gravely.

"It is not!" she exclaimed. "I am many things, Hart, but I am not unwitting! I kissed you back, in case you hadn't noticed."

He stared at her, an incautious joy awakening within. "Why, yes, I believe I did."

"Good." She colored as soon as she'd said the word and he badly wanted to sweep her back into his arms. "I am an equal partner in what transpired here—ill advised as you assured me it was. I never said I wanted to be a lady, you know." She made a great show of straightening her skirts. "Now," she sniffed, "I suggest we forget about trying to determine who was more culpable."

He nodded, smiling. "Agreed. We'd best be back to the house before our absence is noted." He swung into the saddle and turned, offering her his hand, and when she'd given hers into his care, he lifted her in front of him.

She was a cheat, she thought, and as common as she'd always suspected she was and Hart had just tried to convince her she was not. Because she knew full well that except for these next few minutes, Hart Moreland would never hold her again. And she wanted to hoard whatever sensations she could from these brief moments, because she had never felt so much, so intensely, before and she did not expect she ever would again.

So she lay back against the hard wall of his chest, burrowing between the open flaps of his coat, and, sighing softly, turned her head. The warmth of his body toasted her cheek through his thin cambric shirt. His heart beat strongly beneath her ear. She snuggled closer still, and his arm closed more securely about her.

"As soon as we're back we'll forget it happened, shall we?" she asked.

"Oh," he replied quietly, "I don't think I can promise that."

Mercy thanked Brenna for her aid in unbuttoning the evening gown and shooed her out the bedroom door. She was too stimulated to sleep but too preoccupied to chat with the maid. She was a trifle bemused that Brenna had sat up waiting for her. It was late, well past midnight, and she'd been one of the last to leave the party.

She had been an exemplary guest. Even the ever-exacting Lady Acton could not have found fault with her demeanor. She had been entertained and been entertaining. She'd been approachable but not available. She'd been quick witted without being witty. And she'd smiled. Lord, how she'd smiled. At everyone. Her cheeks ached.

She sighed, her shoulders drooping. She only hoped Hart Moreland noticed her sophistication, she thought, self-congratulations fading away in a tide of wry honesty, because she certainly hadn't proven her savoir faire to herself. All day she'd thought of little other than his passionate kiss, his long fingers stroking her body through the layers of clothes; his mouth warm and . . .

Impatiently, she tossed her shawl over a chair and, uncoiling her hair from its loose chignon, wandered over to the vanity. She sat down and slipped off her shoes.

She had tried so very hard to match Hart's presumed insouciance with her own. After all, what was a kiss to a man of the world, particularly one like Hart? So she'd flirted and laughed, hoping Hart would not realize how much that kiss had shaken her. But Hart Moreland knew what he had done. It was there in the amused and all-too-knowing smile she had tried so hard to ignore.

And then, shortly after dinner, as she sparkled with all the brightness the artifice and skills at her disposal allowed, he'd absented himself, leaving her to the company she'd so painstakingly beguiled. As soon as he had left, everything had gone flat, the spirited conversation had become brittle, the gaiety seemed forced. Even Nathan Hillard's urbane wit had failed to charm.

She sat absently brushing her hair out, her thoughts troubled. There had been an echo of Hart's ardor in the way Nathan had watched her. His intimate smile had been a world different from Hart's. Hart's smile had been amused and rueful, Nathan Hillard's had been warm with approval and tenderness. . . .

Nathan Hillard was a handsome and elegant man. Her mother would have found him to be the perfect catch. She shivered and set the brush down. In doing so she tipped over an envelope propped against the bottom of the vanity mirror.

Casually, she turned it over. Her name inscribed across its thick, creamy surface caught her eye. She ripped open the end of the envelope, pulled the single sheet free, and unfolded it. There was no salutation.

I need money, Mercy. Badly. I am in trouble I can't extricate myself from. Do this thing for me, Dearest Sister, get me some cash, at least 5,000 pounds. Don't fail me, I'm begging you. It could not be more important. These men are brutes. They'll stop at nothing. I can give you a week—I think I can convince them to let me have that long to come up with the cash. I'll contact you then.

Will

Blindly, she reached for the discarded envelope. She turned it over, searching for some clue as to its point of origin. Nothing.

Her mind raced. The other notes had been requests for small sums. This was awful. The handwriting was little more than chicken scratches, the sentences jumbled as though written by a frightened hand. Even the affectionate "Dearest Sister" sounded forced, unlike Will.

Hart had been wrong. This wasn't just some young man kicking over the traces. Will was in serious trouble. It sounded as if his life was in danger.

And she'd forgotten him.

She covered her face with her hands, shocked and guilt ridden by how easily she'd lost sight of her reason for being here. *You've been so caught up in Hart Moreland, you forgot about Will.*

She stumbled up from the vanity, mortified. She had to find Will before he was hurt. What if he could not convince these men to grant him a week in which to come up with the money? She had to do something. Now. She could not sit safely in Acton's mansion eating petit fours and playing charades while her brother was in danger of being hurt, possibly even killed.

She spun about, as if in searching the luxurious apartment she would find an answer. She had tried every other avenue she could think. She could not go to Acton. Even if he was willing to brave his mother's disapproval on her behalf, tucked away here on his estate what could he offer her besides consolation? She didn't need consolation. She needed help.

She needed Hart.

The thought of breaking her promise choked her. She smothered the guilt. She couldn't allow herself the luxury of fine principles. She *wouldn't* allow anything to put her brother at risk.

She cracked open the door to the hall and peeked outside. There was no one in the dimly lit corridor. Everyone was asleep. She took a deep breath, summoning her resolution. Hart's room was at the end of the passage, the corner room.

She slipped through the doorway and crept the length of the passage. Her heartbeat drummed in her ears, half in anticipation of being discovered, half in dread of what Hart would do when he discovered what she wanted.

She found his door and grasped the brass knob. It turned noiselessly. Unlocked. Silently, she stole inside.

Accustoming herself to the disparate lighting, she blinked. Bright flames cavorted in the hearth, pitching tall shadows against the walls. The rest of the room was steeped in darkness. She cast about, looking for Hart.

A giant ebony four-poster stood empty sentinel in the midst of the cavernous room. Not a ripple marred the dark brocade counterpane. On a black walnut bench at its foot stood an open trunk. A few articles of clothing lay across the upraised lid. Her gaze moved on to a small battered valise, a scarred pair of boots, a few men's toiletries on a bureau. So little accompanied him on his travels. And there, against the far wall, in the deepest shadowed corner of the room, lay a neatly folded blanket and pillow.

Odd. She frowned, taking a step forward.

The smell of sandalwood and brandy alerted her an instant before she saw him, emerging from the point where the fire's light and night's blackness converged. A tensile figure in an unbuttoned white dress shirt and black trousers, an unfastened white tie draped around his strong throat, broad shoulders and narrow hips, hair that could absorb light or reflect it, moon-dusk skin, and crystalline eyes. Had he been standing there all along, watching her with that inimitable gaze? The thought made her retreat.

"What the hell are you doing here?" he asked.

Chapter 12

He couldn't believe she was here, in his room, in the middle of the night, in the house of his potential brother-in-law. She had to know she risked his sister's future by coming here. One blemish, one whispered transgression associated with his name, and Annabelle could bid adieu to James Trent, Duke of Acton.

He shook his head, trying to clear his thoughts. He wished he'd not indulged in so much liquor after leaving Acton's dinner table. Acton's table? Who was he fooling? He'd been leaving Mercy Coltrane and her smiles and her soft, round American accent and the fact that neither was for him. They had been for Nathan Hillard.

The liquor may have clouded his mind, but there was nothing blurred about the jealousy searing his imagination. Nothing ephemeral about the stark hunger her kiss had bequeathed.

And now she stood here, a slender figure in a

gown that melded with the shadows, her back pressed to the closed door of his bedroom suite, her face veiled by darkness.

She didn't say a word. He could hear her anxious breathing. He stared at her, damning himself for not throwing her out.

"What?" His low voice carried across the room. A log snapped in the hearth and a shower of embers briefly illuminated her face. She looked intent, determined. A woman who would have what she wanted.

But she doesn't want you. The thought goaded him and he responded to his own treacherous longing with anger. Damn her for making him want her, for making him willing to risk Annabelle's future for a few minutes with her.

"I've come about the offer I made the other night," she said.

He laughed, an unpleasant sound. "Did you come to see what you thought to hire?" he asked, his tone harsh, a bitter smile unfinished on his face. "Isn't that the American way? Never buy a pig in a poke."

"No," she whispered, stricken.

Too raw? Too aggressive? Wasn't that what the Coltranes had wanted from him? Aggression? Violence? Was that not what he was all about? Had always been about?

"Yeah. Yes," he said. He jerked his shirttails from his trousers, yanked the remaining buttons free of their holes, his eyes never leaving her face. He pulled his shirt open, exposing his chest, and turned, his arms held rigidly out from his body, palms turned up, presenting himself for inspection.

He wanted to look into her eyes. Because he wanted to know what he'd see when she looked at *his* body. Appreciation? Indifference? Contempt?

But he was as cowardly as he was hypocritical. Even as he stood thus—an animal being considered for purchase—he was afraid. Afraid there would be no approval. Afraid he'd fail her appraisal. Afraid Hillard was the better candidate. Afraid she'd go away.

He was nearly twenty-eight years old and he had had sex so seldom, he could remember each coupling in intricate detail. Twenty-eight years and his near celibacy had never been more than a mild irritation. But ever since having seen her, the irritation had opened into a gnawing wound, a deep gash he couldn't knit back together.

"I'm not here for . . . I'm here because you have to help me. *Please*, Hart."

Her obvious fear plunged him into sobriety. He buried his ardor, banked it deeply, a sizzling ember in a bed of snow. He turned, unwilling to have her see how her words hurt him. Of course she had not come for him. Of course.

"Forgive me," he said. He laughed humorlessly. "I seem to say those words to you on an hourly basis."

He heard her swallow. She came forward into the flickering firelight. Her expression was uncertain, her movements tentative. Her hair hung in a ruby-glazed cloak about her shoulders.

"I'm not going to hurt you. I'm not going to come any closer to you," he said, shame making his voice hoarse. Fool. Regardless of the sweet, budding ardor with which she'd returned his kiss this morning, she was as unfamiliar with lust as he had lately grown accustomed to it. "What do you want?"

"It's Will."

"I told you, forget him."

"I've had a note from him. He needs money." She held a sheet of paper out, suspended from her fingertips.

He took the thing, read it, and returned it. "So? He needs money. I can't tell you how many of these letters I've read."

"From whom?"

He ignored the question. "It does no good to pay them. There's always another letter. Another entreaty. It's a shakedown, Mercy," he said, suddenly tired.

"This one is different. Desperate. He's in trouble. I know it." Her tone was pleading.

"Forget him, Mercy." He took her arm and turned her back to the door, propelling her before him. "Have a fine time here, enjoy the countryside. Go to London, take in a play—"

"Damn you." She jerked free, whirling to confront him. Her eyes, so near his, shone with intensity. "Listen to me. My brother needs help. I'm going to aid him. And you're going to help me."

"No. I'm not."

"Yes." She took a deep breath. Her voice was

low, piercing. "If you do not, I will tell all these people that you were once a gunfighter."

She waited for violence to erupt. She'd pushed him too far and she knew it. But she didn't know any other way. She needed him. And she'd pay whatever price her tactics demanded of her.

His austere features shuttered abruptly, deadened and lifeless. She might as well have been speaking Apache for all the reaction he gave. The firelight limned his lean, muscular torso; like hoarfrost on granite. His coldness was nearly palpable. Only his eyes, gleaming and focused, were alive.

"Is that a threat?" he whispered.

She swallowed. "Yes."

His expression tightened. She realized with a sickening sense of horror that he was smiling. "So much for your word," he said.

"I'd break my word a thousand times for such a cause."

"Some *cause* you've found yourself, Mercy." The word hung between them, mocking and derisive. "What cause? Perhaps your brother is a wastrel who has gambled too deeply." He advanced one step closer. She held her ground. "Or maybe just a pitiful addict in the throes of withdrawal." He brought his hand up, grazing his knuckles along her chin. "Or any other strutting piece of worthless crap who's drunk too much or whored too much or gambled too much. Some *cause*."

Her lips quivered. "I don't care what you say. I don't care what you think. All I know is that you *will* help me find him."

"Will I?" he whispered. Her skin was soft and silky; already he knew too well the chamois texture of it, the graceful delicacy of the bone beneath. She was trembling. The pulse at the base of her neck fluttered wildly.

"Yes." He could barely hear her.

"I'm a ruthless man, Mercy. Conscienceless. I'd have thought you'd realized that. Especially after this morning." His voice flowed over her, low and dangerous, like the purr of a lynx. "And I always get what I want. Are you sure you want to put yourself in the way of my plans, Mercy?"

She was silent.

"You should be afraid."

"I am."

"Good," he said. "Go back to bed."

"No."

He frowned, thwarted. The gentle stroking along her jaw stopped. His fingers brushed down over her throat. With one hand he spanned its breadth, encircling her neck with strong fingers. He exerted no pressure, none at all. His touch was a horrifying travesty of gentleness. His gaze was nearly tranquil. It was far worse than if he had choked her. The potential for violence was itself a violence. And he knew it.

"Yes. Yes and yes," she whispered—whimpered. "Yes, I'm afraid of you, is that what you want to hear? But I need you. There's no one else. You can find Will." The words tumbled from her. "He's in London somewhere. You can make center of the city in an hour. One of his last notes mentioned a place called the Peacock's Tail. You know where to look. The places these people frequent."

"Do I?" Was that a hint of bitterness buried nearly indiscernibly among all that lethal threat? His hand dropped.

"At the least you can find out. I wouldn't stand a chance. You *have* to."

She touched him then. She reached out and spread her hand on his naked chest and filled him with a thousand unvoiced longings and all the while her gaze held his imploringly, beseechingly, without any trace of desire. He stared at her hand, greedy for the sight of her smooth fingers on him. She had no concept of what she did to him. She was unconscious of anything but her need to convince him.

"One week," she said. "That's all I ask. One week, until he writes to tell me where to send the money."

"Just wait for his next note." Somehow he made his voice impersonal.

"A week from now, who knows how much more deeply he'll be involved in whatever trouble he's found? What if he's wrong and these people, whoever they are, whatever they want, will not wait a week? What if they demand the money in three days, or four?"

"They aren't going to kill him, Mercy. You never kill a man who owes you money. I should know."

"They might *hurt* him."

"Probably."

His word dragged an involuntary moan from her, and she swayed where she stood. "Dear God, I can't stand by and let him be hurt, not if I can stop it. Don't you see? You would do the same for your sisters."

His silence answered her.

She bit down hard on her lower lip. If she drew blood, he was lost. He'd sell his sisters' future, he realized with self-disgust, just to keep her from slicing her own lip. She met his gaze, hauling her slender shoulders back.

"It doesn't matter if you do," she said. "You'll go. I'll pay you. I said I would and I will. And if you don't look for him, I'll drop a word to Acton and his mother about your past. Maybe your own sisters . . . Do they know how you earned the family fortune? I didn't think so. You'll go. You'll start tomorrow night."

He drew away from her, as though she were abhorrent to him. He stalked to the door and flung it open. "Oh, yes. I'll go." With a small sob she moved past him into the hallway's gloom. "And you will most assuredly pay."

Chapter 13

$\mathcal{H}$e'd been fool enough to think she had meant to keep her word. Worse than naive: gullible. How long had she honored her promise? A bloody twenty-four hours. He lounged against the morning-room wall, his arms crossed over his chest.

His gaze continued to stalk Mercy as it had all morning, all afternoon, all day. He ignored the curious looks of the other guests who were waiting for the next round of charades to begin. The corners of his mouth turned up in a sardonic smile as she shot another anxious glance in his direction. Of course it was Hillard who finally took her arm and escorted her from the room. Too bad, Hart thought bitterly, the game had lost a consummate player.

Restless now that she'd left, robbing him of the juvenile yet ungovernable pleasure of making her flinch, Hart looked out the window. A pleasant evening she'd picked for him to go searching for her worthless sibling.

Overnight the weather had turned blustery. The sky spat cold rain against the windowpanes, ripped the scarlet foliage from the trees, and pummeled the ground with an angry staccato. It was a fine mirror of his mood. All day he'd fought his attraction to the American extortionist. All day he'd reminded himself that she was using him. All day it hadn't mattered.

He'd still been incapable of ignoring his response to her, both the hardening of his loins as he watched her mouth move or the hardening of his heart when he thought of her lie. He, who'd honed self-control to a razor-edged exactitude, couldn't control the hunger inspired by one lovely, lying American chit.

He swung around, motioning for a servant to bring him a glass of sherry. He had every intention of finding Will Coltrane, and when he did he had every intention of dragging him here by the scruff of his neck and throwing him at Mercy's feet. If there were a just force at work, she might then see what she had abdicated her honor for: a greedy kid with an appetite he could not afford.

He drained his glass and was about to leave when the sound of masculine voices issued from the billiard room. He paused. Acton and his intimates had been sequestered in there for hours. Hours during which Hart had seen Annabelle, a solemn cast to her exquisite features, dogging the steps of the Dowager Duchess.

He'd thought to approach his youngest sister, but he'd been distracted by this . . . *situation* with

Mercy. Acton's voice, booming from the other room, recalled him to his intention. He considered finding Annabelle and asking her what the hell was going on with Acton, but the years of distance and age between them might well make such an overture embarrassing for her. After all, what did he truly know about Annabelle?

He looked around for a member of his family who could shed some light on the stagnating courtship. Richard and Fanny had retired to their rooms during lunch, Fanny's complexion having gone green on seeing the cold collation of jellied eel and stuffed trout. And earlier, Beryl had whisked several leading political hostesses to some private bower. That left Henley. He was across the room, sipping tea as he listened to one of Baron Coffey's monologues.

Hart caught his brother-in-law's eye and motioned him over. With a sullen tensing of his narrow face Henley made his apologies to the Baron and joined him.

As he approached, Hart studied him. It had been a year since Hart had been in England. That year had not been kind to Henley. There was a petulant twist that sat too familiarly on his long mouth. His gaze shifted about the room, and his smile was too quick for spontaneity: It bespoke anticipation.

"Hart, I haven't had the opportunity to thank you for all you've done," Henley began, "both for Beryl and myself and my career. I am fully cognizant of the debt I owe you. I know that my way in the House has been smoothed—"

"My pleasure," Hart cut in, waving away Henley's gratitude. The other man flushed.

"I want to know what the blazes is going on here," Hart said. Henley's gaze shot to meet his. The russet flush that had mounted his cheeks drained away, leaving him colorless. He wet his lips. At least this time his dark eyes did not waver from Hart's.

"What do you mean?" he asked, placing his teacup on a nearby table.

"Annabelle. What the deuce is going on between Acton and her?"

Henley released a barely audible sigh. "Oh. Annabelle."

There was an odd hint of disappointment in his tone, as well as relief. What the deuce was going on with the man? "Yes, Annabelle," Hart said. "Beryl led me to believe that Acton was pressing his suit, that an engagement was all but announced, and then I arrive to find nothing of the sort. Acton gives no appearance of being on the cusp of offering for her, and Annabelle, rather than putting herself out to be gracious, has adopted the most extraordinary demeanor."

"Yes?"

"Yes. Can you explain the situation to me? I certainly wouldn't like to think that I have returned to England just to attend a country house party."

"Wouldn't you?" Henley asked with a touch of

asperity. But his eyes dropped before Hart could properly read the emotion in them. "No," he muttered. "Of course you wouldn't. And we wouldn't have asked you. We know what you want and what we owe you."

"Owe me?" Hart repeated. That was twice Henley had used that term. He acted like a servant, for God's sake. Indeed, his attitude was that of a man who was about to seek a reference. Hart was in no mood for such nonsense. "A damned peculiar thing to say, Henley. You owe me nothing . . . except to keep me informed as to my youngest sister's suitors. And even that is more Beryl's obligation than yours. I simply want to know how matters stand."

Henley nodded, his combative posture dropping away. "I don't know," he said. "We, all of us, thought Acton was on the point of declaring. And Annabelle seemed extremely happy about it. But since we've arrived Annabelle has become even more subdued than usual, and Acton has been not so much aloof as ambivalent. It is as though something—or someone—has seeded his intent with doubt."

"Someone?" Hart asked.

Henley took a deep breath. "He is obviously quite smitten with Miss Coltrane."

Acton, Hillard, Major Sotbey . . . himself. "Damn it to hell."

Henley shifted uncomfortably. "Well, she is an arresting woman."

"Isn't she?" Hart returned dryly. First she had

blackmailed him and now she was sabotaging Annabelle's future as the Duchess of Acton. What had she done to ensnare Acton's attention? Had she visited his bedchambers in the middle of the night too?

Hard on the heels of the bright, searing jealousy came a subtler pain. She could not possibly dream that someone with Acton's antecedents would ever offer for her. To pursue such a fantasy could only bring her unhappiness.

"What has she done?" he asked.

Henley looked up, surprised. "Done? Nothing that I can see. She's simply so dissimilar from Annabelle. Or any of our English ladies, for that matter. I think Acton finds her . . . refreshing."

"Refreshing," Hart said. "You mean novel."

"Yes."

"And she is being courted because of her *novelty*. God, Acton sounds like a dim-witted boy," Hart said in disgust. He turned from Henley and stared out the rain-lashed window. "Has he not learned that novelty is merely a function of inexperience?" he murmured. "What happens when Mercy becomes familiar? He acts as though she were a toy. Not a human being."

"If you have such a contempt for novelty, why do you always seek it?" Henley asked. "Why would you travel so much, if not to experience the new?"

For a moment Hart had forgotten Henley was there. His brother-in-law was watching him curiously and Hart was reminded of how perceptive he'd once thought Henley—though the man had given scant evidence of it since his arrival here. Nevertheless, he did not want to awaken Henley's sympathies by telling him just how very tired he was of all his much-vaunted travels. "It's not the same thing at all. One can abandon a vista without causing it harm, either emotionally or socially."

"I see."

"Well," Hart said, displeased he'd given voice to such private musings, "we can only hope Acton comes to his senses."

"Yes," Henley said.

"And when he does, we shall see if Annabelle is still interested in him. You must ask Beryl to discover her feelings on the matter."

"I will."

"Now, if you'll excuse me . . . ?" He nodded curtly and left his brother-in-law studying him from above the rim of his teacup.

Chapter 14

$\mathcal{T}$hroughout dinner Hart watched Mercy divide her attention between Hillard and Baron Coffey's youngest pup. He was too far away to hear what she said. As the Earl of Perth he had been seated near the head of the table while Mercy, untitled and unclassifiable, had been positioned near the far end.

He should have been pleased. Down there Mercy could not compete with Annabelle for Acton's attention. Though, Hart noted, more than once the Duke's gaze slipped in her direction. Not that he could blame him.

Dressed in shimmery midnight-blue velvet that draped elegantly and closely about her bosom and hips, she was riveting. Wide, marigold-colored bands edged the narrow sleeves and gathered back the heavy train, revealing a richly brocaded garnet underskirt. As intricate as the dress was, it was nearly severe in comparison with the other ladies' countless tiers of pastel ruching, myriad nosegays, and layers of glass beads encrusting their bodices.

Cynically, Hart wondered if she had adopted such restraint only to enhance her individuality. Was she aware of it? Did she play on it? He shook his head, refusing a dish of rum-stewed apricots.

"No, take it away," the dark-haired young matron on his right said as the servant offered her the same. "I cannot accept one more morsel, no matter how skilled Acton's chef. Isn't he skilled, Lord Perth?"

"Very," he said, turning politely. He'd barely noticed her before. But now that she'd addressed him, courtesy required he make the requisite small talk.

"I'd give much to have a healthy appetite, but I fear I have too delicate a constitution to enjoy food." The woman—Lady Jane Carr, was it not?—glanced at Mercy and Hart followed her gaze. Unaware she was being observed, Mercy popped a piece of capon in her mouth.

The currant glaze clung to her lower lip. The tip of her tongue appeared and licked it clean. He felt his body quicken in response.

"You have traveled extensively, have you not, Lord Perth?" Lady Jane asked.

"Yes, ma'am," he responded, refusing to look at Mercy's lips, Mercy's eyes, Mercy's porcelain smooth shoulders devoured by the night-sky-blue velvet.

"You have doubtless seen many extraordinary sights since the last time we met."

"Yes." Good Lord. Had they met before? He racked his brain. Of course. At Beryl's wedding three years ago. He remembered her as being a sweet-faced girl, charmingly enraptured with her first season out. The three years were not reflected on her smooth countenance. There was nothing marring her features, though nothing to recommend them either. He cursed himself for comparing her to Mercy.

"Have you visited the Far East?" She tilted her heart-shaped face. "I have always been fascinated by antiquities. Unfortunately Donald is averse to traveling abroad." She peeped at him to see if he was attending. "Donald is my husband."

"My congratulations to him." Hart inclined his head. "You are newly wed, then?"

"Oh, dear, no. I have been married a full two years now."

"Then you are but a bride," Hart said chivalrously, watching her turn a delicate coral color. "And where is your lucky groom?"

"In Scotland. Hunting." She lowered her lids, touching the linen to her clean lips. He'd never seen anyone eat so daintily. It was an unusual accomplishment. "Donald is always hunting. Quite keen on it, he is. But I'd much rather hear about your travels. Have you been to eastern regions?"

He nodded.

"I have heard they are unearthing wonders in Egypt," she said.

She was a perfect English lady: her expression composed, her voice serene, her appearance unexceptional. Her hands retreated modestly to her lap when she spoke. They did not execute arabesques in the air to diagram her words as Mercy's did.

"Very many wonders, Lady Jane," he answered. "There are tombs in Egypt that still hold the treasures buried in them three thousand years ago."

Her eyes grew large. "And you've seen them? Would you please tell me about them? I am avid for some distraction."

Laughter, full throated and delicious, teased him. Mercy was responding to someone's comment. The sound of her amusement reminded him she'd laughed at something he'd said yesterday. It had surprised him that she'd found wit where others were quick to read scorn.

But that had been before she'd blackmailed him. Before she'd forced him to her will. Before she'd lied. And after she'd suffered his mouth open over hers, after he'd tasted the honey-sweet warmth of hers, his hands had learned the weight of her breasts. . . .

With iron resolve he smiled at Lady Jane Carr. Poor woman, lonely without her husband, no doubt. "I will be delighted to provide such entertainment as I can for so lovely a lady," he said. And, vowing to ignore his heart's irrational tendency, he spent the rest of the evening doing his damnedest to please.

The scrawny, pint-sized stable boy who'd saddled the green gelding for him met Hart at the entrance to the stable. There was a cheeky grin on his broad face.

"What are you doing up, lad?" Hart asked, glancing at his timepiece. It was nearing eleven o'clock.

"Doin' me job, milord. Very popular place the stables is at night." He winked, touching a grimy forefinger to his brow in a conspiratorial salute. "Very pop-u-lar."

Hart dismissed the urge to question the boy. He intended to make London by midnight. "I need a mount. Something fast. And not that deviled creature you gave me yesterday."

"Sure thing, milord. But you did ask fer somethin' wid a bit of brimstone in it," the boy said reproachfully. He trotted down the line of stalls and returned shortly with a roan mare dancing in her tack.

Hart swung into the saddle, touching his heels to the mare's sides. The boy jumped out of the way as he guided the horse to the stable door.

"London Road joins the east drive a mile out. If you be needin' the names of some sporting establishments, I can be of some 'elp," the boy offered cheekily.

"The Peacock's Tail. Do you know it?"

"Peacock's Tail, ye say? If it's the place I'm thinking on, try Cambridge Circus," the lad said doubtfully, catching the coin Hart tossed him. "But it ain't a nice place, milord."

Outside, the cold wind sucked the air from Hart's nostrils as he squinted into an icy drizzle, cursing the night, the rain, and Mercy Coltrane. He was nearing the front of the house when a dark figure astride a pale horse detached itself from a shadowed copse of dripping hemlocks.

He could not contain a surge of pleasure though it was followed hard by outrage. "What the hell are you doing here?" he asked.

Mercy Coltrane eyed him from beneath the brim of her ridiculous battered Stetson. Her leather-gloved hands were wrapped tightly on the reins.

"Well?" he demanded.

In answer she withdrew a paper-wrapped parcel from beneath the man's overcoat she wore and flung it at him. He caught it one-handed.

"There's two hundred pounds sterling in there," she said hoarsely.

The wretched creature! Actually thinking he'd do this for money— What the hell did it matter to him what she thought? Abruptly, he stuffed the package into his coat pocket. He'd keep it, all right, if only to remind him of what she saw when she looked at him. Not a lover; a hired gun.

"Ah." He couldn't resist paying her back a little for her low opinion of him. "My fee. Good. You're sure it's all there? I'll count it later, you know."

She nodded, her lower lip thrust out.

"Now, just so that we are absolutely clear on

this point, you say I don't *have* to kill anyone?" he asked.

"No!" Even in the dark he could see her grow pale. Good.

"Oh, well." He sighed with exaggerated disappointment and then brightened, as though as some pleasant thought had occurred to him. "I expect I'll at least have to hurt someone, won't I? One often does in these piecework affairs. Should I endeavor to cripple or merely incapacitate?"

"Neither! You don't have to shoot, maim, kill, or hurt anyone. Just find my brother."

"Well, that rather takes the fun out of it, doesn't it?" he asked dolefully.

She blinked at him, her eyes widening with surprise. "You're *teasing* me," she said.

"Am I?"

"Yes." Her lips were parted in wonder and he suddenly remembered too well the feel of her slender body, the music of her heartbeat counterpointing his own thudding pulse.

"Perhaps," he replied, acutely aware of how dangerous teasing Mercy Coltrane was. "All right, Mercy. You've dutifully handed over the money. You can go back now."

"No. I'm going with you."

He shouldn't have been surprised. But then, she had an uncomfortable knack of surprising him. "No, you're not. You're going back to the house."

"I am not. I'm not going to let you ride into London and spend my money on liquor and then return at dawn and tell me you gave it your best try."

"You think I'd do that?" he asked softly.

She lowered her face, hiding her expression. "I'm not willing to take the chance," she muttered.

"You're going to have to," he clipped out, and started past her.

She spurred her horse forward, matching his gait. "Look, Hart," she implored, "I have to go with you. If you find Will, what are you going to say to him? How ever would you approach him? I need to be there."

He didn't bother to reply to that bit of fantasy. He wasn't going to find Will. At least not tonight. Oh, he'd look, all right, but a man who set out to get lost in Soho could stay lost a dozen lifetimes with no more hope of being found than a whisper in a windstorm.

"I've dressed like a man." Her words tumbled over each other. "I'll keep up. I promise. And I'll stay out of the way."

He reined in and swiveled around. Her horse nickered as she pulled it to a halt beside him. He eyed her derisively. The coat hid her form and her hair was tucked up tight beneath her hat. It didn't matter.

"Don't be a fool," he said. "No one in their right mind would mistake you for a man."

"A boy, then."

"Or a boy." Her skin was too fresh, too creamy and smooth. Her lips were too softly lush, her remarkable eyelashes too extravagant, to have been wasted on a male.

"It will be dark," she pleaded. "I'll stay outside."

"Forget it." He turned around, preparing to put distance between them, when suddenly she reached out and grabbed his horse's reins close up under the bit.

"No." Her tone had lost its plea. Anger and obstinacy replaced it. "Damn it. *Damn it*," she said with distinct satisfaction. "You should understand. Of all people, *you* should understand. He's my brother, Hart. My only brother. Think of what you did, what you risked, for your sisters."

"You don't know what you're talking about," he clipped out.

"A fool can see what you've tried to do, if they only know half the story," she spat back. "The clothes, the Seasons, Bentwood . . . you sacrificed everything so that they could have the sort of life you thought they were meant for, didn't you? Lady Acton told me about your father leaving your family without any means to provide for themselves. Beryl filled in the other areas. I know what you did, Hart."

"You're not only intractable and willful, you're melodramatic."

"I'm right," she said flatly.

He kneed the gelding. She refused to let go of the reins and he would not trust himself to lay hands on her to loosen her grip.

"It's no different for me," she said. "I know I

lied to you. I gave you my word and I didn't keep it. But I had no choice."

He made a violent sound of disparagement.

"I didn't have a choice," she insisted. "Just because I'm a woman doesn't mean I don't care just as deeply for my brother as you do your sisters. I have no less an obligation toward my family than you do toward yours. It is not simply that I *will* not abandon my brother. I *can*not."

"You haven't abandoned him," he said woodenly. "You've hired me."

"No. *I* have to go," she said. "If you appear, looking like this"—she motioned toward his rough garb—"he'll think you were hired by the men who want to hurt him. He'll bolt. He'll run and there won't be any hope of finding him then."

Her words were reasonable, too reasonable. He could find no fault with her logic and he wanted very much to find fault with her. He considered her, this woman who knew too much and far too little, who in one breath implored him and in the other commanded him, who'd blackmailed him and forced him to her will. Who'd given her word and then broken it. Whose mouth had melted beneath his and then had seemed to forget it. Her gaze locked with his.

She was, damn it, right. He'd done far more for his sisters than break his word. He'd killed.

"You will stay where I tell you to stay, come when I say come, stand behind me and, above all, keep quiet."

"Yes," she breathed. Without another word he

spurred his horse forward, trotting out from beneath the shadow of the great house onto the alley.

High above, a pale curtain fell silently back across a darkened window.

Chapter 15

Mercy squirmed on the carriage's cracked leather seat. Across from her Hart was looking out the window. They'd left their mounts at a respectable-looking livery near the edges of Soho where Hart had hired the cab. Since they'd left Acton's he'd said no more.

He was still angry with her, probably furious. But after having spent the day walking on eggshells because of his cold-eyed enmity, she'd found herself tired of being frightened. She had never let a threatening posture intimidate her before—even from someone as dangerous-looking as Hart Moreland. If she had, she'd never have survived childhood on the Texas Panhandle.

She sighed and pulled back the dusty curtain that hid the dingy window. They were well within the city of London, a London she'd not seen in her short month here.

Tall streetlights spread a sickly sulfurous cast

across the wet, black pavement. People, more people than she'd have imagined would be afoot at this late hour, milled beneath the eerie lighting. The men were a diverse lot: workers in thick-soled boots, their jackets straining over layers of shirts and sweaters; tradesmen and clerks hurrying along; toffs in top hats and dark cloaks, their silver-topped canes gleaming with bilious highlights, their eyes scouring the crowded sidewalk.

There were as many women as men, but there was a harsh commonality about the women that Mercy had, at first, a hard time identifying. It was more than their garb, though they all were dressed in thick layers of clothing: soiled wool skirts, petticoats with patched flounces hiked above sturdy boots and knit stockings. Only the odd bits of ragged lace and bright silk sprouting from incongruously bared throats and bosoms gave a clue as to their profession. Still it was not the manner of their dress that likened them, it was the dead apathy of their expressions, so jarringly at odds with their loud, raucous voices, clamoring for the attention of the prowling toffs.

"Where are they going? Where do they all live?" Mercy asked.

"Are you serious?"

She hadn't realized she'd spoken until she heard Hart's sardonic reply. His expression was obscured by the dim interior of the carriage, but she could easily enough read the cynicism of his tone.

"Yes," she said. "I've never seen so many people, such sordid surroundings."

"This is nothing."

She glanced outside again. A group of young men were lounging outside a dilapidated corner building, leaning against a window that proclaimed FINE WHISKEY and sneering at the passersby. They were a dirty and violent-looking lot. A dog slunk by and one of them hurled a bottle at it, laughing when it yelped and limped away into a dark passage.

She hadn't realized how menacing a place like this was. She and Hart could be hurt here and no one would interfere. No one would notice.

She gulped. "You're packing an iron, aren't you?"

He stared at her.

"An iron, a peacemaker . . . you know, a revolver," she said in exasperation.

"I know what it is. And no, I am not 'packing an iron.' This isn't Texas, Mercy. Men don't go about carrying guns down here as a matter of course."

She gave him a sour look. "More fool they," she said. "Luckily, I have come prepared."

Her words arrested him in the act of switching down the curtain. "What?"

"I have a revolver in my coat pocket. A Colt .38."

"Damn it to hell."

"I thought gentlemen didn't swear," she said sweetly.

"I told you. I'm not a gentleman."

"So I see."

"And you'd be wise not to forget it."

"You won't let me."

"Now, what the hell is that supposed to mean?" he asked, the revolver apparently forgotten.

"Tsk, tsk, tsk, worse and worse," she said, aware that this was like yanking on the chain of a leg-trapped cougar but unable to help herself. She would, she realized, rather have his anger than his coldness. "It means that I am perfectly aware of what you think of me."

"I doubt that."

She didn't deign to reply to that incomprehensible statement. Her courage built, becoming, she suspected, folly. "And you needn't go reminding me again that you're a dangerous man. It doesn't wash."

His beautiful eyes narrowed. "Meaning?"

"Danger is a flash flood, or a herd of stampeding cattle, or a tornado, or a grass fire. Danger is being caught on a flat prairie in an electrical storm or coming upon five hundred Apaches in warrior's paint," she said haughtily.

"Your point?" he asked.

"I *know* danger, Perth. And it *doesn't* have an English accent."

Impossibly, he burst out laughing, that rich but all-too-rare sound. The corners of his eyes crinkled up, his teeth gleamed in the dim lighting of the carriage. His humor was irresistible, much more dangerous than his ire.

"Touché," he said. "I won't bore you any longer with my qualifications as a threat."

She settled back and smiled. "And perhaps I needn't curse."

The carriage slowed and the driver called down to them, "Cambridge Circus in a minute."

"Grand," Hart muttered. "Now where?"

"You mean," she said slowly, "you don't know where the Peacock's Tail is?"

He sighed. "No."

"But, surely you've been . . . I mean, a man . . . you said that young men sow wild . . . I assumed . . ." She stuttered to a halt.

"I really do hate to disabuse you of your interesting notions concerning me, Mercy, but as I have tried to explain, I have spent the last six years *avoiding* any association with places like the Peacock's Tail."

"You have?"

"I have lived a monotonously virtuous life since I left Texas."

"I'm sorry."

Again, he laughed. "For your mistake or my virtue?"

Heat poured up her neck into her cheeks. The amused light died in his eyes, his mask of cold indifference returning just as the carriage lurched to a halt. Hart kicked open the door and jumped out, leaving her. He tossed the driver some coins as Mercy poked her head through the doorway, looking for the steps. Before she realized what was happening, his big hands encircled her waist. He lifted her with effortless, smooth strength. For a timeless second he held her aloft, captured above him, his gaze searching hers.

Her heart beat dully. Her fingers tightened on his shoulders. His lips parted as though he would speak and then her feet touched the ground and he was backing away from her, his eyes averted, looking down the street.

"Over there," he muttered, motioning toward a dimly lit doorway set deep in a bricked alcove. A stained-glass window in the shape of peacock's tail was set high up in the heavy-looking door.

He pulled her forward, close to him. He smelled of masculine musk and warm, dusty leather but his breath was fresh and clean. "Remember. You don't talk. You don't ask questions. You don't do *anything* but stay close to me."

She nodded and he led the way to the door. It swung open as soon as he knocked. A thick-necked bull of a man with improbable black ringlets and stained teeth answered.

"How much?" Hart asked.

"Depends on what yer want," the man answered in a thick cockney accent, his small eyes traveling over them in a bored fashion. "A room fer you and the kid'll go two quid. The smokin' room'll cost you one. Just ter get in is a crown."

Wordlessly, Hart gave the man two crowns. The man shrugged and stepped back, allowing

Hart and her to pass. "Whatever. Yer can always change yer mind."

Inside, a pungent haze cast a bluish pall over the narrow, unfurnished hallway. Closed doors lined its length. At the end a steep staircase descended into a black rectangle. Occasional laughter drifted up from its depths.

"I can't believe Will would be here. There has to be some other Peacock's Tail," Mercy protested.

"You promised silence." Hart grabbed her by the arm and pulled her close. His face was set and hard, the deep nostrils of his aggressive nose flaring. "Don't say another word," he whispered harshly. "Not one."

Abruptly, he released her and stalked down the hall, anger in every lithe, whipcord inch of him, leaving her to scramble after him. He pulled the first door open and pushed her ahead of him.

She blinked as smoke stung her eyes. Her throat closed against the cloying perfumed air and she squinted. Though richly furnished, the room was seedy and unclean. The red-plush-and-gilt furniture had a neglected air. The thick Oriental carpets were dusted with cigar ash and the dull, sticky-looking tables were scarred and burned.

The few men present were all tricked out in some manner of evening dress. Starched white shirts and high collars, black cutaway jackets and expensive silk cravats. A few of them glanced over before going back to their drinks.

They looked a reasonably well-to-do lot. But

they all wore the same dazed quality about them, an air of sightless preoccupation.

She glanced over at Hart. His cold demeanor had abandoned him. He looked absolutely furious, hard eyed and tight jawed. He pushed her in front of him toward a small raised counter behind which stood a smiling young man with gleaming black hair and acne-pitted cheeks.

"Brandy," he said.

The young man scanned Hart's lean figure from his battered boots up over his heavy, rumpled coat.

"Pay first," he said.

Wordlessly, Hart slapped a five-pound note on the table. The young man grinned and filled two glasses. His thin white hand snaked out toward the note. Hart caught his wrist in an iron clasp. "It's yours for some information."

The young man sighed. "Can't. Against house policy. Never ask a name, never give a name. 'Cept my own. Ned," he said, carefully enunciating each word.

Hart slapped another five-pound note down. "I don't want a name."

Ned licked his lips, his gaze darting toward the door. "What do you want to know?"

"An American has been in here. His name is William Coltrane. Young, well spoken. Is he here?"

Mercy held her breath. The man responded with slight negative shake of his oiled dark head.

Relief coursed through her. She should have known Will would not come to a place like this—

"Was he here?"

A nod. Her stomach coiled tightly.

"When?"

"Couple months. He was a regular until then. Haven't seen him since."

"A regular?" Mercy asked.

Hart cast her a furious glare but she couldn't have held her tongue, not to save her soul. What in God's name had Will gotten himself into?

For the first time Ned looked directly at her. A slow, ingratiating smile exposed little yellow teeth.

"Yeah, sonny," he said. "A regular customer. A hophead." He winked and Mercy recoiled against Hart's side. He was solid and warm and he ignored her completely. Only the veins cording beneath the copper-stained skin of his throat gave a clue he was feeling any emotion.

"Do you know where he went? Where he stays?"

"No," Ned answered, his eyes on the two notes. "I never asked."

"We can pay you more. Lots more," Mercy put in. "We have the money." With lightning speed Hart's arm snaked around her, crushing her to his side and robbing her of breath.

Ned pursed his lips. "Say, now," he said, "you ain't no boy. You're a dollymo—"

"That's none of your concern," Hart cut in. "Do you know anything more?"

Ned shrugged, still apparently eager to help, but for an instant his gaze skittered behind them. Just a small twist of his lips, something hard flash-

ing in his eyes, and he was smiling at them again.
"He was taking up with some swells of late. Maybe
he's gra-dur-ated, if you knows what I mean," he
said, suddenly loquacious. "You could try some of
the houses up by Red Lion's Square. Nice houses
up there. You pays for what you get. Or"—he
paused a fraction of a second and his glance flickered behind them again.

Abruptly, Hart swung around. He grabbed her
hand and strode toward the door, hauling her after
him into the dim, narrow hallway. He stopped,
looking around.

A giggle bubbled up from the black rectangle
at the one end. He started forward again, his aqua
gaze raking the closed doors.

She stumbled after him, panting. His grip on
her was painful. Suddenly the bullish doorman appeared in front of them, blocking their way, a smile
of evil intent on his oily face.

"Damn, he's big," she heard Hart say.

"Too big?" she breathed anxiously.

"Far too big," he muttered, backing slowly up
and hauling her with him.

"That's right, trapped like rats," Ned said from
behind them, the careful middle-class accents
wiped from his voice. "Now, mates, gets the girl
and I'll gets the ready."

Hart lunged for the nearest door and grabbed
the handle. He heaved it open just as Ned and two
other men started down from the hall. He shoved
Mercy inside, leaping in after her and slamming
the door shut. The lumbering beat of footsteps in-

creased as the men outside started running. He snatched a ladder-back chair and rammed it under the handle.

Mercy ran to the closed window on the far side of the room and tugged at it. It didn't budge. In a trice Hart was beside her. With a grunt he jerked it open and glanced outside. Still looking angry enough to chew rocks, he scooped her up and stuck her feet-first out the window. The sound of splintering wood crashed around her ears.

He pushed. She fell.

She landed awkwardly, collapsing on the gravel, tearing her breeches and skinning her palms. Panting, she was clambering to her knees when a heavy body careened into her shoulder, knocking her back down onto the pavement. She turned her head. Hart.

"Damn it," he growled, his hand beneath her arm, "get the hell up and run!"

"I'm trying!" She staggered, stumbling twice more before he managed to snatch her upright, an epithet forming on her lips.

"Run where, guv?" Ned asked, his breathless voice echoing hollowly in the cramped, wet alley.

Low snickers met his query. She looked up. Four men stood outlined in the bilious yellow glow at the end of the alley. She swung around and her heart missed its beat. There was nowhere to run. The other end of the alley was a blank brick wall.

Chapter 16

"*J* said run!" Hart shouted angrily.

"Right," Mercy shot back. "Do you suggest I run to that big ox or would you rather I ran to our smiling friend with the oily hair?"

"This isn't any time for sarcasm," he returned.

"Right again," she said sarcastically. "Once more and we'll have to see about a trophy."

"Look," he said, shoving a finger under her nose, "if you hadn't been so damn eager to inform everyone in Soho that we were carrying cash, we wouldn't be in this mess."

He was right—yet again—but it only made her angrier. She wouldn't have been surprised to learn he'd *tried* to land on her when he jumped out the window.

"If *you* had asked the right questions in the first place—"

"'Ere now," the hulking figure of the doorman

said in a confused voice. "You two off yer blinkin' rockers?"

"Daft as two-headed dogs," one of his cohorts said.

"Bickerin' like me an' me old lady and them but one jump away from Old Nick's trident," another added.

"Oh, *do* shut up," Hart flung out.

"You stupid buggers!" Ned spat, shouldering his way past the men and advancing toward them. "They're just playin' fer time, 'oping the coppers'll show. Well, ain't no copper goin' to show 'ere, *laddy*," he sneered, pulling a short, stout cudgel from his rear pocket and dancing its heavy-looking head up and down in his palm.

"God, I hate fisticuffs," Hart muttered, shooting her a condemning glare. "And this time you'd damn well better run when I say run," he added.

The men prowled forward, their faces intent, splitting into two factions and flanking Hart and Mercy. Ned swaggered ahead of them, quickly closing the gap between them.

"Don't move!" Mercy shouted, fumbling in her coat pocket. She made certain her voice carried, each word distinct. It was the tone she'd used when shouting "git" at a coyote scouting the henhouse. It had the same effect.

Or maybe it was the sight of the Colt revolver she pulled from her coat pocket that brought the group—including Ned—skittering to a halt. It didn't really matter. Their mouths dropped open, eyes widening with uncertainty. Even Hart was staring at her.

"Forgot I had it, didn't you?" she asked him.

"Yes. I must admit I did." She could have sworn that he gave a short, rueful smile.

"And"—she continued to address him, her eyes fixed on the shuffling, scowling ruffians a few yards before them—"I suppose we can safely be said to have rethought our stand on it not being necessary to 'pack an iron' in London?"

"Hm."

The men looked to Ned for some clue as to how to go on. Ned was otherwise occupied. He was staring at the gun four inches from his forehead so intently his eyes were crossed.

"Now," she said to the men, watching Ned's sweating face, "unless you want to find out what an American *lady* does when confronted by ruffians with untoward designs on her person, I suggest you leave." She offered a prayer of thanks that she wasn't stuttering with fear. Regardless of how steady her hand was, her knees felt as though at any second they would start banging together.

The men peered at her assessingly. Mercy lowered the gun barrel ostentatiously toward another part of Ned's anatomy. "Git!"

"Ah, she'd never—" the ox started to say.

"Yes, she would!" squeaked Ned.

"I think so too," Hart said encouragingly.

Still, the other men didn't look convinced. She sighed dramatically. "Look, even if you are willing to sacrifice Ned—and after my short association with him I can certainly empathize should that be your decision—these things"—she waved the gun barrel and Ned made a choking sound—"are riotously noisy. And I daresay gun blasts are enough of an oddity here that even your most incurious policeman will be bound to investigate."

"She's right!" Ned sputtered. "Back off!"

"Ah, shit," the ox grumbled, turning with a disconsolate air. Without another word or glance to either side he lumbered past his mates. The others fidgeted a second or two before disappearing after him.

"Now get moving, Ned. At a decorous pace." Mercy motioned in the direction of the alley's opening. "And do not make the mistake of thinking you and your friends can dog our steps and take us at a more opportune moment. Percy"—she nodded at Hart and had the satisfaction of surprising an expression of incredulity on him—"is a *notoriously* dangerous man. I shan't be accountable for what he does if he even *thinks* you are plotting something."

Ned scowled but cast a worried glance in Hart's direction. Hart, resigning himself to his role, lifted his lip in a snarl.

"Right-o," Ned said, his shoulders and bravado deflating in an instant, leaving him looking exactly what he was: a young man with bad skin, too much hair oil, and—in spite of his painstaking imitation of middle-class mannerisms—no hopes of ever leaving the sordid streets that had bred him. "Ned Bright ain't no fool. We had a go. We failed. No hard feelings, what?"

Mercy almost laughed at the incredible cheek of the young man. But the memory of his hard, speculative eyes and the pointed tip of his tongue wetting his lips when he'd discovered she was a woman killed her humor. They were at the entrance of the alley now. Hart held up a hand and prowled forward, looking either way before motioning them on.

Ned started past her but Hart caught his arm. The man flinched. Hart looked at him impassively, all animation having died on his countenance. An arctic wind would have been a balm compared to that harsh gaze.

"Where is he? Where is Will Coltrane?"

"I don't know. I swear," Ned said, squirming. "You knows how they are. They comes and goes. Willy-boy, he had an appetite, he did. It takes some of 'em like that. And I told you true before. I'd look up ter Red Lion's Square way. Chinee houses, most like."

Hart thrust him out of the alley. Ned broke and ran until he was swallowed by the Peacock's Tail's dark recessed alcove.

"I think we should—"

"*You* be quiet," Hart said.

"But I—"

"One more word and I swear to God I'll leave you here," he ground out before bellowing at a cab just pulling away from the corner. It rocked to a halt and he bundled her forward, all but shoving her into its moldy-smelling interior and slamming the door shut behind her.

Once alone in the dark relative safety of the decrepit hansom, Mercy's fear, held at bay during the last half hour, found purchase. She shivered uncontrollably.

They could have been killed.

She could *still* be killed, she thought humorlessly. She wouldn't be surprised if Hart strangled her. And what had their escapade gotten them? The name of another place like this and the promise of another confrontation with evidence of her brother's debasement. God. What had become of Will?

And, seeing an image of Will's face superimposed over the greedy eyes and furtive manner of "Ned," Mercy buried her face in her hands and cried.

———◆———

He was simply going to have to scare her witless, Hart decided as he stood outside and gave the driver directions. But if he was going to find her damned brother, it was going to have to be without her tagging along.

With a start he realized that he was, indeed, going to find Will for her. Her fierce loyalty and determination had won his respect in spite of her lies, manipulations, and—he bit down on his teeth as he felt the thick wad of cash in his inner coat pocket—even her damned "two hundred pounds sterling."

Nevertheless, she couldn't go with him again. Though he'd admit she had saved the situation tonight, there wouldn't have *been* a situation if it hadn't been for her. She was too eager for some clue, any clue, of where Will was. She hadn't yet learned patience when dealing with her heart.

He hoped she never did.

He tossed the driver a quid as an added incentive to get them quickly back to the stables and rounded the hack's ill-sprung body. He had to make her so damn afraid of him, she wouldn't even consider following him again. She could get hurt down here.

His hand knotted at his side, his expression bleak. She *would* get hurt as soon as her facile mind unraveled Ned's slum-cant and she realized her brother was a *hophead*. An opium addict.

He shifted his shoulder as though redistributing an uneven burden and paused at the carriage door, staring at it. He couldn't do anything about that pain, but at least he could keep her physically safe.

Steeling himself to play the part of the bully, to force her to see him as a far greater threat than any slow-witted behemoth or brain-rotted addict with an unctuous smile, he snatched open the carriage door.

She was crying.

All the air abandoned his lungs in a single breath. He climbed in, pulling the door shut after him. She didn't notice. She was hunched forward, her slender back shaking. Her hair spilled in a dark tangle from under her hat, half shrouding her face as she muffled her broken sobs with her palms.

"Mercy," he said softly, helplessly.

If she heard, she gave no sign. He didn't know what to do, what to say. But he couldn't sit here and watch her cry. Not to save his soul. He reached out and brushed the nape of her bowed neck.

Without hesitation she turned and flung herself against him, wrapping her arms around him as though she would never let go. Her damp face burrowed against his neck, hot and sticky. Impotently, he stared at the dark hair spilling across his chest.

He had never had a woman seek comfort in his embrace. Hell, he had never been held by a woman with any object other than sex in mind. And God knows, for the last three days he'd been as randy as a virgin adolescent. But not now. Not now.

Now there was nothing but this overwhelming need to soothe, to ease her pain and shelter her from grief. To hold her as though by doing so he could absorb her anguish. It was a shattering sensation. His throat ached and his body bowed over hers in a shielding posture.

Lightly, he smoothed her hair, his fingers shivering on the thick mantle. She nestled closer and awkwardly he set his arms around her. When she did not reject him, he settled her nearer still. She was ravishingly compliant in his arms, her sylphlike body narrow and fine boned and strong beyond conception, and when her breath fanned his skin, he lost his own.

He didn't have any words. He was struck dumb by the tenderness she wrested from his arid, arctic soul. He had no right to hold her like this and he knew it—even if she didn't. Still, he thought with a shred of black humor and blacker self-knowledge, there was nothing in the world that could have made him relinquish her.

For long minutes she cried, spending her strength in sorrow until gradually her breathing quieted and she relaxed, limp and spent. Like a thief he brushed his cheek against the delicately shaped head tucked beneath his chin, masking the caress as a movement preparatory to pushing her away. She murmured something incomprehensible and clung more tightly. He swallowed and gave up.

Abandoning himself to the unaccustomed role, he pulled her wholly onto his lap, tucking her legs up over his, cradling her there. She sighed, a sound of utter release.

His head fell back against the stained leather headrest. Gazing at the blackness overhead, he damned himself for a fool even as he hoped the driver would ignore his instruction to hurry.

———◆———

"We're back." Hart's voice roused her from sleep and Mercy lifted her head. The wonderful warmth that had surrounded her had vanished. It

was cold. She shivered, looking about as she tried
to adjust her vision to the murky interior of the
carriage.

"The stables?" she asked in a sleep-hoarse
voice.

"No. Acton's estate."

"But the horses—"

"Hitched to the back." His voice sounded indifferent. "We're at the gate."

She'd forgotten; he was angry with her. Regardless of the fact that he had allowed her to find
a haven in his arms, his remote tone made it obvious it was only a temporary one. The realization
brought fresh tears welling up in her eyes.

Fool, she thought. *He kisses you and you all but
offer yourself to him. He offers a consoling pat and you
fling yourself in his arms. And when he doesn't dump
you on the floor you assume . . . you hope . . .*

She turned her head away. She wouldn't embarrass him again. She wouldn't have him witness
her crying again.

He opened the door and jumped from the carriage. She struggled upright, still disoriented. Before she could act, he plucked her from where she
swayed at the entrance and carried her to her
horse. He lifted her up into the saddle.

He was a gentle man, she thought muzzily, for
all his dangerousness. His hands lingered a second,
ensuring that she was secure. And then he was
stepping back.

"You're all right?" he asked.

She nodded.

"How are we going to get you back into the house?" he muttered, swinging into his own saddle.

He was impatient to be rid of her, impatient to be rid of her duplicity and blackmail, impatient to have her gone from his life. True, he'd said he admired her, but he did so grudgingly, as one admires a coyote for its relentless opportunism.

That was all she was to him—a coyote raiding his manor house, she thought in despair. And how could she blame him? She represented everything he wanted to forget: violence, deceit, vulgarity.

For God's sake, she thought on a bubble of feverish laughter, she was blackmailing the Earl of Perth! What did she expect from him? An invitation to the opera? She dashed the dampness from her cheeks with the back of her hand.

"I've made arrangements," she said, and spurred her mount away from him and all she could never hope to have.

Chapter 17

"*M*iss Coltrane, you slept well I trust?"

Mercy started at the sound of Henley Wrexhall's voice. She was tired and uncertain and filled with an overwhelming desire to see Hart. A desire she wasn't about to examine too closely.

"I had a perfectly restful evening, Mr. Wrexhall," she answered. "And yourself?" He wore his usual bland smile but there was an assessing quality in his eyes that was not at all pleasant. Had he seen her come in last night?

Nonsense, Mercy thought. Brenna had sneaked her in through the servants' entrance. There was not a soul the wiser. She'd stake her reputation on it. In fact, that is exactly what she had done.

He shifted on his feet. "Perfectly."

Then why, she wondered, *are there pouches beneath your eyes?* Her own mirror had reflected similar dark areas this morning when she'd made a hasty toilette.

"Pleasant morning, is it not?" she asked, fumbling for a topic of conversation. Wrexhall, if she remembered correctly, was a member of the Liberal party and a rising young politician. Which knowledge left her no more certain how to proceed than before. She hadn't the least acquaintance with England's politics.

"Your brother-in-law appears absent this morning."

"Tending Fanny, I expect," Henley replied. "It's become rather a full-time job for the poor chap. Though I doubt whether he begrudges her it. Richard never did like crowds. Much happier on his estate."

Richard? Of course, Mercy remembered, the other brother-in-law. "Mrs. Wrexhall enjoys house parties, then?" she asked. "Lucky woman to have so indulgent a spouse."

"Oh, dear, no. Fanny is most strained by the prospect of parties. Always worried someone will expect her to say something clever."

Mercy frowned in perplexity. "Then why ever did they accept the invit—" She stopped, abashed by her rudeness. "Forgive me."

Henley smiled, and this time the expression made it to his eyes, a sardonic gleam, true, but more than his usual social expression, which was a tightening of cheek muscles as meaningless as it was ubiquitous.

"Quite all right," he said.

"Actually, when I asked you about your brother-in-law, I was referring to Lord Perth."

"Oh." His dark eyes went flat. "I'm afraid I don't know where Perth is. Probably busy with his machinations." If his smile was an attempt to rob the words of criticism, it failed. "Not that we aren't indebted to Perth," he hurried on, "but it might be for the best if Annabelle were to enter any . . . permanent association with a certainty that she herself was the main factor in its evolution."

She stared at him in bewilderment, at a loss as to how to respond to such an extraordinary statement. She was saved from having to by the arrival of Nathan Hillard.

This morning he looked in fine spirits, rested and genial. His golden hair was polished to a deep shine, his dress was elegant and subdued. He was, she thought objectively, a very handsome man.

"Miss Coltrane," he greeted her, "I trust you spent a restful evening? These morning rides of yours are not taking a toll, I hope. You must remember, we are not keeping rancher's hours here. Take care of yourself, m'dear."

His concern was slightly proprietary. Mercy felt a rush of shame under his scrutiny.

"Lovely, thank you, Mr. Hillard." That was the second man who'd studied her rather too closely. She would have to see if Brenna had any powder to conceal the circles beneath her eyes.

Henley, obviously relieved to have been extricated from his indiscretions, welcomed Nathan with a clap on the back. "Nate, I haven't had the opportunity to thank you for your support in the boroughs last year."

"It is not only my pleasure but my duty to do anything I can to advance the economic and social conditions of our country, Wrexhall. And seeing you made a member of the House is certainly a step in that direction." It was a munificent statement, but rather than giving Wrexhall pleasure, it seemed to have the opposite effect. He flushed deeply.

Hillard turned to her. "And how do you propose to spend this lovely day, Miss Coltrane?"

"I haven't given it any thought," she replied. Beyond finding Hart and charting their next move, she'd made no plans.

"Ah. Well, perhaps I might interest you in a ride in the country or a trip to Fair Redding? It's an extravagantly picturesque town."

"Perhaps some other day, sir." She had other matters to see to today. As delightful as it would probably be, she couldn't afford to waste time seeking her own enjoyment while Will needed her. The decision felt suspiciously like a reprieve.

Henley snorted. "And what would you know about picturesque towns, Nate? I confess, I'm surprised you're here at all. Didn't think the country was your cup o' tea."

"It depends on who is in the country," Hillard responded, his brilliant blue eyes resting on her. She had never seen such eyes; the crystalline blue irises dominated them, all but swallowing the pupils in gemlike color.

"You must miss the hustle and bustle of London, Nate," Henley went on, either missing or ignoring Hillard's byplay. "The amusements, the parties, the society . . ."

"I'd forgotten you were a permanent resident of London, Mr. Hillard," Mercy said. "So many of the people I have met have a country address as well as a town one and I must confess, I find it all very complicated."

"So many of the people you have met have the means for two residences," Hillard said with a self-deprecating smile.

Immediately, her cheeks burned with the enormity of her faux pas. "I beg your pardon, Mr. Hillard," she exclaimed, mortified.

"No need, Miss Coltrane. The circumstances of my address or lack of one is simply a temporary condition. Who knows, next year perhaps I'll own four country houses."

"And why would you want to?" Henley asked, his usual smile absent. "Great encumbrance, if you ask me."

The bitterness in the words was obvious, and Mercy was reminded that the Wrexhalls lived on Hart's ancestral estate, which Henley managed during Hart's prolonged and successive absences.

"Too true, Henley. I have no desire to *own* property, I merely wish to have the occasional use of it."

"You enjoy living in the city, Mr. Hillard?" Mercy asked, an idea forming in her mind. Perhaps she need not embroil Hart in her plans after all. Plainly, Hillard was . . . interested in her and as such might be sympathetic.

"Nate is a gadabout," Henley said. "He knows everyone, everything, and everyplace in London."

"Hardly," Hillard demurred. "I simply enjoy the company of my fellow man. I am, I admit, a social creature."

"Perhaps you have met my brother in town, Mr. Hillard."

"Your brother?" Hillard's smooth forehead creased. "Ah, yes. The mysterious Will. I recall your mention of him when we were first introduced in London. Quite intent on discovering his whereabouts, you were. And have you found your elusive sibling?" he asked.

"No. I haven't."

"Oh! Forgive my flippancy, Miss Coltrane. I assumed you—" He stopped, turning his hands up apologetically. "I am sorry to say I haven't had the pleasure of meeting your brother. How long has he been in the city?"

"He's been in England for nearly a year. I suspect he's spent most of that time in London."

"Suspect?" Henley asked. "You mean you don't know?"

Mercy smiled, aware it was a brittle attempt. "No. I don't. He is apparently kicking over the traces as young men are wont to do—or so I've been told," she added with a dark thought to Hart. "I wish to remind him that he has a doting family."

Nathan studied her with approval and tenderness. "Might I be so presumptuous as to ask after him for you?"

"Oh, would you?" she asked eagerly, leaning

forward. "I'd be so grateful." She considered naming the places William frequented but recalled the Peacock's disreputable air and even more disreputable bartender and decided against such a course. It could give Hillard a bad opinion of Will, make him renege on his offer of help.

Perhaps just having him ask among his acquaintances would net results. He might know someone who knew someone. . . . After all, many of the men at the Peacock's Tail had been as fashionably dressed as those here.

"I'd be delighted," he said. "But I feel obliged to say that if your brother is determined to remain elusive—especially a lad who is intent on establishing his independence," he added with an indulgent smile, "—there is little hope of finding him. London is a big city."

"Oh, I'll find him," Mercy said stubbornly. "However long it takes, I will find him. He's my only sibling, you see. I must find him."

"With such resolution I wager you'll succeed," Hillard answered in a soft, considering voice.

"What is it you're wagering now, Hillard?" Acton hailed them. Mercy turned to find her host bearing down on them, his broad ruddy face wreathed in smiles. Annabelle Moreland glided at his side, a vision of loveliness in pale lilac muslin and tiny orchid-colored satin bows. "You aren't challenging Miss Coltrane to another contest of marksmanship, are you?" Acton demanded in a bluff tone.

"Good Lord, no," Hillard said. "I wouldn't stand a chance."

"Good, because I've just been to see the gamekeeper and I have my own suit with which to press Miss Coltrane. I had him set out some three hundred pheasants in the meadow yesterday. Today"—he rubbed his hands together—"would be splendid weather for an afternoon shoot."

"I'm afraid I don't hunt, Acton," Henley said.

Acton glanced at him as though just realizing his presence. "Oh, Wrexhall. Quite all right. But for those of us who do, it shall be marvelous." He turned to Mercy. "I was hoping you'd grace us with your skill, as well as your delightful company, Miss Coltrane."

Mercy cast about for some way of refusing. Since provoking Hart into that contest, Acton had become her most ardent fan. It was a bit wearing having to live up to his exaggerated—and romanticized—image of her.

"The other ladies will be attending?" she asked.

He smiled. "Oh, none of the other ladies can hope to match your skill, Miss Coltrane. I'm sure they will be content to spectate from the carriages."

Not if Annabelle were an example of such contentment, thought Mercy. The young girl was regarding her frostily. There was a definite ripple of discontent across the seemingly impenetrable pool of her serenity.

"Do you shoot, Miss Moreland?" she asked.

"No, Miss Coltrane. I am not a sportswoman," Annabelle said.

"Course you aren't, Miss Moreland," Acton said. "Perhaps you and some of the other ladies can arrange a *déjeuner* alfresco?"

"Certainly. Would you like to start with cheese and fruit?" the girl snapped. "And what beverage? Lemonade? Hot chocolate? Perhaps you'd like me to see that the linen is properly ironed?"

Startled, Mercy looked at her.

"Ah, that won't be necessary." Acton's mouth looked a trifle slack.

"And for the main course?" Annabelle continued. "Meat pies or sausages in pastry?"

Mercy could have sworn one dainty foot was tapping beneath the four tiers of laced ruffles.

"Anything," Acton squeaked, and cleared his throat. "Whatever Cook provides."

Wrexhall grinned. "Quite partial to sausage myself, Belle," he said.

"I'll arrange it immediately." Annabelle twirled, her frothy lilac skirts billowing out as she strode away, probably off to inform her brother of the suspected insult.

"If you gentlemen would excuse me," Mercy said, marking Annabelle's progress through the small groups of people.

"Of course, dear Miss Coltrane," Acton said, bowing forward at the waist. "We'll see you later on."

"Yes," she murmured, waiting to see which door Annabelle exited through.

"You'll be shooting, then?" Hillard asked as she started forward.

"Yes, I expect so." She'd lose sight of Annabelle if she didn't hurry. "Good morning, gentlemen." She hastened across the room, arriving in the wide, gleaming hallway just as Annabelle was about to turn the corner.

"Miss Moreland!" Mercy called.

The girl obviously didn't want to acknowledge her. But it would have been ridiculous to pretend she didn't hear her. They were the only two people in the hall. She had stopped but not yet turned. Mercy could see the tension in the set of her narrow back.

Good manners won out. Annabelle turned, a small questioning lift to one golden brow. She waited until Mercy was close enough so that she didn't need to raise her voice. Point for Annabelle, Mercy thought wryly.

"Miss Coltrane?" she asked politely. "There is something you wanted? An item added to the luncheon menu, perhaps?"

Mercy laughed and Annabelle's lovely eyes widened.

"No, Miss Moreland. I am looking for your brother. I have a—a book he wished to borrow."

It wasn't a very good lie, but Annabelle's breeding once more held on, if but by a tenuous thread. "Do you?" she said. "Well, I'm afraid you'll have to wait until later to give it to him. He's gone."

"Gone?" To press Annabelle for more information was unforgivably vulgar and if Annabelle had had even a year of seniority over her, Mercy was sure she would have given her the set-down she was obviously trembling to contain. Thank God for English governesses.

"Yes," Annabelle said. "At breakfast this morning he mentioned he would be in London for the day. Business. Is there anything *else* you want to know?"

London, Mercy thought. He'd gone to find Will by himself. *Damn him, he's left you behind like a lame dog.*

The thought cut deeply. After she'd made clear how important it was that she be the one to approach Will. *After he'd held you. After you'd imagined he might have some feeling. . . .* She refused to follow the thought further.

"No, Miss Moreland," she said faintly.

"You're most welcome," said Annabelle, and, with one last superior glance, left.

"Bully!" shouted Major Sotbey as the pheasant plummeted from the sky in a flurry of feathers. "Grand sport, what?" he asked, beaming at Mercy.

"Delightful," she returned perfunctorily.

"That's a fine-looking firearm you have there, ma'am," he said.

"Thank you, Major. Lovely, isn't it? It's a Winchester."

"You carried your shotgun from America?" the major asked.

"No, sir. His Grace had it in his collection. He gave it to me after the, er . . . exhibition between Lord Perth and myself." Hart's face flickered across her thoughts. She forced it away. He'd left her. Even now he was in London, searching for Will while she stood here, useless and abandoned.

"Did he, now?" The retired major's voice took on an interested tone.

Mercy fixed him with a severe gaze. "Yes, sir. As a *consolation* prize to the losing participant."

"Didn't really lose, though, did you?" the major asked. "Just left Perth the field."

"No, sir. I forfeited because I could not repeat his shots."

"Well, young lady, you'll have a hard time convincing Acton of that."

"Convincing me of what, Major?" Lord Acton asked, appearing beside them.

"Convincing you that Miss Coltrane here isn't the best shot in the county."

"Too true," Acton declared. He beamed at Mercy. "Miss Coltrane, you haven't fired yet. Is there something amiss? You dislike your gun?" His face fell.

"No indeed, Lord Acton. It is a very nice gun. Everything is very . . . well orchestrated," she replied.

"I know what the problem is," Acton said, snapping his fingers. "These fellows are so set on impressing you, they haven't given you a clear shot."

"Really, that's not the—"

"Here, now! Gentlemen!" he called. The other members of their party stopped their slow progress through the waist-high grass that still gallantly held on to a vestige of summer's green. "We'll let Miss Coltrane have a go, shall we?"

"That's not necessary," Mercy protested, but Acton was bound and determined to showcase her expertise.

"Course it is," he said. "Pull up, lads."

The other men complied, shouldering their shotguns and waiting patiently for her to shoot something. Fighting back a sound of resignation, Mercy pushed the safety button on the gun and waded out into the grass. Acton wouldn't be content until she'd downed at least one pheasant.

She looked over her shoulder to the small oak-tree-covered knoll where open carriages, festooned with bright ribbons and more brightly clad ladies, were parked. All except Annabelle, who was standing a bit away from the carriages, watching her with that impassive chill so like her brother's.

Mercy wistfully regarded the relaxed, convivial—well, mostly convivial—group. They were sipping punch, nibbling on cakes, and droning on to each other like autumn-drunk bees while she staggered over hummocks and rodent holes as beaters drove the fields a hundred feet ahead.

She narrowed her eyes against the sun. She would have freckles tomorrow. Unless Brenna had some magical concoction that took care of those too.

Suddenly, to her right, a pheasant rooster exploded from a gorse thicket, cackling raucously as it beat its wings skyward. With a tinge of regret Mercy shouldered her shotgun. At least it was a clean end. One second flying upward, the next falling lifeless to the ground.

She pulled the trigger.

A deafening roar shattered her eardrums. Agony ripped up her hands through her arms. The world buckled beneath her.

And then it was she, not the pheasant, that fell to the ground.

Chapter 18

Hart rounded the stable and headed for the front of the house, weariness slowing his pace. He'd spent an entire day in London, choking on the fumes in countless gin houses, "private" clubs, and dens, and still he was no closer to finding William Coltrane than he'd been when he set out this morning. And no closer to ending Mercy's quest.

The memory of her lithe young body, so supple and vulnerable, relaxing into his embrace, stirred a deep yearning in him. He bit it back. There would be nothing she wanted from him now, except possibly his head on a platter.

The thought wrung a rueful smile from him. She would be mad enough to spit because he'd left her behind. Not that he'd had any choice. Since he hadn't been able to bring himself to frighten her into staying behind, he'd simply sneaked away. Now, as soon as she discovered that he was back, she'd doubtless treat him to a display of American vitriol. He picked up his stride. If she insisted on a scene, he wouldn't disappoint. He even looked forward to it. Her energy, her passion, were magnetic.

He sniffed at his coat. Even after three quarters of an hour in the open air the faint odor of opium still clung to it. He started to shrug out of the battered ulster and grimaced as he felt the knife wound over his ribs protest this treatment. He looked down. Beneath the concealing coat his shirt was ruined, stained with blood. His thoughts clouded with the memory of the two men he'd left unconscious in the squalid Soho side street.

Six years and he'd not once lifted a finger in violence, and then Mercy Coltrane appeared and awoke every brute instinct he'd thought he'd destroyed. He had snapped one of those men's wrists with no more remorse than he'd buttered his toast. And God help him, he'd do worse if the situation should call for it. If *she* needed it.

There was still a dangerous animal lurking beneath the surface calm, testing the bars of self-restraint, prowling along the trenches, waiting for its opportunity to be free. He closed his eyes. She was pushing him toward some fatal union of past and present, some volatile and explosive combination of impulse and act.

He entered the house, intent on avoiding conversation, to find the foyer crowded. Some sort of disturbance had upset Acton's party. White-faced ladies cast surreptitious glances up the staircase, troubled-looking gentlemen clasped their hands behind their backs and murmured.

". . . disastrous," he heard Baron Coffey say.

". . . never heard the like in me life."

". . . couldn't believe the damn thing exploded!"

What, Hart wondered bitterly as he wove his way toward the staircase, *the pastry chef's soufflé?* He'd spent a day among London's lost and destitute. He'd no sympathy for whatever disaster had momentarily interrupted the pleasurable pursuits of Acton's house guests.

"Poor Miss Coltrane . . ." Lady Carr was saying.

He halted, swinging around and scowling at her so fiercely that she stepped back. "What of Miss Coltrane?" he demanded, his pulse quickening.

"You haven't heard?" she asked.

"No. I wouldn't have asked otherwise," he bit out. "*What* of Miss Coltrane?"

"Her shotgun . . . the barrel exploded when she was shooting at—"

"Where is she?"

"They've taken her to her room. But you can't—"

He shouldered his way past her, barely aware of her gasp of indignation. He took the stairs two at a time, his heart hammering, his body tense, a fire of urgency setting his pace.

In the upper hall Beryl detached herself from a group of ladies and came toward him, her lean face full of sympathy. She stretched out a hand to stay him.

"I know she means something to you—" she began to say.

"Get out of my way."

"My God, Perth, you can't just—"

He shook her off and strode to Mercy's door, reaching for the knob. Fear made his hand tremble. *God, don't let her be maimed. Don't let her be dead.*
He wrenched it open.

". . . so please, Lord Acton, don't dismiss your gamekeeper," Mercy was saying.

She was alive.

He closed his eyes, nearly slumping to his knees, fighting to regain the blessed numbing coldness, not wanting to feel these things. Not wanting to sob with relief. He forced his eyes open and looked around the room.

Hillard and Acton were perched on low ottomans beside an ornately carved four-poster in which Mercy lay, propped against a half dozen pillows. Near the bed's foot Lady Acton sat in a wingback chair. All three stared at him in open astonishment. But Mercy . . . her hands lifted toward him. It was only a fractional movement, a matter of a few inches, but it was telling.

He almost went to her then. Almost gave in to the overwhelming need to meet her unspoken entreaty. Almost.

"Hart," she whispered.

He ignored her, swinging on Acton. "What the hell happened? They said there was an explosion."

"Yes." The Duke stumbled to his feet, chagrined and red faced with guilt. "The barrel of her shotgun split. Luckily, she was only thrown by the concussion. The doctor assures me she is fine—"

"*Only* thrown by the concussion?" Hart demanded. "Men have died from such shock, Acton." His gaze raked the other man's face.

"Here now, Perth—" Nathan Hillard said. Why was *he* here?

Hart ignored him. "Whose shotgun was it?"

"It was hers." Acton burned a brighter scarlet. "That is, one I had given her."

"Good God, man," Hart bit out. "Doesn't your gamekeeper check your firearms before handing them out?"

"Perth, it wasn't his fault," Mercy said.

"Yes, it was, Miss Coltrane," Lady Acton said. "You are our guest and therefore our responsibility. I have been remiss in my duty. How remiss is only now"—her autocratic gaze touched Hart—"becoming apparent. I cannot tell you how very much I regret our negligence."

Mercy stirred among the flounced and ruffled covers. "The gun was fine," she insisted. "I checked the action myself before the hunt. It was in perfect working order."

"But, my dear," Hillard crooned, "surely there was some small defect that would have escaped the hobbyist's eye but should not have been missed by the gamekeeper."

"No," Mercy said, a stubborn set to her mouth. "I am not a hobbyist, Mr. Hillard. I am well acquainted with firearms. I have had to be. There was nothing untoward about that gun when I returned it for loading."

"An undetectable weakness in the metal, perhaps?" Hillard offered. "Or the shell was improperly loaded?"

"That must be it," Mercy said with a grateful smile. "And as it was undetectable, no blame can be ascribed. So as I was saying, please do not dismiss the gamekeeper."

"If that is your wish, dear valiant lady," Acton said. Hart felt his lips tighten.

"It is." She looked over at him. "I'm sorry you have returned to such a commotion, *Mr.* Perth. I heard you went to London. On business." The light in her eyes took on a harsher cast.

Ah, he thought, *she knows where I have spent the day and wants to question me about what I've discovered.* She'd already dismissed her accident as inconsequential and was once more intent on pursuing news about her brother.

But even though she was satisfied with the explanation of why her gun had exploded, he was not. Acton wouldn't own any but the finest firearms.

"I trust your trip was productive?" she asked, pushing herself more upright in the bed and glowering at him.

"Not particularly."

"How unfortunate. Things did not go well?" she asked.

The others in the room swung their attention back and forth between them.

"The party I was hoping to meet did not show up."

"Ah. You will *have* to find the time to tell me about it," she said. "I insist. I am so interested in English business practices."

No, he would not find time to tell her anything. He would not spend one more moment alone with Mercy Coltrane. She was blackmailing him—even if he understood her reasons for doing so. She was an impediment to his youngest sister's marriage— even if she was unaware of it.

But most of all, she threatened all the years he'd spent buffing the chill that encased his heart, all the years he'd spent trying to subdue those feral tendencies.

Being with her simply risked too much.

———————————•◆•———————————

Outside in the hall Beryl fell into step beside him. "Good Lord, Hart. I would have told you the girl was all right if you'd only paused long enough to listen. Whatever can you have been thinking? How on earth do you suppose it appeared to Lady Acton and her son when you burst into her room like that?"

"I don't give a bloody damn," he answered.

She snagged his sleeve, stopping him. She glanced around. They were well away from the in- terested gazes of the others clustered around Mercy's doorway.

"Well, you'd better start giving a bloody

damn," she said in a low, tense voice. "Your actions may well jeopardize Annabelle's future."

He ground his teeth. She was right. He'd acted like some gauche, ridiculous knight errant. The Dowager would doubtless be asking herself what had given him the right to storm into Mercy's room and act so possessive. Mercy—as well as Annabelle—could only suffer as a result of his rash act.

"How could you, Hart?" Beryl went on. "Acton has been growing more and more indifferent and Annabelle is beside herself with anguish, the poor lamb."

He narrowed his eyes on her. He would accept blame, but it was time that some things were made clear. "If Annabelle is beside herself with anguish, it isn't discernibly different emotion from her rendition of jubilation."

Beryl gasped. "Hart—"

"No, not 'Hart.' Annabelle. Good God, Beryl. If the chit has a *tendresse* for that blustering oaf, she has a damn odd way of showing it. Padding about like some wan ghost."

"Hart, what has happened?" Beryl asked, troubled and anxious. "This isn't like you. Annabelle is a dear, sweet child."

"Perhaps Acton wishes to wed a woman," he said, his thought unerringly refocusing on Mercy.

She blinked at him in consternation. "Please, Hart. Don't be like this. Remember, you're the head of our family."

"No, Beryl," he said intently, "Henley is the head of your family."

"Yes, of course," she said, turning pink. "But you've always . . . accomplished things. Annabelle needs your help."

Annabelle. He had to think of her.

He was exhausted, his side throbbed, he stank of opium, and Mercy's image imbued his every thought; Mercy, yielding to him; Mercy, laughing at him; Mercy, defiant and fierce; Mercy, pale and slight among white lace pillow shams. He scowled. Something about the gun's explosion disturbed him. Ridiculous. First a shot in the woods, now this. Accidents did happen. Even twice in as many days. Even to Mercy.

He must force her from his thoughts. Whatever his preoccupation with Mercy, it did not exempt him from his duty to his sisters. "All right, Beryl. I'll make amends somehow. Smooth things over."

She nodded, satisfaction marching alongside her obvious relief. "And, Hart, there's something else. . . ." Her gaze skittered away from his.

"Yes?"

"Henley. He is having some problems."

"What sort of *problems*, and where *is* Henley, anyway?"

"Political problems," she said. "That's why he was gone today and yesterday. He was in Town meeting with various House leaders and some of his constituents." Her mouth crimped unhappily. "Oh, Hart. They abuse his dedication horribly. Sometimes these meetings go on well into the evening. Often he has to stay in town overnight."

Henley was having political meetings in Town?

During the off-season? It was highly unlikely. No one stayed in Town when Parliament was not in session. Yet one look at Beryl's intent face and he realized she believed it.

"And what do you want me to do?" he asked.

"I want you to use your influence to smooth Henley's way so he needn't work so hard. See that he knows the right people."

He shook his head. "As I've told you before, Beryl, *I* don't know the right people. I have no connections, Beryl, whatever you think. I'm rarely even in the country."

"But you're the Earl of Perth," she insisted doggedly. "People listen to you. Even Henley says so."

He narrowed his eyes on her. "Did Henley ask you to make this request?"

"No," she said, refusing to meet his gaze. "No. He would be angry if he knew I had. It is my idea. Being the Earl of Perth's brother-in-law has always lent Henley a certain cachet. I thought . . . that is, I had hoped that you would be willing to actively exert yourself on his behalf."

"Beryl," he said wearily, "my interference wouldn't do any good. Henley is a brilliant man. He will succeed or fail on his own merit."

Her fine-drawn vulpine features took on a resigned cast. "As you say, Hart," she murmured, and left, her shoulders bowing, her face for one brief moment stark with unhappiness.

Henley Wrexhall, Hart thought, had some explaining to do.

Chapter 19

"*W*ell," the Dowager Duchess said as soon as she had shooed the others from Mercy's room, "what was that all about?"

"What?" Mercy asked.

The Dowager pursed her thin lips so tightly, they all but disappeared. "Don't play the innocent with me, young lady. Nothing is going as I'd planned. The Earl of Perth storms in here, demanding explanations in the most proprietary manner. Nathan Hillard looks like a little boy who's had his sweet taken from him, and my own son, after having arranged this elaborate house party, does nothing, *nothing*, to conclude his courtship with that young chit.

"Add to that the Whitcombes closeted in their adjoining room—I won't even begin to tell you the coarse speculation *that* must be provoking; then young Annabelle Moreland inexplicably finds not only a backbone but one made of steel; and Beryl

Wrexhall attends every function without the benefit of her husband as escort. And it is all centering about you, Miss Coltrane. I won't have it."

"I'm sure I don't know what you mean," Mercy murmured, pleating the lace edge of her bed jacket, her thoughts fixed on the Dowager's initial charge. Without a doubt Hart's audacious conduct had landed her in a thicket. Still, a treacherous elation welled up within her. He might not like it, but he cared.

"Have you been doing something you oughtn't?"

The Dowager's question caught her off-guard. She dropped the bed jacket's hem. "No!"

The Dowager gave her a hard look before muttering, "Well, see that you don't. I have a responsibility to you and Lady Timmons. And I mean to do it . . . no matter how painful." She lifted her chin, fixing Mercy with an odd, defiant stare. "I was hoping to avoid this, but it is obvious we need to have A Conversation. You, Miss Coltrane, need guidance."

You can't possibly know how much, thought Mercy as she meekly replied, "Yes, Your Grace. I am grateful for any instruction you would be kind enough to offer."

The Dowager sniffed. "Very pretty, child. I am sure your manner with the gentlemen has been just as circumspect." She fixed Mercy with an expression that made it clear she was not at all sure of anything of the sort.

The memory of slipping into Hart's bedchamber caused heat to ignite in Mercy's cheeks. The Dowager's brows climbed. "Oh, dear," she breathed. "Worse than I'd expected. We must salvage what we can."

"Your Grace, really, you misunderstand—"

"I am an elderly woman, Mercy. I have lived a long life, during which I have witnessed too many women ruined because they gave their hearts the whip hand."

"Ma'am?" Mercy asked.

The Dowager nodded. "We women, Mercy, are by nature foolish, gentle creatures," she lectured. "We are malleable, trusting, at the mercy of our tender emotions. Altogether sweet and childlike, totally unfit to guide our own destinies."

"I see," Mercy murmured. She could almost hear her mother's voice in the Dowager's recitation. *Pliancy, Mercy, is our gift to the world. It is a woman's duty to temper the harsh practicality of men with our innate gentleness.* But how often, Mercy wondered, did simple impotence masquerade as gentleness? Pliancy certainly wasn't going to find Will and bring him home. The thought seemed a betrayal of her mother.

"Mercy, do try and attend. I speak only for your own good. Being an American you are doubly handicapped. Your womanly sentimentality is compounded by your American frivolity."

"Madam?"

The Dowager frowned. She obviously found this frank manner of speech distasteful, but just as obviously felt the need for it. "You American girls

are so audacious, so animated, yet so *innocent*," the
Dowager said with something like surprise. "Especially compared to our serene, self-effacing English
girls. Clearly, you have been encouraged to indulge your ebullient, labile emotions to an exces-
sive degree.

"Not that you aren't perfectly charming, my
dear," she added, "and I do not mean to wound
you, but you do want to be a lady, do you not?"

Again, the words were so familiar, Mercy
nearly blinked. Familiar and yet it seemed as
though she were truly hearing them for the first
time. Perhaps it was because this was only the
Dowager Duchess of Acton speaking and not her
mother and so she could for the first time hear beyond the disappointment to the content.

Her mother had spent her life hoping Mercy
would achieve the dreams she herself had abandoned. But now, listening to the Dowager, it struck
Mercy that her hostess was very much like her
mother. Neither had really relinquished her own
aspirations. They had simply bequeathed them to
their children.

An idea pricked at Mercy. She had unquestion-
ingly received the burden of those dreams and
from the first she had failed to fulfill them. Always
before she had been certain that some inherent
quality within herself—something unworthy and
unwomanly—had resulted in that failure. But perhaps that wasn't true. Perhaps her mother should
not have expected her to achieve secondhand
goals.

The idea wouldn't be ignored. And, Mercy was stunned to realize, instead of guilt she felt a sense of relief, something akin to emancipation.

": . . but your ebullience may give rise to unfortunate talk," the Dowager was saying. "Our English gentlemen may misunderstand you. As the Earl of Perth—and perhaps my own son—has obviously done. And then where are you, m'dear?" she asked.

"I have never acted improperly," Mercy said distractedly, still overwhelmed by her newfound conjecture.

"Would you even know it if you had?" the Dowager went on. "Society is based on subtlety and nuance, Miss Coltrane. Perhaps unwittingly you have encouraged these gentlemen's attentions or expectations." Mercy met her gaze. The Dowager's did not waver. "I am loath to say this, but their expectations cannot be ones you would welcome."

"I don't understand."

"My point exactly." There was a hint of bitter triumph in her tone. "You must not think for an instance that your charm and wealth will overcome generations of exclusivity and breeding."

"Ma'am?"

"I am forced into being unbecomingly coarse," she said, her face tightening with distaste. "Acton finds you vivacious and intriguing. It is only to be expected. He has had scant intercourse with a woman of your upbringing and subsequently has developed all the signs of becoming besotted with you. But mark me well, my dear, he is, when all is said and done, the Duke of Acton."

My God, Mercy thought, *she is warning me off Acton*. That bluff, fusty, sweetly incompetent man! "Your Grace . . . !" Mercy blurted out in a agony of embarrassment.

The Dowager lifted her hand, waving down her words. "I do not care that the Duke of Manchester's son has married an American heiress. His profligate behavior had already precluded him from marrying any decent Englishwoman. Not to mention that his mother danced the cancan at a music hall with the Prince." She sniffed, some mental image offending her. "What more could one expect of her offspring? But that is not the case here, Mercy. Acton has impeccable antecedents and a tradition to uphold."

Mercy's sense of humor saved her at the last minute. The Dowager had sat back a little and was watching her expectantly, if compassionately, obviously expecting Mercy to wail with despair that she wasn't going to be allowed to wed her son. Mercy simply did not have it in her to disappoint such maternal confidence.

"Oh!" She managed to turn a laugh into a shaky breath and bowed her head, her lower lip trembling.

"I know, dear," Lady Acton said. "But it had to be said. One can only hope that your heart is not already too deeply engaged. Acton can be most charming."

Mercy sniffed. Three sniffs seemed adequate.

"I'm nonplussed, madam. But I shall strive to overcome my . . . disappointment."

The Dowager fidgeted. It was so uncharacteristic, that Mercy abruptly left off snuffling. "There is something else, ma'am?"

"Yes." The Dowager stiffened her spine and edged forward, sitting regally erect, composed and autocratic. She did not flinch from meeting Mercy's eye. "I am further compelled by my obligation as your hostess and chaperone to warn you that neither is the Earl of Perth a potential suitor. No matter what his extraordinary behavior a few minutes ago."

She was blindsided by the Dowager's words. She had not expected to have half-formed dreams, dreams so tenuous and fragile she had not even acknowledged them to herself, so brutally discovered and dismissed. She had no defense against the other woman's words, she could only stare at the Dowager's stern face, feeling more exposed and vulnerable than she'd ever been before.

The blood pounded dully in her temples. The room seemed suddenly too large, too cold. She should have expected this, but she'd been intent on deluding herself, experiencing each moment in Hart's company as a separate thing, without past or future, refusing to acknowledge the emotion that grew each time she saw him.

Love.

God help her, she was in love with Hart Moreland, a man to whom titles and privilege and English society were so important he'd spent a decade serving them for his sisters' sake.

Fool, she thought bitterly, telling herself Hart cared, quivering with joy when he'd stormed into her room, storing away the memories of his heart beating beneath her cheek, his arms effortlessly lifting her, the scent of tobacco and wool, his lips opening over her own with something she'd foolishly called desire. . . .

"Perhaps Mr. Hillard might entertain notions of forming a permanent alliance with you, Mercy," the Dowager went on after a moment. Mercy nearly wept. "He is, after all, an intimate of our Prince, a man who is reported to be quite besotted with young American girls. And Hillard has no title to consider."

And then the tears did fall, hot and bitter and uncontrollable. She dashed them away, her face averted, staring out the window.

"My dear," the Dowager said, stiffly reluctant. "Perhaps a Hungarian count. Or a French *duc* . . . their titles are mostly formalities anyway."

"Please, just go," Mercy said.

"Well. My heavens." Indignation that she'd been so summarily dismissed filled her tone. Mercy heard the Dowager's heavy skirts rustle, heard the click of heeled slippers cross the room.

"I will leave you to compose yourself." There was heavy criticism in her voice.

Mercy almost laughed through her tears. No, indeed, she wasn't acting like a lady, not at all. But a lady probably wouldn't allow her heart to be shredded on an icy facade and an ancient title.

"I will see what I can do for you. Perhaps when we return to London, I can arrange an introduction to one of the Russian princes. Or an Italian count," the Dowager said. The door hissed open and quickly shut.

Mercy buried her face in her hands. The Dowager could parade titles and coronets and medals and estates by her until the end of time. She did not want a title.

She wanted a gunfighter.

———◆———

Hart stared out of his bedroom window as dawn, still a filigree of silver, traced the horizon. He hadn't slept much. Not that he ever did. Rather than attend dinner last night, he'd gone back to London. There he'd scoured the Soho district, looking for some trace of William Coltrane.

He hadn't found Coltrane but he had found others: lost eyes and ruined dreams, men feeding a hunger for oblivion and women feeding an irrepressible hunger to survive. Desperation, remorse, and resignation. He'd seen the like before, in North African tent villages and overflowing Eastern seaports, in American cattle towns and in European capitals. He saw the like every time he looked in the mirror.

Finally, a few hours after midnight, a glassy-eyed dandy had told him that he'd shared a pipe with Will Coltrane a few days before. Hart had pressed him. A day to an addict is no more than a notion. But the man had insisted he knew Will well.

Charming chap, for all his American accent, the man had said. Too bad he'd been bankrupted. Rather changed his personality. Became unpleasantly insistent. The man had paused to squint at Hart in perplexity. Why, the dandy had wondered aloud, hadn't Will's mentor extradited him from his financial troubles?

Mentor? That had caught Hart's attention. What mentor? Who was he? "The mentor" was discreet, well spoken, English. Maybe tallish, maybe broad, always wore a slouch hat, didn't know what color his hair was. The dandy couldn't say any more than that. He hadn't paid that much attention.

Hart had returned to Acton's estate with his thoughts racing. Who was guiding Will through London's sordid underbelly? And, more important, who was responsible for Mercy's accidents? Because the more he considered the matter, the more inexplicable those accidents became. And try as he might, he could think of no one more likely to want Mercy dead, and her inheritance forfeit, than her own brother. A desperate man, Hart knew full well, was capable of any betrayal.

But how had Will Coltrane managed these accidents? Could he somehow be at Acton's estate? It seemed impossible that his presence wouldn't have been noted.

There was only one thing Hart was certain of: he couldn't tell Mercy his conjectures. She wouldn't believe him and, knowing her, it would only send her racing into potential danger.

When he'd finally stumbled to his blankets, Hart had been hounded by dreams as relentless as they were familiar. But this time images of Mercy's body, torn and brutalized, were superimposed over all the other horrific visions. He'd woken, sweat drenched and shivering in the cold winter darkness, and stood sentinel at midnight's gate, waiting for dawn.

Madness, he thought, finally turning away from the ash-colored vista. How had he allowed Mercy Coltrane to become so thoroughly entangled in his heart? When had he let her past the wall he'd so carefully constructed?

Let? he asked himself grimly, *allowed?* His heart had not asked permission to love Mercy. He had simply taken the only course open to him. To deny himself this love, however ill fated it might be, would be like asking a blind man to relinquish an hour of sight.

But like that blind man, there was a price to pay for the sharp, painful reawakening of his heart—brief, tantalizing, so acute it burned.

For there was no chance such a love could find expression. He lived by sheer will on the near side of madness, hounded by night terrors from which he awoke howling like a dog, chased by unnamed specters that could set him trembling for days on end.

What could he offer her? A man whose hand sometimes shook so badly he could not hold a glass of water without spilling it? The custodianship of a madman? Sometimes only his fury and disgust at his weakness kept him from sobbing like a babe. God, even his name was not his own to give.

And, too, there were others to consider. He snagged the blanket from the floor and flung it to the bed. He could offer but one thing: he could find her damn brother.

For all the joy it would bring her . . . or him.

Chapter 20

"*I*t's delightful to see you up and looking so well, Miss Coltrane," Nathan Hillard said the next day as he joined her at the dairy barn's door. It was late morning and Acton was taking them on a tour of the home farm.

"Thank you, Mr. Hillard. And thank you for your consideration yesterday," Mercy replied. Hillard had apparently been the first one to her after she'd fallen. He—so she'd been told—had carried her to the house, shouting orders for her immediate care. Now, his unusual eyes shone with a soft, concerned light.

"I trust your unfortunate accident yesterday left no lasting impairments?" he asked.

"None in the least." She had responded to countless such queries since she'd appeared at breakfast. By and large they had been solicitous. Except, that is, for the unmistakable tincture of gratification coloring Annabelle Moreland's gratis inquiry. As though she had supposed something unseemly was bound to occur to any woman who infiltrated so masculine a province as hunting and was happy to have her suspicions confirmed.

Mercy hung back from the rest of the guests peering into the barn. Hart stood a short distance away, Annabelle's hand resting in the crook of his arm, his austere features approximating interest. The Whitcombes were beside them, Richard tenderly supporting a puffy-faced Fanny. Only Henley and Beryl's absence kept the group from presenting a perfect tableau of family affection, Mercy thought, suddenly wishing fiercely that Will were here, with her.

She found herself studying Hart's drawn face. He knew something, she would swear to it, and he was keeping it from her. All morning he'd avoided her, making polite conversation with the other guests, placidly dogging his sisters' steps—in other words acting totally out of character. Perhaps Lady Acton had had A Conversation with him too. The thought hurt. It hurt more that he'd apparently taken it to heart.

Well, he needn't concern himself that she would embarrass him by reading anything into his appearance in her room yesterday. She knew now what she had seen: a man she'd coerced into extending his protection to her; a man to whom responsibilities were sacrosanct.

She didn't need his protection. She needed him to find Will. She would think only of her brother.

Liar.

"I was so very worried about you," Nathan said in a low, warm voice, interrupting her thoughts. "Your welfare has come to mean a great deal to me."

His fixed study of her face brought warmth creeping up her throat.

"Miss Coltrane, I cannot stay silent any longer. Surely you must be aware of my regard—"

"Sir, please," she broke in, remorsefully recognizing the ardor in his tone. "I am unable to think of anything other than finding my brother. I cannot think of myself while he is lost."

"Of course." Nathan inclined his head, masking any affront or pain her words might have caused. He was so perfect a gentleman, even without a title or money; he was exactly the sort of man her mother would have wanted for her . . . urbane, gentle, polished.

"But soon the matter of his whereabouts will be resolved and then—"

"Soon?" She leapt on the word.

"I have had the first responses to those inquiries about your brother I made for you," Hillard said quietly.

"You did?" He must have received word among the morning's posts.

"You were very naughty, m'dear." His gaze touched her tenderly. "You should have told me your brother was involved in activities beyond the pale."

The hint of patronization set the hair pricking on the nape of her neck. "Is he?" she asked.

"So my friends say. But then"—a light, charming smile—"people are given to exaggeration."

"Do you know where Will is?"

"Alas, I do not. Your brother seems to have disappeared. Perhaps he has gone to the Continent."

She frowned, troubled. If she could not find Will here, what chance had she to find him in France, or Austria, or Italy? No. She didn't believe it. He'd said he would write again at the end of the week. She still had three days. "I don't think so, Mr. Hillard."

"Well, rest assured I shall do everything in my power to find him for you."

"As will I," she said smiling, feeling guilty for her churlishness when he obviously wanted only to help. She allowed him to take her hand and squeeze it encouragingly.

"I must warn you, you might not like what you find."

"I'll take that chance," she replied. "Will is not an evil boy. He is perhaps too easily led. But someone has done the leading. I only wish I knew who," she ended tightly.

"Perhaps. But then, perhaps he has found his own way."

"I will not believe that," she said.

"As you say, m'dear."

"Miss Coltrane!" Acton suddenly called to her from the front of the party. "Miss Coltrane, I would appreciate your opinion on my cows."

Mercy grinned at Hillard's surprised expression. "Because I'm a rancher's daughter, Lord Acton thinks my understanding of cows is neigh well omniscient. If you'll excuse me, Mr. Hillard?"

The other guests opened a path for her to Lord Acton's side. He was standing beside a brown Swiss, patting it awkwardly, beaming with pride. The heifer rolled its eye.

"What do you think?" he asked when she was beside him. Lady Acton, on the other side of her son, had gone rigid with disapproval, her eyes frosty with warning.

Damn be to Lady Acton! Mercy thought, suddenly angry. *Damn be to her arrogance and insensitivity and cautions.* She was tired of being made use of as a means of assuaging the ennui of Lady Acton's friends, as a collectible American oddity, as the unwilling receptacle of the Dowager's indiscreet confidences—confidences revealed to her not because she was trusted but because no merit would ever be ascribed anything she might recount. Her nationality—and concomitant lack of breeding—robbed her of credibility with these people. And most of all, damn Lady Acton for her "obligation" to warn her off her son—and Hart.

Mercy turned, clasping her hands in front of her heart and smiling up at Acton. "What do *I* think? Why, I think that these, sir, are prettiest stock I have ever had the pleasure of viewing. I have never seen such bovine beauty. Look at those clear eyes, those shining coats, those splendid feet!"

Acton puffed his chest out with pleasure.

Someone chuckled and Mercy swiveled. Hart was smiling at the ground. She studied him suspiciously. His smile was so beautiful. His teeth were white and even. A long dimple scored one lean cheek and a lock of thick brown hair had fallen over his brow.

"Why, thank you, Miss Coltrane," Acton said. "Did you note their udders? Not that I know that much about udders, but I am told that these have lovely little—"

"Acton!" Lady Acton cut in. "I think we've had quite enough of the barn." Her eyes, beneath aging hooded lids, pierced Mercy with a look of pure dislike and more. Beneath Lady Acton's imperious manner Mercy glimpsed an extraordinary vulnerability.

Her gaze fell away from Lady Acton's. What right had she to determine Lady Acton's priorities for her? If the purity of her family lineage was so important to Lady Acton, so be it.

Clearly, the Dowager saw Mercy as a threat to everything she cherished and in her worst nightmares envisioned her ancient name being used to provoke titters at dining tables or, worse, pity among her intimates.

Mercy's anger evaporated. She would never fit in here. And she was punishing Lady Acton for that.

"Ah, er, of c-course, Mother," Acton stammered. He offered his arm to Mercy.

"Your Grace," she said, "I still feel some of the effects of yesterday's accident and I would not like to hold back the rest of the tour. It's far too informative. Please continue without me. I'll just amble along at my own pace."

"You're certain?" Acton asked, casting a troubled glance at his mother.

"Quite."

"Do get on with it, Acton," Lady Acton said coolly. "We are having an early luncheon."

With an apologetic smile Acton moved forward. The rest of the party slipped by her, heading out of the barn. Not knowing what else to do, she trailed behind until she found herself standing at the paddock gate a short distance from the Morelands.

Annabelle took one glance at her and, with a slight tightening of her small, bowed lips threaded her way toward the opposite side.

If my popularity continues along this course, Mercy thought, *I'll be wearing tar and feathers to Acton's country ball.*

" 'Splendid feet'?" Hart whispered. She could not control the start his voice—low, modulated, incredibly sexy—caused her. No more than she could control the sudden acceleration of her heartbeat.

"You really are incorrigible," he continued. "Teasing Lady Acton like that."

Her cheeks warmed at the laughter in his voice. She did not want to look at him. He was far too appealing, particularly in this gentle, cajoling mood.

"Oh, the dears!" Fanny flew by her, swooping toward a stack of hay bales near the fence and snatching a tiny, furry bundle from a crevice. Eyes shimmering with tears, she held the tiny kitten to her face, rubbing her cheek up and down along its back.

"Oh, the little love!" she said. "It's a baby! A teeny 'ittle babekins! Isn't he the sweetest 'ittle t'ing?" She thrust the kitten into Mercy's face as if for confirmation. The kitten slashed out with a tiny, needle-spiked paw.

"Delightful," Mercy said.

"Isn't it?" breathed Fanny. "It just a teeny 'ittle sweet 'ums." She spun and held it up for her husband's approval. Mercy sidled a step closer to Hart.

"Don't tell me," she said in a low voice. "You never allowed your sisters to have a cat."

"Cat?" he asked. "Of course they've had cats. The creatures are epidemic in the country. Push over a hay bale, you find a cat."

For some reason her implied criticism had touched a nerve. Good. He had her feeling more than raw. His very presence was an abrasion, making her too aware of her body, her pulse, her breathing, a dull ache in her lips that only the pressure of his could assuage.

"Why would you think I wouldn't let them have a cat? Really, Mercy, you have the oddest notions of me and what I—"

"If you don't do something soon," she said calmly, "there'll be one less cat plaguing Jolly Ole England."

"What?" He looked beyond her at his sister. Fanny was clutching the kitten to her bosom. It hissed and yowled, struggling fiercely to avoid being literally smothered with Fanny's affection. "Oh, for God's sake, Fanny, let the poor beastie go!" he said.

"But, Hart. I just want—"

"Let the kitten go, dearest," Richard cooed. "It wants its mother."

"Oh!" Hastily, Fanny tucked the kitten back in the straw pile.

Something in her stricken face, in the tender regard with which Richard watched her, alerted Mercy. *Fanny,* she realized, *is pregnant.* She should have known. All the pieces added up: Fanny's tempests of tears, her puffy face, her moodiness, her absence at meals . . .

"Come along, dearest," Richard said. "We'll return to the house for a nice spot of custard." He tucked his wife's hand through the crook of his arm and led her away.

"You know, Hart," Mercy said thoughtfully, "it really isn't good for a woman in her condition to indulge in all those sweets."

"Excuse me?"

"Pregnant women shouldn't get fat. And I do hope she's stopped wearing corsets. I am sure they are accountable for any number of birth complications— Whatever are you staring at me like that for?"

"No reason. I just usually don't stand about paddocks discussing my sister's breeding habits with young, unmarried women. Of course, no genteel woman would broach such a delicate subject but then again, we're—"

"Not talking about a *genteel* woman," Mercy finished for him, still raw from the Dowager's censure.

He met her angry gaze with an implacable light in his turquoise eyes. He lifted one hand. A heartbeat of a pause. He dropped it. *"If you say so."*

"Are you mocking me?" she asked, tilting her head back.

"I'm trying to help you," he answered. "Lady Acton is a breath away from having you shipped back to London."

He'd caught her off-guard. Her eyes widened, stricken. If she lost Lady Acton's patronage, she had no one else to whom she could turn for social entrée. "But why?"

He shrugged. "For interesting her precious son. Or for Hillard's public pursuit of you, or for making her potential daughter-in-law look vapid in comparison, or for refusing to be an obedient and worshipfully grateful little houseguest," he said, his voice growing colder each minute. "Or for me, because I stormed into your room without any right to do so."

He paused as though steeling himself for what he would say next. "Or for pestering her guests with inquiries about your reprobate brother. Leave it, Mercy. He's an addict. The proof is incontrovertible."

She was bruised by his words, stung by his scorn. "Will is not! You don't know that. Have you seen him? Talked to him? No. I can see you haven't. You're making suppositions. Guessing. Well, I will not forget Will. I promised my mother myself. And I'll do anything—anything!—to find Will. Use Lady Acton. Use her son. Use Hillard—or use you!"

He pinned her with a harsh, unreadable glare. "You have made that clear. But if you want to stay here, and *use* me to search for your damned brother, you'd best behave." He leaned forward, his lean predatory features intent. "And don't give me any crap about not knowing how. You have every grace at your disposal when you've a mind. But you have decided that English society is silly and inconsequential and you are going to thumb your nose at them."

She made to turn away, but he caught her hand, spinning her around and holding her wrists captured between them so no one could see. There was nothing she could do, shy of making a scene, to free herself.

"Have a care, Mercy," he went on in a low, taut voice. "Lady Acton will not allow her son to become involved with you. And she is a far stronger opponent than you give her credit for. If she needs to destroy you to wean her son from his infatuation, she'll do so. And she can. Mark my words."

She turned her head from him. He saw too much, too clearly. She couldn't allow him to see anything else.

Abruptly her wrist was released. She heard his

footsteps, breathed the scent of bruised hay as he departed. Her shoulders slumped. She'd lied.

She had not thought of using Hillard or Acton or him. She had not thought of anything when he'd been with her but the sheen of his mink-brown hair, the fatigue bruising his clear skin, the lean, hard length of his masculine body. After all her promises she'd forgotten Will.

But worse, Hart had not.

Chapter 21

❧❧❧

The evening's entertainment, a performance by a troupe of London-based actors, had ended. The players had left the temporary stage that had been erected in the ballroom and the guests were patiently waiting for the cold collation that was being set up in an anteroom.

Hart could not say if the production had been good—he would have been hard pressed to say what had been performed. He'd spent the hours in the dimly lit ballroom watching Mercy.

Even from this distance her allure was nearly tangible. Her slender figure was draped in some softly antique gold fabric. A jet necklace was nestled in the sweet, shadowed valley between her breasts.

She was trying to be good, he noted dispassionately, apparently having taken his admonitions to heart. She was dividing her conversation, her notice, and her restrained laughter impartially among those clustered around her. She never fixed her attention on any one man for too long. She smiled demurely at her lap, her eyes lowered, a model of maidenly virtue.

It was only Nathan Hillard who was allowed to stay with her longer than was strictly seemly: their heads bowed too near each other as they spoke in hushed tones, their gazes level and earnest, the subject of their conversation obviously serious.

It was infuriating.

And, he thought, it wouldn't do any good. Mercy had made an enemy of her hostess. She hadn't played by Lady Acton's rules. She had shown Lady Acton how vulnerable her ancient bloodlines were and worse, made Lord Acton aware of her as a desirable woman, perhaps even a matrimonial prospect. Lady Acton would never forgive her.

Mercy glanced up and their eyes met across the room. *Oh, no, my dear,* he thought in answer to her silent demand. He wasn't going to tell her what he'd found out about Will . . . or what he suspected about his involvement with her accidents. Not until he knew exactly what this brother of hers was or had become. He'd try again tonight and every night until he found out.

All afternoon she'd been looking for an opportunity to have a private word. He'd made sure there was none. He knew that she considered their conversation at the barn incomplete. She would want to hear everything he knew, hear every piece of evidence that had led him to his assertion that her brother was a drug addict. But if she'd taken his warnings about Lady Acton to heart and gone to pains to present a blameless facade to these people, so must he. They would not be found closeted together. Damn it, he would save her from her impetuous heart.

"Hart." The sharp snap of a fan opening drew his attention. Annabelle stood beside him, the breeze created by her fan agitating a profusion of pale ringlets.

"Annabelle," he greeted her, dismayed that her appearance didn't ignite the swell of pride it once had. All that white was a bit much. White lace, white flowers, white flounces, white feathers. "Have you ever considered wearing an indigo-colored gown?"

She blinked at him.

"Not that I know much about lady's fashion," he continued, "but I think you'd look very nice in something dark blue. Maybe velvet."

She took a deep breath. "I really don't understand you, Hart. *Dresses,* for heaven's sake. I am assured by my London modiste that I am most *à la mode.*"

"You have a London modiste?" He wouldn't pay the next bill. Rigging Annabelle out so she looked like some giant spring lamb. All those frizzed curls—

"I didn't come to discuss fashion with you, Hart," she said. "I need to speak to you—alone." There was a decisive note in her usual dulcet voice.

She looked about. "The conservatory will do as well as any other place."

He nodded and followed her into the adjoining glasshouse. Once inside, she turned around.

"There will be no announcement of forthcoming nuptials between Acton and myself at the ball," she said. "Please, let me finish. I know this is a great disappointment for you and I am very sorry you have had to return to England for nothing, but I did not recall you lightly. I"—her voice wobbled—"I sincerely believed Acton would offer."

"I am not disappointed, Belle," he said, studying her. "Don't concern yourself with me."

Her little mouth puckered as though she were containing a deep-seated anger.

"Belle, I am only concerned for you," he said.

"Well, you have a fine way of showing it," she suddenly snapped. "I haven't seen you in a year and when we do meet, you act like a stranger."

He was taken aback by the vehemence of her tone. She quivered with . . . *irritation*, he realized in surprise, not the hurt he'd expected.

"Instead of spending time with your family," she went on in a low, furious voice, "you flaunt your infatuation with that American interloper!"

She might as well have slapped his cheek.

She went on, ignoring his stiffening posture. "*You* saw to it I was raised as befitted our class and social position," she said. "Why, *now*, on the eve of settling my future, have you ignored the axioms you have had me schooled to and indulged this vulgar whim?"

"Whim?" His voice was careful, composed.

"Yes. What else can it be? You are the Earl of Perth, you would not seriously consider a mésalliance with that person."

"Would I not?" God, how little she knew him.

"No," she said flatly. "I may be young, but I am not green. Beryl has told me the sorts of . . . impulses that lead men to pursue certain types of women. I don't care about your base inclinations. I only care that those inclinations have affected my future."

"I see," he said, biting back other words, as appalled as he was despairing. Because, when all was said and done, she was correct.

He had had her groomed and polished and primed to be the perfect English lady. He had hired the finest governesses and tutors. He had even stolen a title to give her entry into the most exclusive society, assuring her—assuring them all—the life their father's abandonment had nearly forfeited.

He looked at her, nearly regal in her irritation. She'd achieved every criterion he'd set for her. She was utterly his creation.

His stomach coiled. She was also insufferable, arrogant, contemptuous, and disdainful, hiding it all beneath a bland mask of pretty indifference.

He smiled bitterly. He had made her . . . or rather paid to have her made. He couldn't decry his accomplishment now.

"What would you have me do?" he asked tautly.

"I've been thinking." Her silky little brows puckered with consternation. She'd never doubted for a minute that he would do what she asked, he realized. He added manipulation to the list of skills she'd honed. Her regret that she'd "failed him" had been phrased to produce an answering guilt in him.

Very nice, he thought. *Very effective.* He could not help but compare her subtle maneuvering to Mercy's blatant blackmail.

"I believe if Mercy Coltrane's attentions were fixed on one man the rest of the gentlemen would lose interest. Acton could go back to the business of choosing a wife and forget his preoccupation with acquiring a paramour."

His head snapped upright. "You think that is what he is doing?"

"Hart," she said in exasperation, "the one thing I would never have called you is naive. Of course. That is what all the gentlemen are doing. She has money, yes. And some looks. But for God's sake, she is an American rancher's daughter."

He stared at her. He'd never considered the possibility that these other *gentle men* were courting Mercy as a potential mistress. Naive, indeed.

"You're already well ahead of the pack in engaging her interest, Hart. All I ask is that you monopolize her for a few more days. It's too late to do anything about the engagement ball, but perhaps my future can yet be salvaged."

"You love Acton so much?" he could not help asking.

"I will make an exemplary duchess," she replied. "And besides, Hart, if you *have* developed some sort of fondness for Miss Coltrane, you will be doing her a service."

"How is that?"

"Well, if you don't want her as your mistress, at least she'll not be hounded by those who do."

She smiled. Docile, sweet Annabelle. "Please, Hart."

There was every reason to agree. He could not alter what Annabelle had become and he could not refuse to help her achieve the ambitions he'd helped foster. He would not use the term *dreams*. He doubted Annabelle thought of her goals in such fanciful terms.

And—if what Annabelle said was true—he might save Mercy from some potential insult. His jaw throbbed. Damned if he wouldn't make it crystal clear to any interested parties that she wasn't to be used lightly.

And, too, you can be with her.

"All right, Annabelle."

"Thank you, Hart." She exhaled with satisfaction. "I knew I could rely on you, despite your extraordinary behavior over the last few days. We have *always* relied on you, dear brother." And, having achieved her goal, she left him.

He stood for long minutes, accustoming himself to his new perception of his sweet-faced baby sister as a pitiless, heartless manipulator. He thought of all the things he'd wanted so desperately to give his sisters, all the things his father had taken when he'd abandoned them: money, position, security.

He'd tried to get it all back. And where had it led? Beryl was miserable, struggling to keep up appearances while her absentee husband did who-knows-what; Annabelle had become a vociferously ambitious, covetous doll; and Fanny was a puddle of maternal tears. God, how he'd failed.

"Lord Perth?" Lady Jane Carr spoke from nearby, startling him from his preoccupation. He looked down to find her petite face angled up toward his. "Why it *is* you, sir!" she exclaimed.

"Lady Jane," he acknowledged.

Her pink mouth curved as she looked around at the plants and flowers frosted by moonlight streaming in through the glass roof. "You've come to seek a moment's tranquillity? I understand. It can be tiring, being around so many people all the time," she said.

What was she doing here? Hart wondered. Now that she'd discerned his identity and realized she was alone with an unrelated man, she should leave. But instead, she gazed about her, in no apparent hurry to depart.

"The other evening you were telling me about all the wonders you've seen on your travels," she said, sidling closer. "I've been in England all my life. I fear I will never be free to cater to my taste for the exotic." She laid her plump, small hand on his arm. "I would love to have . . . an adventure," she purred.

He tiredly gazed down into her rapt, feline little face. He hadn't seen this coming either. His eyes had been filled with Mercy Coltrane. They still were. He didn't feel the least tincture of arousal when she hooked an arm through his and pushed her small breast against him.

"Maybe you can convince your husband to take you on a tour."

Her eyes widened, more with consternation than affront. He almost laughed, albeit ruefully. Was he accounted such easy game?

She smiled doubtfully. "Oh, no. Carr will never leave England. He's always too busy with government issues. But your brother-in-law is one of Carr's associates, is he not?" she asked. "I will have to speak to Carr about Wrexhall's prospects."

Hart regarded her with chill silence. She must have recognized that her lure had fallen shy of its mark, for her skin turned dusky.

"Not that I see Carr often," she said, switching tacks. "I am so often left to my own devices. Alone."

"Unfortunate. Would you care to rejoin the party now, Lady Carr?" He motioned her before him. She didn't move. Instead, she placed one hand on his chest. The other crept around his neck, clinging there as she gazed into his eyes.

"You, too, are often alone, are you not, Lord Perth?"

"I enjoy my solitude," he answered, trying to think of some way to get rid of the woman. The amusement her contrivances had provoked had disappeared. He felt only a slight disgust, an encroaching ennui.

"Perhaps"—she pulled at his neck, lifting her mouth to his—"we can enjoy the solitude together?"

"I don't think so."

She frowned. Firmly, he pulled her arms from him, holding her away. She stared at him, her face made ugly with embarrassment.

"You have a reputation as a cold, bloodless man, Perth," she said. "I see it is true. I wish you joy of your . . . solitude."

He stepped back, bowing formally. "Good evening, Lady Carr."

She sniffed contemptuously and left him once more, as always, alone.

———————◆———————

I am not watching for him, Mercy thought. *I am not.*

She couldn't help it if she happened to be looking in his direction when he'd followed Annabelle to the conservatory. When Annabelle had left and he had not, she had merely been glancing that way. And witnessing Lady Jane Carr duck into the dark glasshouse had been a matter of happenstance. And when . . . that woman . . . had reappeared, her color high, her eyes bright, patting her hair and licking her lips nervously . . . *damn, damn, damn him!*

He entered a few minutes later and the breath

caught in Mercy's throat, painful with jealousy and longing. He was far too attractive. The black evening jacket was stretched across his wide shoulders in stark contrast to his snowy-white dress shirt and starched collar. He looked completely at ease, even coming from his assignation, utterly composed, elegant; in short, an aristocrat with blue blood, she'd been reminded, that would never flow in her veins.

He caught her studying him and she tossed her head, turning back as Nathan Hillard returned from the buffet tables with a plate of delicacies.

"I recommend the pâté. Goose heart, I believe. Or the salmon *en croûte*," he said.

"Thank you, Mr. Hillard." His fingertips brushed lingeringly across her knuckles as she took the proffered plate.

"Anything I can do for you, Miss Coltrane?"

"How chivalrous," she mumbled, all too aware of Hart's intent study. She did not want Hillard witnessing her agitation. "Would you be so kind as to get me a glass of punch?"

"Of course," he said, and hurried back into the anteroom.

How dare Hart look at her like that? Mercy thought furiously, noting the other guests' awakening interest. Had he not done enough already? Lady Acton had not said a word to her since this afternoon, Annabelle Moreland quivered with enmity, and Acton was sulking like a child because she'd refused to sit next to him during the play.

All day Hart had avoided a single moment alone with her, stymieing her intention of finding out what he'd discovered about Will. Now he lounged against the wall, his arms folded across his chest, his light eyes tracking her slightest movement.

She lifted a buttery canapé from her plate, raising it to her mouth only to see his lids lower and his gaze grow hotly vulpine as he stared at her lips. She dropped the blameless crust as though it scalded her. A lazy smile turned the corners of his wide, sensual mouth.

Heat rose in her cheeks in answer to his leisurely perusal. It wouldn't do. He could not ignore her one moment and publicly ogle her the next. Already she thought she detected the murmur of speculation among the others present.

A dark thought arose. Perhaps, that was his plan—to provoke so much comment that Lady Acton would ask her to leave. He would be rid of her then, rid of her demands that he find her brother, and rid of her interference with his sister's courtship. Perhaps, the dark musing uncoiled further, he hadn't been going to London to look for Will at all. Perhaps he'd been meeting Lady Carr or some other poor besotted woman.

The flush of sexual awareness became the heat of anger. She *would* have her conversation with him, she *would* learn what he'd found out, and she *would* find Will. Then she would leave this place, these people, and him. But until she had, she would stay here, an absolute picture of decorum.

Shortly after the buffet ended, Hart disappeared. As soon as decently possible, she made her own regrets, intent on following him. She knew where he was going. Back to London.

She raced to her room and donned her boy's clothes, sneaking down through the servants' entrance and running out to the stables.

Too late. The stable lad smirked at her, cheekily telling her she'd missed Perth by a good hour.

Frustrated, she sneaked back and pulled a chair to the window overlooking the front gate and settled in to wait. When Hart returned, she would confront him. But hour chased hour, and the fire in the hearth died and her eyes grew heavy.

She awoke to a room as cold as it was dark. A few embers glowed fitfully in the fireplace and ice frosted the windows. She bolted upright.

He must have returned by now. Grimly, she wrapped herself in a blanket and crept down the hushed hallway toward his room. She paused outside his door, holding her breath, listening for any sound.

He was awake. She could hear his footsteps crossing and recrossing the floor. She turned the handle and entered. It was black except for the dull illumination of the embers gleaming sullenly in the hearth.

She looked around, had an impression of

movement beyond the fire's reach, of a shadow prowling the darkness. She saw him then.

He was pacing along the edge of the light on the far side of the room, his strides quick and mechanical, as a caged panther prowls its cage, automatic and sightless, reaching the far wall and pivoting, pacing back.

He was shirtless, bare chested, seemingly impervious to the deep, penetrating coldness of the room. She caught her breath. He heard. He dropped into a crouch, spinning around, his right hand flagging his hip. She stared at him, aghast. His eyes were glowing in the half-light, feral and ferocious. She dropped the blanket, frightened by the lack of recognition in his eyes.

Slowly, he straightened. His gaze, hot and passionate, riveted on her face, consuming her, hunger and anguish inexorably entwined. For one unguarded moment he stood utterly vulnerable, exposed. He was haggard and exhausted and hunted. Shadows scored his lean cheeks, masked his eyes, and she had to go to him.

She took a step forward and he backed away, turning from her, quivering with some nameless emotion. She stepped closer, uncertain of what to do, what to say. She had never seen such pain. Helplessly, she looked around for some clue as to its source.

His few pieces of luggage still sat open on the floor near the bed, their contents still within. He'd not even bothered to unpack. His shirt lay on the smooth counterpane, his boots near the foot of the bed and on the floor against the far wall—she stared. Blankets were crumpled there. The single pillow still held the imprint of his head.

It suddenly came to her. The Earl of Perth slept on the floor.

Chapter 22

"What happened to you?" she breathed.

He turned and she shuffled back from the violence she saw in his haunted gaze. He stopped, disoriented, and peered at her, as though trying to place her. "Mercy?"

"Yes. It's me, Hart."

"God." He laughed and her heart pitched at the bitter sound. He lifted his hand, groping for the mantel and, once finding it, leaning heavily forward. She stared at his naked back licked by the firelight, so broad and masculine and oddly vulnerable.

"Go away." His voice was muffled, strained. He made no move to face her.

She couldn't. Nothing could have made her leave him, could make her abandon him to whatever tormented him.

"Hart, why are those blankets on the floor?"

There were some terrible things associated with those bolts of wool tangled in the shadows.

"Go away!"

"No," she said, apprehension making her voice quiver. His dangerousness—so vaunted, so valuable, so prized by her father, by everyone who'd used him—had never been more apparent. Some horrible inner tension coiled his body into an unnatural rigidity. His torso was cloaked in a sheath of glistening moisture and dark ribbons of sweat-drenched hair clung to the nape of his neck.

"No." Her voice gained strength. "Not until you talk to me." She stepped forward and touched his shoulder. He was hot, on fire.

He flinched away. No. He shuddered—as though her touch were exquisitely painful. But still, he would not turn to face her. He flung his head back, turned it up to the black vaulted ceiling above, his eyes clenched against the sight of her.

"Hart," she pleaded. "Please."

She tugged at his arm, trying to turn him, to force him to see her, to talk to her.

"My God. Tell me. *Why do you sleep on the floor?*"

He swung on her so quickly that she stumbled back. He snatched hold of her, keeping her from falling, and glared, furious she was pushing him, so angry he propelled her back against the wall. She stumbled and he grinned, feral and bitter.

"You want to know?"

God, how had she ever thought this man unemotional? His skin was dark with suffused blood, flushed a hot bronze in the molten light. Golden glints in the stubble of his beard sharpened the angle of his jaw and his eyes were starkly blazing.

"Must you know?" There was an awful victory, an eagerness, in the demand.

"Yes."

"I have slept there or on a floor like it for eight years." The words, once started, tumbled out, self-violence rife in the low, choked monologue. "I am *afraid* to sleep in a bed." He took one deep breath and exhaled, his gaze climbing over her, touching her throat, her hair, her mouth . . . anything but her eyes. "Amusing, isn't it? The gunslinger, your daddy's hired killer, the Earl of Perth, cowers in the shadows each night?"

"My Lord."

"My Lord, indeed." Another laugh, brief and corrupt. "No act goes unpaid, Mercy. Retribution comes in myriad guises. Sometimes no guise at all. That may be the worst."

"But why do you say 'coward'?"

"Not enough yet? You need everything? All right. I can only sleep with my back against a wall. I've been like this"—he lifted his hands in a despondent gesture—"ever since Africa."

"Africa?"

"Yes, Africa! Those holes in the desert. They were the only safe place," he said, as though she were being deliberately obtuse.

"But this is England—" she began in stunned confusion.

"I know! Damn you, do you think I haven't tried to sleep in there?" He pointed at the four-poster, raised like an altar amid luxuriant tapestries. "And in any other bed . . ."

His voice faded. He could no longer see clearly. The image of his childhood bed was superimposed over this one, and then, suddenly, he saw a lice-ridden blanket, bleached by the African sun. The past twined dizzyingly with the present and he moaned.

He gripped Mercy's arms more tightly. She was solid and real and supple in his grip and her fragility was a lie. He'd never felt anything more potently alive, more vital, stronger, than she. She was a lifeline tying him to the present and, God, he needed her.

God, don't let her leave. Not her.

"I couldn't. I can't," he choked out, hating himself for this recitation but discovering he'd do anything to keep her here, letting him touch her. "If I lie on that bed I can feel a bullet sever my spine, or explode my skull. In the pits, on the ground, they can't shoot you. Even in your dreams."

She trembled, her expression pitying and understanding. Impossible. She couldn't understand. She wouldn't look like that if she did.

"Don't you understand? I'm a *coward*."

"Why do you punish yourself like this?" she cried.

"I don't. God has already seen to that. I have to live with my weakness. Sometimes months will pass and I think I've won. I think maybe I've been strong enough to beat this miserable cowardice. But then it happens again.

"I've tried, Mercy." He panted. "God, I've tried to tell myself it's nothing more than a nightmare, a child's terror of the dark. It doesn't help. I can't stop the sensation, no matter what I tell myself. I'm too damn weak to master my own thoughts."

"Weak?" she repeated in astonishment. "You're the strongest man I know. I remember how you faced that man in the way station. You didn't flinch. You were brave. Incredibly so."

"Killing isn't hard, Mercy. Dying is even easier. It's living that offers a unique challenge." His insouciance was ruined by the hoarse timbre of his voice.

"Why, Hart?" she asked quietly, intently. "What is the challenge?"

"I wake sometimes without knowing where I am." He wasn't speaking to her now; the words, held back for nearly a decade came out low, harsh, confused. "My heart pounds so hard, I think it will burst out of my chest. My own breath chokes me. I want to run, but I don't know from what. I don't even know what it is I'm afraid of. There's no image. No face, no memory. Sometimes I think it's just my soul, afraid of its own blackness."

"No." A tear slipped from beneath her lashes. He watched it follow the curve of her cheek, concentrated on its course, clung to it as an anchor against the internal panic still clamoring for release.

"Yes," he said tonelessly, staring. "Either that or . . . or I am nearer madness than sanity."

"You're not mad, Hart. You've been wounded. In here." She touched her cool fingertips over his heart. "Who wouldn't be? Who *couldn't* be?" Her sorrow was overwhelming.

He wanted to believe as she believed. He could see it in her eyes. That belief nearly wrung a sob from him. He was undone by it.

She lifted her hand and brushed her fingertips against his cheek and all he could do was stare at her, trying desperately to read what was in her mind.

Her fingers drifted near his temple, hesitated and passed over his cheeks again, traced his jaw with gossamer delicacy. He watched intently as a flicker of surprise crept into her gaze; a hint of apprehension, but not fear. Not yet.

She shifted and he became aware of how close she was, how his body hindered her escape. She was supple curves, scented skin, and glossy hair, so utterly feminine and thus so utterly mysterious that he felt suddenly clumsy, too big, too heavy.

She moved and the jut of her hip brushed against the jointure of his thighs. He gasped at the chance contact, immediately becoming aroused. She looked at him, startled by his involuntary hiss of pleasure. Her hands fluttered past his mouth. He snapped his head around, capturing one tardy finger between his teeth, licking the salty tip. He heard her sharp, indrawn breath, felt her shiver translate itself to her fingers. She tugged her hand back, shocked at this intimacy, and he released her finger. She stared at him, transfixed by whatever it was she read in his expression.

He took advantage.

Slowly, he lifted his hands and bracketed the sides of her face, his thumbs resting near her parted lips, his forefingers grazing the downy hair at her temples.

Stop. Now, before you scare her. But he could not.

Her eyes widened. The gold-ash irises glinted in the firelight. Her lashes fluttered, sweeping feathered silkiness against his fingertips. He moved closer, oblique and cautious, his breath shallow, trying not to alarm her, thief that he was.

It was so easy.

She tilted her head and he stooped over her and kissed her. It was as ravishing as he remembered. His lips touched a silken brow, each lid, the corner of her soft, trembling mouth. She sighed— sweet, sweet sound, delicious and erotic—and he grew rock hard and full with an urgency he'd never before known. He found her mouth, aware in some appalled recess of his consciousness that his restraint had vanished but unable to call himself back from the edge of the passion engulfing him.

She was here and while he could hold her, devour her with hand and mouth and breath, she held back the night, her sweet body offered a sanctuary. His heart raced and his thoughts spun blackly, panic gibbering futilely in the corners of his mind while he felt her supple curves, tasted the salty tear, breathed the hot, excited scent of her. Panic couldn't compete with this. It didn't stand a bloody chance.

She started to speak and he closed her mouth with his. He would not let her speak, would not let her breathe, would not let her say no. He kept his mouth over hers, molding her lips against his, tasting and moving and touching the plush softness, the yielding warmth, until he was light-headed.

He dipped and caught her behind the knees, swinging her up into his arms. She was light and tensile and her breasts, covered in that ridiculous boy's shirt, were unbound. He could feel the voluptuous mounds crushed against his chest. She whimpered and lust careened through him. She clung to him, overpowered by his insistence, her ardor, his passion.

He strode with her to the great, dark-curtained bed and laid her upon the dark, shimmering counterpane and followed her down. For an instant he hung above her braced on his arms, his stiff sex against her belly, the last vestiges of restraint shredded upon the ever-sharpening edge of his need.

He bent his head, nuzzling open her collar, his mouth prowling the forbidden flesh of her neck. He fumbled between them, finding her breast. It was soft and lush and he cupped the swell, lifting it and kneading it and stroking it and, God, oh God, her nipple beaded against his palm.

He wrenched the shirt away, exposing her young, supple body. Her round, pale breast jiggled ripely. He moaned, dipping his head and taking the dark nipple into his mouth and wetting it with his tongue. She gasped, arching, and the flexion thrust her breast deeper into his hungry mouth. Her hands flew to his chest, his throat, his face, seeking a bastion on which to cling.

He suckled harder, holding her shoulders down, pinning her beneath him. She panted, surprised passion in each staggered exhalation. He could taste pleasure on her skin, scent hot excitement on her. His body quaked with an uncoilable skein of shame and exultation as her hips lifted fractionally in a tense, instinctive response to passion.

With a harsh, triumphant sound, he rocked back on his knees, settling between her legs, and jerked her breeches open. She gave a startled mewl. He ignored the sound, the blood ran thick and insistent in his body. He was only here now. With her. The night terror was a spectator, waiting without as the predator within took precedence.

He yanked her breeches off as she stared at him with moon-dark eyes, her breasts pale and clean in the shadowed corridors of the bed, her lips parted, her hands curled into fists on either side of her face.

He fumbled with his own trousers until he felt himself spring free. With a low growl he sank onto her, hissing when he felt the crisp, silky curls against his sex. His forehead fell against her throat, his head spinning with the sheer pleasure of it. She was so damn small. He'd never been more conscious of his own weight, his size. He must crush her and yet, and yet, God help him, he only wanted to sink deeper onto her, *into* her, to absorb her. Take her. Bind her to him.

She moved and every conscious thought was devoured by instinct. He was nearly there. His hardness was shoved against the jointure of her thighs, a slick, warm sheath enveloped the very tip him—exquisite sensation. So close.

Her legs tumbled wider, nestling him, opening to him. He tangled his fists in her hair and found her mouth again, thrusting his tongue in, desirous, willing her to catch fire, to want him and . . . and God! . . . he was in her, gripped in a velvety fist, pressing against some smooth, hot barrier.

She arched, whimpering, and he shoved his hands beneath her buttocks—pleasure too intense, softness filling his palms. And then, God help him, he felt it. Despair and fury pulsed in equal parts through him as he held her still, realizing what he pushed against. Her maidenhead.

She moved, clutched his shoulders, squirmed beneath him. He swore. He was going to explode.

He tried to withdraw. God, he would swear he tried. But she surrounded him, tight, hot, and each small movement she made rippled through her body, ending in a contraction about him, wringing tears of effort from him. He strained above her, teeth clenched, jaw knotted, and lust rode him even as he rode her, spurring him with killing blades. Nothing had ever felt like this. Nothing had ever been so compelling. And he would have it.

With a thick moan he thrust deep into her, past the thin web, drinking the startled gasp from her lips and giving back his own hoarse cry. He moved, closing his eyes, his hips convulsing with the unbearable pleasure of each thrust.

Breath no longer mattered. The blood pounded in his temples, pounded in his loins, surging through him, and he could feel her own blood coursing, feel the frantic rhythm of her pulse, feel the tightening of her body. His senses exploded, burst upon him, engulfing him, shattering him with sheer intensity, washing through him and leaving him eviscerated.

When it was over, he laid his forehead against hers, spent and exhausted. Slowly he became aware of her heartbeats, still a rapid staccato. Her breath came in tiny pants. Her skin was damp and hot. Beneath him her body felt terrifyingly vulnerable and slight. He rolled away from her, awareness of what he had done banishing the lethargy, remorse cutting as sharply as passion had but seconds before.

"Did I hurt you?"

"I'm not sure." Her voice sounded stunned and faint.

"Jesus." He stared at where her pretty breasts were chaffed by his beard, pink where they should still be virginal pale. Her nipples were swollen and bruised-looking. His gaze slipped lower to the boy's breeches tangled about one ankle and returned with a gut-knifing sense of dismay to her thighs.

Dark stains laced their delicate inner flesh. He rolled away and stood up, his back to her. He yanked his trousers up and fastened them. He heard the rustle of the coverlet behind him and closed his eyes.

"What can I do?" he whispered, knowing there was nothing. "Mercy, whatever can I do? Anything."

He did not know what to expect from her and found to his amazement that this was his greatest grief: he did not know her well enough to anticipate her thoughts, her emotions.

He hazarded a glance over his shoulder. She was curled on her side beneath the satin brocade. Her hands clutched the glowing fabric to her waist, as though to protect herself from further invasion.

Too little and far, far too late.

"I'm sorry. God, I am so . . ." He would not offer her weak self-recriminations. She deserved more than a litany of self-blame as useless as it was hypocritical. "Mercy. I . . . God, I hope I haven't hurt you. Shall I send for the maid?"

"No!"

Of course not, fool! he thought savagely, turning and staring down at her stricken face, her imploring eyes. She would not want this broadcast.

"What can I do?" he begged.

She swallowed, the working of her throat looked painful. Her gaze drifted away from meeting his. "I . . . I don't want to be alone. I . . .

please." She sounded proud and vulnerable and lost. "Don't leave me alone."

He raked a hand through his hair. She should be in the tender embrace of her husband. This should be her wedding night. There should be lace and flowers in vases and light; much light. She should have been taught lovemaking in sunlight, on white Irish linen, with the windows open and a heather-laden breeze caressing her.

She should not be huddled under a dark counterpane in a cold room, a boy's shirt hanging open across her sweet, soft breasts, her hair gnarled by his fists, tears streaking her flushed face.

"I'll stay here. I'll watch over you." He made to turn. Her hand darted out, snatching his wrist.

"Please."

"Could you . . . would you hold me? Like you did in the carriage?"

She could not want him. Not after what he'd done, he thought in bewilderment. But then—the bitter thought bloomed with malevolent logic—who else did she have? What had he left her?

He'd taken the worst advantage of her. She was alone, without family or friends in a strange country, and he'd all but raped her. *Yes*, he thought, forcing himself to acknowledge the word. *Rape.* When had he given her the opportunity to say no? When had he done anything but press her, force her, overpower her?

He sat down wearily on the bed and pulled her, wrapped in that damn coverlet, over. She clung to him, seeking some solace. From him. And as ironic as he knew it to be, he would find some comfort to give her.

He leaned back against the headboard, carrying her with him. Her hair spilled across his naked chest, coiling along his rib cage in cool satiny ribbons. Her breath trembled against his throat. Her fist lay like a hard stone on his chest. She did not move again.

Fatigue and an odd, bittersweet contentment weighted his limbs. He inhaled. She smelled musky with exhaustion and lavender soap and the subtle, evocative fragrance their bodies had made. He closed his eyes, exhausted.

She nestled closer. Her breath slowed, became a warm rhythm. Her fist relaxed until her hand lay slack over his heart. He drifted for minutes, then longer ones, finding comfort where he'd sought to give it. Finally, lulled by the sweet weight in his arms, the face pressed to his naked chest, the unexpected ease with which she slumbered, he yielded to his own fatigue.

And for the first time in eight years, the Earl of Perth rested as well as slept.

Chapter 23

"*H*art, for heaven's sake, where are you? The maid here said she knocked but you didn't answer and Richard is waiting to go and Fanny refuses to leave until you say good-bye— Oh, my God!"

Hart fought his way up through thick shrouds of lethargy. Muzzily, he searched for the source of the voices.

Two feminine figures stood in the doorway, outlined by a nimbus of early morning light. He squinted and shook his head. Annabelle and some maid. He heard his sister gasp before he could form a word. With a snap of whirling skirts she disappeared.

"'Scuse me, sir!" the maid sang out. The door slammed shut and Mercy, snuggled against him, stirred.

With a growing sense of despair Hart stared down at her. The coverlet had slipped during the night and the sun, angling low in the autumn sky, streamed across the bed, bathing her naked breasts in golden, soporific light. Her hair rippled in a tangled veil over his naked chest. Her hand splayed intimately across his chest.

For an instant he closed his eyes and tightened his hold on her, savoring the pleasure of sheltering her in his arms, however illusional he knew that to be. She made a soft, objecting noise. A smile touched his lips and died. He would give his soul to hear that grumbling complaint each of the rest of his dawns.

"Mercy, wake up."

"What?" Her voice was husky. She lifted her face. Her skin was flushed pink. She looked so damn young and fresh and innocent. . . . He wanted to howl. "Hart?"

"Yes." There was no time to talk. Each minute counted toward rectifying this unrectifiable situation. "Mercy, you have to go back to your room. People are starting to rise. They'll be in the corridors soon."

She pushed herself up on her arms. Comprehension sharpened the soft cast of her features. She looked down at her open shirt and her hair fell forward, veiling her expression from him. She jerked away from him, sitting back on her heels. He ached to haul her back into his embrace. With unsteady fingers she began buttoning her crumpled shirt.

"I'll send for you," he said. "Within the hour. We have to talk. But not now. Annabelle was just here. She saw you."

"What timing!" Her voice shook. "It's a wonder she doesn't tread the boards."

"Damn it to hell," he muttered. She blanched. *No time.*

"You have to go *now*, Mercy." He stood up, pulling her to her feet beside him. She moved away from him and for the first time he noted that her feet were still encased in their soft leather half boots and this, of all the acts he'd perpetrated on her virgin body, seemed the most monstrous: he'd taken her maidenhead while she'd still had her boots on. She moved carefully and he cursed when he realized what made her wince with each footfall.

"Jesus, Mercy. I am so—"

"Do *not* say you are sorry." She wheeled around, her hand on the doorknob. "I could not stand it if you were to say you were sorry."

"But—"

"You are not some animal at the mercy of your impulses, Hart," she said in a tense, savage voice. "You knew full well what you did. You could have stopped. You could have."

He went rigid, stung with a razor-tipped lash.

He'd thought he endured a full measure of torment before. That he'd tasted a complete portion of despair when he'd questioned his own sanity. He nearly smiled. He had only dallied with anguish. But now, *now* he would learn its full embrace.

She hated him. And with every reason.

Somehow he managed to nod. She was right. He could have stopped. But he hadn't.

"And dammit," she continued in that low, furious voice. "I'm not an animal either. I could have said no. I *could* have stopped you. So do *not* say you are sorry."

He stared at her, amazed.

"Not now. Not ever," she said. "It's too late to wish you hadn't indulged yourself and far too late to wish that I'd stopped you."

She snatched the door open and without glancing either way, marched into the hall, leaving him stunned with disbelief.

———◦◆◦———

The clock on the marble mantel struck eight times and Mercy, who'd been waiting for the chime, rose from her bedroom window seat. Lady Acton was expecting her. The Dowager's note, delivered an hour after Mercy had returned to her own room, had been specific.

In a way it was a relief. Nothing could have been more torturous than hours—perhaps days— of anticipating the aftermath of, of— God, what did one call what had happened last night? Maelstrom? Vortex? Cyclone?

It had certainly not been the fulfillment of the secret, tender expectations she'd harbored. Those had been gentle imaginings; this was fierceness, an urgency she'd never dreamed possible. Passion. They'd made passion.

She smoothed her hair back with shaking fingers and pinched color into the cheeks she knew were far too pale. She made her way to the hall, aware of a dull ache between her legs, an ache that had less to do with pain than tangible memory.

Hart had been *in* her last night. His hard, tense body had lain over her, pressing down on her, and then he had been in her; a thick, hard presence that had been uncomfortable and compelling and shatteringly intimate. She would never be the same.

She almost laughed at the melodramatic summation as she made her way down the interminably long staircase. But it was true. Beyond anyone's ability to argue, last night had changed her life, her body, and her heart.

And—she bit down hard on her lip, forcing tears away—the hell of it was, she had no idea what it had meant to Hart. He'd not said a word besides his near apology. God, how could he? Didn't he want to know what she *felt*?

She paused outside the morning room. Tipping her chin at a defiant angle, she pushed open the heavy mahogany door and went in.

She was unprepared for the number of people therein. *Good God*, she thought, feeling the floorboards tilt slightly beneath her feet, *she'd been called to a tribunal*. Was it really necessary for Lady Acton to have an audience at her denunciation?

The Dowager was ensconced in a chair near the fire. Her spine did not touch the upholstery. Her gaze narrowed on Mercy and Mercy understood. She, impertinent pretender to the Acton coronet, was once and for all to be revealed as the brazen, lowborn creature she was. It was to be a lesson for Lord Acton.

Seated at Lady Acton's feet was Annabelle Moreland. Her head was bowed, her expression hidden. Behind the two women, hovering near the fireplace mantel, stood Acton. He looked up as she entered. Reproach and embarrassment chased each other across his blunt features.

And in front of her, facing them, his back rigid, was Hart. His hair, she noted irrelevantly, was too long. It curled against the acid whiteness of his shirt collar. It was thick hair. She knew firsthand just how luxuriant. Warmth washed up her throat.

Hart, following Acton's gaze, turned. When he saw her his mouth—Lord, had that mouth touched her so boldly, so intimately?—parted only to snap shut. His expression, always unreadable, seemed even more remote. The very color seemed leached from his beautiful eyes.

"Miss Coltrane." Lady Acton beckoned her forward.

Mercy started. Lady Acton's voice revealed not only a deep revulsion but grudging pity as well. For the first time Mercy realized how society would see her.

Ruined.

This is how it would be. Lady Acton's flat, superior regard or the disappointment in Lord Acton's gaze, even the shamed hint of curiosity with which Annabelle glanced at her, they would all become familiar, echoed in numberless faces.

"Come in, Miss Coltrane. It appears we have

much to discuss." Lady Acton's rings glinted in the sunlight as she gestured to the settee across from her.

Mercy did as she was bid, took a seat upon the edge of the cushion, and hid her twining hands in her skirts. Her stomach was knotting and her heart raced. She was afraid.

"I believe this . . . situation would be best served with frankness." Mercy glanced at Hart. He was watching Lady Acton silently, an odd, controlled readiness about his posture.

"It is too late to express shock," Lady Acton continued. "Whatever respect due my home or my feelings or the feelings of my guests"—her gaze touched Annabelle's blond head—"apparently has not influenced you."

Mercy closed her eyes for a second, fighting for composure. Hart took a step forward and Lady Acton met his movement with a quelling stare. "Or you either, sir."

"I don't give a damn—"

"Obviously," Lady Acton shot back.

"Here, Perth," Acton interjected, stepping to his mother's side. "I'd have you remember your manners, sir."

"If he'd remembered his manners, we wouldn't be having this discussion!" Lady Acton snapped. "To be caught by his own sister . . . in Acton Hall!"

"*Manners?*" Mercy stared. *Is that all that had happened last night, a breach of etiquette?* Was she ruined not because she'd lost her virginity but because she'd been foolish enough to be caught?

"Good God," she said, hearing the rising hysteria in her choked laugh, "I must write Woolsey's School for Exceptional Young Ladies immediately!"

"What *are* you talking about, Miss Coltrane?" Lady Acton asked.

"I shall insist they offer more discussion on the Social Graces. Manners! Who would have made the connection? To think my . . . *downfall* may have begun with something so seemingly inconsequential as using the fish fork in place of the shrimp trident!"

Her mockery was met with absolute silence until, impossibly, Hart laughed. It was a fullthroated, appreciative sound and it echoed in the quiet room.

"For my friend Lady Timmons's sake I will assume you are overwrought," Lady Acton said, the skin whitening on either side of her nostrils.

"Kind of you," Mercy answered. For the first time since she'd woken, she felt herself. Lady Acton could have broken her. Had the Dowager accused her of disgracing her family, her mother, her upbringing, Mercy would have been reduced to as pliant a material as Lady Acton could have wished.

But to dismiss what had transpired between Hart and herself as a social *infraction*, one whose gravest consequence was that it might put Lady Acton in a unflattering light . . . ! But then, to these people social transgressions were the only real sin.

She knew what she must do.

"As I was saying," Lady Acton went on, "whatever the failings of others, I know my duty. And I shall do it. Your welfare is my responsibility, Miss Coltrane. That responsibility does not stop at mere physical considerations. It includes your social health as well."

Hart's gaze narrowed on Lady Acton. Lord Acton cleared his throat. "Well said, Mother. And I . . . I am fully cognizant of my own part in this . . . misfortune."

Oh, God, thought Mercy, trying to stifle another burble of hysteria, *how could he possibly conceive himself accountable for last night?* It was absurd!

Unless, she thought, he believed that in her wretchedness at discovering he wasn't going to offer for her she'd thrown herself at the nearest available Title? Or rather into The Title's bed.

"And what part would that be?" The Title Himself asked, and by God, if there was not a glint of rueful amusement in his eyes.

Acton cleared his throat again. "Mother—and Miss Moreland—have pointed out to me that in attempting to bolster Miss Coltrane's self-confidence"—Hart snorted. Acton blushed profusely—"well, I encouraged the gel to have an inflated sense of her own importance. Undoubtedly, she was led to expect—"

"Expect what?" Mercy asked.

Acton pulled his collar away from his throat

with one finger. Her refused to meet her eye. "I . . . possibly . . . led her to think herself socially invulnerable. I am sorry, Miss Coltrane. There are, when all is said and done, rules."

This last was said with such remorse that Mercy found herself pitying him. Hart, apparently, did not share the feeling. All humor had died on his lean face. He surged forward only to stop suddenly, as if checked by an invisible cord.

Annabelle peeked up at her, triumph in her pale eyes.

"That doesn't matter now," Lady Acton said. "What does matter is how we will deal with this situation. And we *will* deal with it, as distasteful as it must be to all parties involved, in the only honorable way open to us." She turned to Mercy, antipathy in the jerk of her head. "Perth will make it right, gel."

"How kind of him," Mercy said. She refused to look at Hart.

"Kindness has nothing to do with it. You are fortunate that you are in the Duke of Acton's house. Fortunate or perfidious."

Hart quivered where he stood, but remained silent. Mercy felt herself grow chill. "How so, madam?" she asked, her chin hitching higher.

"I will have no scandal attached to my house, my name, or my guests. You knew this. We will not allow our ancestral home to be used as a brothel by light-skirts and profligates."

She would not break eye contact first. She would not give this woman the satisfaction. Her hands trembled in her skirts and still she met that imperious glare with her own brand of hauteur.

"You had best watch *your* own manners, madam." Hart's voice was low, calm, and deadly. "You are addressing the future Marchioness of Perth."

Annabelle's head snapped upright and she gasped.

Little fool, thought Mercy. *Hadn't she seen this coming? It had been obvious from the first where this conversation must end.*

"Hart. You can't! Our family . . . the title. . . . You're the Earl of Perth!"

"Be quiet, Annabelle," Hart said coldly. "You should have anticipated the results of your . . . divulgence. Did you imagine that Lady Acton would *demand*"—there was an odd emphasis, nearly a sneer, on the word—"anything less? God, you are a fool."

"Here now, Perth—"

Hart ignored Lord Acton. "Lady Acton is Mercy's chaperone, *her surrogate guardian*, for God's sake." His lips spread in a biting, humorless smile. "Though it will doubtless comfort you to know that I am certain Lady Acton is even more chagrined than you by the contingency which necessitates an earl marrying an American."

He was right, Mercy thought. Damn him, she could read the truth of what he said in the harsh, indignant line of Lady Acton's countenance.

"Perhaps Miss Coltrane does not wish to wed?" Annabelle made the suggestion wildly, frantically. As one, each of them looked at her, waiting for her answer.

"Oh, but she does. For now," Mercy said. She was not going to act the fool, no matter how much her pride demanded it. She would not bring an unnamed babe into the world. She would play along with this farce as long as she had to.

"Well, then," Lady Acton said. "I suppose we can announce the nuptials at the ball. Though such a hasty courtship will provoke comment."

"No," Mercy said.

"Miss Coltrane?" Lady Acton asked, eyes narrowed.

"I said no. You are correct, Lady Acton. An announcement at your ball will serve no purpose other than to awaken idle speculation. We will wait until next month."

Lady Acton and Annabelle traded confused glances. Hart regarded her for a second before understanding sharpened his already keen glance.

"Well done, Mercy," he said.

"I think so, sir," she said.

"I don't understand," Annabelle said, glancing about as though she expected some further horrendous ramifications to announce themselves. Her pallor was severe, and Mercy realized with some surprise just how very much Annabelle was stricken by the notion of having to welcome her as a sister-in-law. Though *welcome* was hardly the word for it.

"Why, Annabelle. Miss Coltrane here is doing what I believe they call 'covering her bases.' "

"Bases? What rubbish are you talking, Perth?" Acton asked.

"It's a game they play in America, called baseball. 'Covering your bases' refers to protecting as many contingencies as possible."

"Well, I still don't know what the blazes—sorry, Mama, Miss Moreland—you mean," Acton said.

Mercy noted his omission of her name. A small slight, inconsequential, but the cumulative effect was too much and, damn, damn, try as she might she could not control the quiver of her lower lip. Hart took three ground-eating strides to where Lord Acton stood.

"If you ever show Miss Coltrane the least amount of disrespect again, I shall see to it that you are personally and very, very physically involved in a scandal that shall have society hissing for years."

Acton listened in open dread to the dispassionate promise and backed away, mumbling under his breath. "Didn't mean any offense, I'm sure. Miss Coltrane, beg pardon."

"What did he mean, 'covering your bases'?" Annabelle persisted.

Mercy studied her a moment. "Your brother suspects that I'm not sure this is the best offer I can come up with. He is correct."

Annabelle gasped with outrage.

"But," Mercy continued, anger driving her now, "as I do not yet know if I have—how to say this?—a bun in the oven?" Annabelle's hand flew to cover her mouth. Lady Acton touched her hand to her heart. Vulgar did they think her? She would *bludgeon* them with her vulgarity—"I shall simply wait and see. If I am, ah . . . about to find pups? I expect I'll make do with His Lordship here. But if I haven't, er . . . swallowed a pumpkin seed? Why, then, the field is still open and I shall certainly aim higher than a mere earl. One month and I shall doubtless know if I'm to, hm . . . wear the bustle backward? The royal family is extensive, is it not? I'm sure I'll have numerous opportunities. Now, if you'll excuse me, I have some packing to do. I would not wish to blemish Lady Acton's ancestral home with my presence. I will be leaving this afternoon."

"You can't leave, Miss Coltrane. Think of how it will look—"

"I don't give a damn, and yes, madam, I can. And I will." Without waiting for a reply, she rose and swept from the room.

Chapter 24

$\mathcal{H}$art bit out instructions for his sister and Acton and strode into the hall, intent on following Mercy. He looked around. She was already gone. Her very absence in the hundred-foot-long corridor confirmed his suspicions; her demeanor had been nine tenths bravado. As soon as she'd left the room she'd run. For sanctuary.

She wasn't going to find any. Not from him. Not yet. They had to talk. When earlier this morning he'd found Annabelle closeted with Lady Acton, he'd demanded Mercy be sent for. Lady Acton had understood his intent. And though she'd obviously hated it, she been honor bound to support his proposal. Annabelle, however, had been dumbstruck.

He trotted down the hallway and up the stairs, ignoring the curious glances of the other guests. If only he had been able to cling to the notion that what he felt for Mercy was simple lust. But last night had shattered any hopes of that. She'd ferreted out what little was left of his soul. She'd made him . . . *feel* things. . . .

She'd told him he was not mad. She'd touched his shivering body, his face. God, she'd *looked* at him. Into him. And she hadn't shrunk away.

His fingers clenched convulsively. Before, he'd hungered for her body—a constant state to which he'd become accustomed over the short week—but now, now he wanted the impossible. He wanted her heart.

His lips curled. How tenderly he'd demonstrated his regard. He'd fallen on her like a starving man on a feast, brutal in his rapaciousness. He'd taken her as though by forcing himself into her body he could absorb a part of her soul. And then, not content with that violation, he'd lashed her spent body to his side all night long, imprisoning her in his embrace, keeping her with him . . . until they'd been discovered.

It would be easy to tell himself he'd simply fallen asleep, but he knew it for a convenient lie: He hadn't "simply fallen asleep" in eight years. No, he'd willed himself to unconsciousness. At some deep, insidious level he'd done everything in his power to bind her to him.

Because he must have her. He'd had to have her since he'd seen her across the room, since she'd recalled to him the sound of his own laughter, had seared his cold heart with her passion, had believed in him. How sweetly he'd repaid her faith, he thought as he approached her suite.

He did not pause outside. There were too many who'd crack their doors to see whether she allowed him entry and, if she refused him entry, too many witnesses to Acton's door being kicked down.

He was amazed to find her door not only unbolted but unlatched. He entered silently, stopping as his vision adjusted to the sunlight-flooded room. He spied her sitting in front of a huge, ornate vanity. He froze.

She had unknotted her heavy chignon and was untangling the dark red hair as she stared at her reflection in the mirror. How could she be casual— how could anyone be casual—about something so exotic, so pretty?

He could not move. Unexpectedly confronted with her femininity, he was confounded by it. He stood in the shadowed doorway, oppressed and floundering in the purloined intimacy. In his entire life he had never seen a woman comb her hair.

Her fingers held the comb as delicately as a violinist would a bow. Each graceful movement, each smooth pass of the ivory teeth, each second she sat gazing heedlessly at her reflection, overwhelmed him.

She was artlessly, carelessly, exquisitely feminine. He could only watch, dumb, wrung wordless by the simple act, separated by the welling hunger—

"What?" She caught him off-guard. Her reflected gaze met his shadowed countenance in the mirror. He moved into the light, up behind her. Their gazes tangled in the silvered glass.

"If you've come to apologize, I will kill you," she said. "Maybe not today. Maybe not tomorrow, but someday, somehow, I'll shoot you."

Strangely, it was her very fierceness that lifted some of the darkness from him. "Then I won't apologize," he said, "as I have no intention of patting down your wedding dress searching for that damned pistol of yours."

"I doubt that will be necessary." How could she sound so calm? The blood was pounding in his ears. He wanted to sink to his knees and twist his fists in her hair and breathe in the womanly sweet-warm scent that played across her skin. Didn't she know what she did to him?

No. She wouldn't be staring at him so expectantly if she did. Little fool. Hadn't he proven what he was capable of?

"Why is that?" he asked hoarsely.

"I wasn't in my proper phase."

"Phase."

"Yes. You know. *Phase.* The timing. The— Don't look at me as though you haven't any idea what I'm talking about."

"I don't," he replied honestly, watching in amazement as her face turned a bright shade of pink.

"I'm most sorry to offend," she grated out, "and I'm sure you'll just hitch your impressive aristocratic nose higher in the air, but I don't know what a *lady* calls being in season so I can only assure you I wasn't *it* last night!"

"Aristocratic nose?" he repeated.

She sighed with exasperation. "Why is it men are incapable of dealing with the crux of a conversation?"

"You're the one who mentioned my nose."

"Yes, yes, yes," she said in the tone of one capitulating to a demanding child. "Your nose; a great, bold brute of a nose it is. Most decidedly aristocratic and most decidedly it was elevated to aristocratic heights some few minutes ago. But, as I have been trying to point out, you needn't worry about bequeathing such a magnificent specimen to my unworthy descendants, as *I do not believe I am breeding!*"

"Oh." She didn't like his nose. He quelled the impulse to lean over her shoulder and examine it in the mirror. True, it was large but it hadn't any unsightly crooks or— Damn and blast! How had he gone from self-castigation to dry-mouthed lust to fretting over his *nose*?

Because of *her*, he thought. Because this is what she always did to him. From the moment he'd seen her, she'd harried him from the cold, dark place to which he retreated, the stronghold from which he'd attempted to hold on to his sanity. But sanity, it appeared, was better served with fire and wit and passion.

She was regarding his reflection with a rueful twist to her plush lips. Only flushed cheeks betrayed that she was not as composed as she would have him believe.

"*Oh?*" she parroted. "I would think you'd be a bit more enthusiastic over your 'stay of execution.' And would you kindly leave off admiring yourself in the mirror and attend to me? You *did* barge in here."

The accusation was a lie, she thought. He'd slipped into her room like a fire-limned shadow, haunting her dreams, her thoughts. . . .

"Certainly there is nothing I'd like better to do than attend you." He smiled wolfishly.

"Why are you here?"

"I know the most pressing reason for you to marry me is to legitimize any offspring we might have made last night—"

"I told you; I don't think it is a concern." She dropped her gaze and began toying with the silver-backed brush. He reached over her shoulder, his hand grazing her collarbone. She might as well have been naked. His touch electrified her. Even through the staid layers of wool and cotton and batiste she could feel a jolting physical awareness. He didn't appear to even notice.

He wrested the brush from her frozen fingers. With odd hesitancy—she would swear he held his breath—he began brushing her hair. She could only stare at her hands, her own breath shallow and uneven, afraid he would stop.

What did he want? She had been so sure he had come to regretfully inform her he was withdrawing his offer, that he would not be manipulated by Lady Acton.

"There are other matters to consider, though," he said. His hands worked soothingly over her head, the bristles prickling her scalp before he pulled the brush firmly through each long tress.

His tenderness was hypnotizing and yet, and yet, he hadn't said he *wanted* to marry her. "Nothing else matters," she said.

"I know you don't think so right now, Mercy." His voice was soft, reasonable. "But you're angry. And with every right to be. You are alone, vulnerable, and yet you were seduced and betrayed and now you are being driven toward a marriage you do not want. I'm amazed you haven't used your pistol." He smiled crookedly, and in spite of the fact that everything he said was true and damning of him, her heart felt wrung by the bleakness she glimpsed behind his calm facade.

"Don't think I haven't considered it," she said gruffly to cover her confusion.

"Mercy, please listen to me. I swear I will try to act in your best interest. I will attempt to give you objective advice. There is a matter of honor at issue. I will be honest. Not only yours but mine. There are also reputations at stake, once again mine as well as yours. I know you don't think mine is worth much, but to certain people . . . to my sisters . . . it is essential my reputation be unscathed."

She'd expected it, so why did it hurt so damn, damn much? she thought. His hand touched her shoulder and she jerked away. No, not kindness. Not from him. He could save his thoughtfulness for those damned sisters of his.

"How eloquent. Too bad you didn't listen to your own advice last night. Still, I am hopeful that your sisters will somehow recover from *my* downfall. Comfort them with the assurance that I shan't taint the Perth bloodlines."

"I'm afraid," he said, "that our *not* wedding will create a far greater scandal than otherwise."

"Come now," she said, and he closed his eyes.

Bitterness had been replete in her words. He'd never heard bitterness in her tone. Such a fine betrothal gift, he thought.

She went on. "It's quite clear that Lady Acton and Acton and your sisters look on a union between us with the same degree of relish as they would sitting down to dine with a talking dog. So why can we not just forget it happened?"

"Could you 'just forget'?"

Her cheeks burned and she bit down on her lip. No. She could not forget. How could she? His body over hers, his muscles slipping beneath her palms, his skin sleek with heat and sweat, the urgency of his possession, the feeling of tumultuous pleasure building toward some unseen peak . . .

"I will try."

His pallor became obvious, but he did not waver. "Well, my dear, unfortunately society lacks your purpose or your will. And as for hoping it goes unnoticed—I am sure that within the week half the guests will know where you spent last night."

"How?"

"The chambermaid. She was with Annabelle. Belowstairs gossip quickly finds its way upstairs. No. I'm afraid the only course that will satisfy society is for us to wed."

"I don't give a damn for your society! And I meant what I said. Brenna will be in to pack my bags immediately. I've already sent for a carriage."

"Don't fool yourself, Mercy. English and American society grow closer each year. We trade money, merchandise, and *aristocrats*. You will eventually feel the consequences of last night. Or your family will."

"*My* family now." It was all too much. She did not know what to think anymore. With each reasonable statement he pressed her toward marrying him. His rationale was honorable and clear sighted and well thought out. "How droll," she murmured.

"Mercy?"

"Here I am being offered a coronet and the only person who would find that gratifying is dead. She might finally have been proud of me."

Abruptly, he ceased brushing her hair. She felt his hand hover an instant and then he bent over her, deliberately placing the brush beside its mate. "I would hate to disappoint you—and your dear, departed mother—but I'm afraid there may be no coronet."

Chapter 25

"What do you mean?"

He turned and stood in profile to her, his strong-boned face and bold nose, the clean, sharp angle of his jaw and sensual lower lip, backlit against the window.

"I returned from Africa shortly after my mother had died," he said offhandedly.

So much control. What sort of tyranny did he exercise over his emotions that he could speak so calmly of his mother's death?

"Some months before I'd received word that my father had perished in a yachting accident off the coast of New Guinea. I cannot claim to have been overly affected by either loss. He was a libertine and a wastrel. And after he abandoned her, my mother stopped caring. About anything."

"Hart . . ."

"I wouldn't bore you with this, Mercy," he

said, "but since you must at least consider marrying me, even if under duress, you need to know.

"My homecoming was greeted with a mountain of papers from lawyers and tradesmen and my
relatives' creditors and—" He stopped. "Forgive
the histrionics. It was all rather overwhelming and
I was not feeling very well at the time." He slanted
a sardonic smile at her. "But then, you've seen the
manifestations of my indisposition. Suffice it to say
that at that time they were worse."

She saw his nearly indiscernible flinch as he
looked away. *Worse?* The thought that he'd had to
endure so much, so young, wounded her. When
he'd returned home had anyone held him when he
shivered? Had any voice called him back from the
haunted landscape of his imagination? No. There'd
only been more responsibilities, more demands.

"The only thing of any value I was bequeathed
was my great-uncle's title. His estate was in ruin,
as was the sordid little rubble pile my sisters had
been reduced to living in. They'd been raised to
think of themselves as ladies and I hadn't the
wherewithal even to buy them shoes. I didn't know
what to do."

He turned his palm upward in a gesture of unconscious apology. She raised her hand to take his.
He stared at her bleakly. His fingers curled into a
fist and dropped to his side.

"I developed one skill during my tenure with
the army. I learned that I was a very, very good
shot. I'd heard from some of my comrades that a
marksman—one without too much conscience or

too much curiosity—could find lucrative work in the more lawless territories of your country. I had nothing to lose and I certainly met the criteria. And before you ask, no, the thought of killing men didn't bother me. I'd killed plenty in the war . . . and they weren't even men. If I could shoot a boy,"—his teeth clenched around the word—"why not a thief? Or murderer?"

"I *didn't* ask," she said. "But it sounds as though you have asked yourself that question. Scores of times."

"Damn your pretty eyes," he said dispassionately.

"Go on."

"You know that part of the story. I was more than good. I was the best. I commanded an exorbitant wage for my services. Later, I became a partner in a few cattle operations. I grew rich. More than rich. I've thrice the wealth of your father, Mercy. So, if you agree to marry me, you won't lack for material things."

It did not entice her in the least. She flew to the point that did interest her. "What is the 'other part' of the story?"

He nodded as though something had been confirmed. "When I returned to England, I set about arranging my sisters' entries into society. I was determined they would have every advantage my father's desertion had ripped from them. Every family heirloom he'd pawned, I bought back. Every piece of my mother's jewelry he'd sold, I found and purchased. Every bank account he'd drained, I filled ten times over. Every social chasm he'd created with his pandering and licentiousness, I spanned with my title and my wealth and my blameless reputation."

"And then . . . ?"

"And then, about a year after I returned, he wrote me a letter."

"Your father." The words fell between them and Hart nodded.

"Do you want to hear something amusing? He'd never even been on the damned yacht. He'd been in Africa and had only just learned of my inheritance and wasn't it a grand joke, me having assumed a title that he had inherited?"

"I don't understand."

"Of course you don't, but *I* did. Too bad, he wrote, that I had assumed the privileges as well as the title. I would doubtless be loath to give them up. But he was the legal heir to the title. I was the Earl of Perth only if he was dead.

"And as for my sisters! *Think* of the scandal! But then, they'd have their father back soon to guide them through society." Hart's words came too quickly, slurring over each other as though he could not expel them fast enough.

"My God."

"Of course, perhaps it would be best if he just stayed in Africa. He was ill, you see, having contracted some tropical disease, and it would be very hard for him to travel. If he just had enough cash he'd just as soon put off his reappearance in society." His tone was unemotional. "I sent him ten thousand pounds. Four months later I received a similar letter. Once more I sent money. I kept receiving letters and I kept paying him off until finally I grew so sick of his taunts and complaints and threats that I had an account set up. I wrote him, telling him that I would make a yearly deposit and nothing more. I have done so for the past four years."

"And what does he say now?" Mercy asked.

Hart shrugged. "That was the last contact I've had with him. I don't even know if he's still alive or how or even if he uses the money I send. I don't give a damn. So you see, Mercy, any day he may appear and demand his title, his estate, and his daughters. There may be no coronet."

It suddenly made horrible sense. "That's why you said you'd seen the like before."

"Excuse me?"

"The letter from Will. You said that you'd seen its kind many times. You were speaking of your father. You thought Will was doing to me what your father had done to you. Extortion."

He frowned at her and she could not ignore the pity she saw in his expression. "That's what your Will *is* doing, Mercy."

"No." She stood up, needing to tell him he was wrong. She plucked at his arm. "Will isn't like that."

"He's an opium addict, Mercy." His tone was harsh.

"No," she said, and hearing the frantic quality in her denial, she forced her voice to a more normal

level. "He's just experimenting. You said so yourself. Young men like to kick over—"

He grasped her shoulders in his big hands,
gave her a little shake. His blue eyes were stark in
his face. "That's before I knew where he was going.
Before I knew what he was doing. *He's an opium
eater, Mercy.* The Peacock's Tail is an opium den."

"No!" She gasped. "Will isn't like that. He's
not much more than a boy. He's gotten in with a
bad lot, but as soon as I—"

"Can't you see? *You* can't do anything," he cut
in. "You never could. You aren't to blame for your
brother's actions. Now or ever."

"Yes, I am." Her head bobbed in jerks. "I
wanted Will and my father to be at odds. I didn't
want them to like each other. It's all my fault and I
have to make it right."

"Mercy," he whispered, brushing his knuckles
against her cheek, "you were a little girl looking for
approval. You give yourself too much credit. You
can't fix what you didn't break."

"Oh, God, that's rich coming from you. You've
spent a decade trying to make reparations for your
father! Trying to make it right for your sisters!"

He didn't recoil from the accusation. "Then
we're both wrong. Let him go, Mercy. Before you
get hurt."

"I'm not going to get hurt." She tried to jerk
away, but his hold was too firm.

"Will isn't the same boy you knew, Mercy. You
don't know what he's capable of now."

"You're talking nonsense," she said, fright making her voice strident.

"An addict doesn't have a conscience, he only has an insatiable animal that lives where his soul used to be. When it gets hungry, the addict can't control it, he can only feed it, by whatever means necessary."

"I don't know what you're saying." She wanted to plug her ears, to shut her eyes, but his voice went on, cruel in its sympathy.

"Will needs money, Mercy. Opium is expensive and the amount it takes to satisfy the animal is always growing."

"What the hell are you saying?" she demanded shrilly.

"If you die, who inherits your father's money?"

She stared into his eyes. She could see her own face mirrored in his black irises, her mouth twisted with anguish, her lips chalky.

He'd taken everything, her peace of mind, her body . . . damn him, even her heart, and he hadn't left anything to fill the emptiness . . . except his sense of obligation and his bloody coronet.

And now he was taking Will.

She slapped him hard across the face. He didn't even blink; he just held her with his hard, implacable gaze as she stared in horror at the red imprint of her hand on his cheek.

"You can strike me as many times as you like. It isn't going to make it any less true. I wish it would."

"You don't know what you're talking about. You don't know Will." She panted, her back stiff, her eyes glittering. "You're lying."

He shook his head. "No. You've been shot at. You narrowly escaped a serious, perhaps even fatal, injury when your gun exploded."

"Accidents!" The word rang out too fast, betraying the fact that she, too, had questioned those incidents. That somewhere in some dark corner of her mind, Will's name had risen in connection with them. Pain clouded her vision. She nearly hated him for making her admit it to herself.

"You've been here ten days, Mercy," he went on. "Ten days and two 'accidents.' There is no one who would benefit from your death besides your brother."

"Annabelle," she whispered. "Lady Acton. Either of them would do anything to protect their precious Duke from me."

"Mercy, you don't believe that," he answered.

"Don't I? Why is that so much harder to accept than your assertion that my brother is a cold-blooded, heartless fiend?"

"Because Will is an addict."

She raked her hand through her hair, turning away from him. "I won't believe that. I won't believe anything you say. You'll see. When I find him—"

"No!" he shouted.

"Yes!" Then the tears began, spilling from her eyes and blinding her.

"Mercy." He caught her damp chin between

his fingers and forced it up. "Don't try to find him." She tried to twist away but he wouldn't let her. His voice was low, urgent. "I'll look. No, wait. Listen to me. I swear I'll find him for you, bring him to you. Just do not risk yourself. Promise me. Promise!" he demanded.

"Why should it matter to you?" she flung out.

"Because if you are hurt, Mercy, I . . ." He closed his eyes and his mouth shut for an instant, barring her from seeing what his gaze held.

"Because *you're* the only one allowed to hurt me?"

His eyes snapped open. He stared down at her, through her, and when he spoke, it was with a deadly calm. "Yes. I'm the only one," he said, and spinning around, left as though chased by devils.

Chapter 26

"My heavens, Hart," Beryl exclaimed as he pulled her into an anteroom and closed the door; "whatever is going on? I just left Annabelle. She is working herself into a conniption fit."

"Impossible. She doesn't have enough real emotion in her for a pique, let alone a fit."

"The same has been said of you, Hart," Beryl said. "And, like you, she has very strong emotions indeed. Occasionally *she* gives voice to them. Like now. She claims you're about to ruin her by forming a mésalliance with Mercy Coltrane."

"I've asked Mercy to marry me," he said. "Whether she'll accept or not is another matter."

"Marriage?"

"Yes, Beryl, *marriage.*"

"Oh, dear." Beryl let out a little whoosh of breath and sank onto a chair. "I'd supposed from the way Annabelle was carrying on that you'd intended to set the girl up as your mistress. But marriage . . ."

"You can save the protestations for someone who is willing to listen to them. Annabelle has already made quite clear how disastrously she expects this will reflect on all of you."

"Oh, Hart—"

"No," he broke in, unwilling to listen to her beg him to reconsider. "You will listen. And then you will relay this information to Annabelle, and after that you and Henley will repair to whatever hotel Mercy is presently hieing herself off to and act as her damned chaperone whether she wants it or not!"

"Yes, Hart."

"If I can convince Mercy to have me, have me she will."

"Do you love her, Hart?" Beryl asked.

"Love?" Her question took him by surprise. His mouth twisted around the word.

"Does she make you happy? Can you imagine life without her?"

He paused and for one brief instant considered describing for her what he imagined life without Mercy would be like. But he had no words for what he envisioned and, being ever a private man, kept that imagined anguish as his own burden.

"If you're asking whether I can live without her, yes." *I can survive without her.*

Beryl's brow knit. "Then why would you risk so much? Society will be severe in its judgment. Oh, certainly there are those who would accept her simply because you are the Earl of Perth, but there are those who will not."

"Society be damned," he said. "If you or Fanny or Annabelle chose to attach your happiness to society's whims and dictates, then the more fool you. I have tried to give you everything and in doing so I have robbed you of that which is ultimately invaluable. The truth."

She twined her fingers in her lap and he went on then, determined to tell her everything. When he was done, Beryl would have at her disposal every fact, every bit of history, that affected her, whether directly or indirectly. She could then determine her own actions.

Mercy was right. He had been arranging his sisters' lives, he'd made a bloody mess of it, and he was done with it.

"First, our father did not die in a boating accident," he began, and, once started, he spoke for over an hour.

Mercy descended the grand staircase into the lobby of Browne's Hotel and restrained a surge of frustration. Beryl Wrexhall rose from her station near the door.

"Miss Coltrane?" The tentative smile on the older woman's dark face nearly undid Mercy's resolve to act cool. Whatever Hart had said or done to force Beryl into shadowing her every move had been effective, she would grant him that.

She could not leave her suite without bumping into Mrs. Wrexhall. She could not appear on the avenue without a shiny carriage, the Perth coat of arms emblazoned on its side, lurching to a stop beside her and a liveried driver leaping to her side and asking where she would like to go. She could not walk down a street without Hart himself—ridiculously and improbably attended by the maid Brenna, of all things!—pacing silently behind her.

Hart she could, and did, ignore. Beryl with her worried and conciliatory air was beginning to trouble her conscience. It was not Beryl's fault she'd been bullied into acting as a duenna.

She sighed. "Mrs. Wrexhall."

The woman's smile brightened so much at that scant encouragement that Mercy felt another tug of guilt.

"Miss Coltrane, would you . . . could you care to take tea?" Beryl asked, pitifully eager.

With a silent curse for Hart, who'd placed them in such an onerous position, Mercy nodded. She allowed Beryl to take her by the arm and lead her to a discreet alcove where a silver swan-necked teapot and delicate china service awaited them.

They took their seats and Beryl poured out tea as a waiter slipped a plate of cakes and sweet breads in front of them and disappeared. For long minutes they sat in strained silence, munching and sipping and regarding each other covertly over the rims of their cups.

"This is most unnecessary," Mercy finally said.

"Miss Coltrane?"

"I don't know what pressure Hart is using, but you really needn't concern yourself with me."

Beryl gave her a gently dissenting smile. "Miss Coltrane. You are alone, unchaperoned, and possibly, from what Hart says, my future sister-in-law. It is my duty to see that you are not made the topic of conversation among polite society."

"I don't give a—"

"Exactly what Hart said you'd say. But, might I add, my duty is also my pleasure."

Mercy drummed her fingers on the linen-clad table. "Mrs. Wrexhall, let us be candid. I remain in England for one reason and one reason alone. To find my brother. As soon as I am successful in this I shall return to America, where I shall endeavor to forget all about London, polite society, and your brother."

"Really?"

"Really."

Beryl's brows dipped in consternation. "You won't marry Hart?"

"No. I will not. There is . . . no need." She felt her face grow warm.

"I see." Beryl sat back in her chair and dabbed at her perfectly clean lips with a napkin. "Well, I suppose I can understand your aversion to marrying him."

"How perceptive of you."

"I mean what with him shooting you and all. . . ."

Mercy gaped at her, caught completely off-guard. "You know?"

"Oh, yes." Beryl nodded, helping herself to another slice of bread and generously slathering it with butter. "He told me all about it. And about Father's blackmail. And the title. Yes," she went on in response to Mercy's stunned expression, "it was initially rather overwhelming, but it makes sense of things I'd wondered about for years: why Hart never settled down, his isolation, his aloofness. He's had rather a burden to carry, hasn't he?"

"Yes," Mercy snapped, unable to keep herself from responding to the unfairness of it.

"Just imagine," Beryl ruminated, "all those years of trying to do what was best for us and never considering himself."

"Apparently it's a hard habit to break."

"I'm not sure I understand."

"He's doing it again, with me. That is what your presence here is all about, don't you see? Trying to make things right?"

"Really?" Beryl tipped her head, considering her remarks. "I don't know that I agree. I think Hart is finally doing something for himself. But then if you must hate him for having shot you—"

"I don't hate him for shooting me," Mercy denied hotly, sitting forward in her chair, her hands palm flat on the table. "He saved my life."

Beryl raised one black brow, making Mercy immediately aware of the belligerence of her pose. She settled back and lifted her teacup to her mouth. The liquid shivered across the surface. She banged it down on its saucer, furious anyone could think Hart's actions less than heroic.

"Oh," said Beryl. "Then why *do* you hate him, my dear?"

When had they gone from "Miss Coltrane" to "my dear"? Mercy wondered an instant before realizing what Beryl had asked.

"I *don't* hate him," Mercy protested. "Not at all."

"Oh." Again that slightly puzzled frown. The expression was suddenly replaced by one of enlightenment. "Ah! Then it is a matter of your heart not being engaged. I understand. You cannot force an affection where there is none. Please, allow me to finish. I have to admit I was rather hoping it might be otherwise. I asked Hart if he loved you, you know." She glanced at her.

Mercy had stopped breathing. She couldn't have spoken had her life been threatened. *Could Hart love her?*

"I don't suppose you'd like to hear what he said."

Mercy blinked.

"I will tell you. Perhaps it might prove instructional for you in regard to some future relationship." She smiled. "Hart said he wouldn't know what the word meant."

A dark, chilling despondency settled over her thoughts. She tried to reach for her teacup but her hand refused to act. It lay limply in her lap. She could only stare, numb and despairing, at Beryl.

"I find that rather amusing, don't you?" Beryl continued blithely on. "I mean, here is a man who has endured things I doubt he'll ever relate, who has sacrificed his childhood and much of his adulthood, who has struggled to give so much, saying he does not know what the word *love* means. You know what I think?'' Beryl leaned forward confidingly.

Mercy managed to shake her head.

''I think Hart knows quite well how to love. I don't think Hart knows how to *be* loved.'' She sat back, smiling as though quite pleased with her assessment, as though it were no more than a curiosity that had plagued her and now was settled, as though what she'd said did not mean more to Mercy than any few words she'd heard in her life.

''I mean,'' Beryl went on, chattering as though they were discussing a play or a book and not a living, breathing man, ''when do you suppose was the last time Hart heard the words *I love you*? I wonder if he ever has. . . .'' She screwed her mouth up. ''Mother was always so involved with Father: adoring him, hating him, berating him, and later mourning him. We girls had each other to bolster. But Hart . . .'' She shook her head. ''He was the eldest and a male. He was sent to school when he was eight and then he went to war. He wasn't more than a boy when he enlisted, but he was a man when he came back.

''As far as I know, there has never been a paramour or even a mistress who would have said those words. A shame. But then, knowing Hart, I'd imagine that purchased words would have repelled him. You know, I don't believe Hart would know *how* to ask for love. I don't believe it would ever even occur to him *to* ask."

Please, Mercy thought, *please, let that be the reason he didn't ask me about my feelings: He was afraid of my answer.* For a man like Hart to have let down his guard so far he'd lost control over his emotions, his subsequent actions would have been horrifying. *That* could be why he hadn't said anything to her in the library, in his bed, in her room. He'd assumed she was as appalled by his loss of control as he.

If only she was right. The thought, having found root, took hold. If only Hart wanted her love as much as she wanted his.

"But I've bored you long enough. Please, allow a fond sister to indulge her doting brother. He wants to protect you, my dear. Is it too much to ask that I be granted your company now and again? It isn't that much of a sacrifice, is it?"

"No," Mercy mumbled, shaken.

"You'll doubtless soon find *your* brother and be off." She smiled her sweet, sad smile. "I've just rediscovered mine. I'd like to please him in some small way, if just for a while."

Hart waited in the dark interior of a hired hack and watched the front door of the brothel. It was in a very respectable, middle-class area of town, one hardly to be suspected of housing a high-priced bordello. But then, that was the greater part of its appeal.

Already Hart had seen a judge, an alderman, and two conservative lords make use of its plain front door. He didn't give a damn for them. He was waiting for another, the man he'd seen leaving Browne's Hotel and had followed out of an idle curiosity that had turned into a cold anger. He settled back in the seat.

It must be nearing midnight, he noted, his thoughts turning unerringly to Mercy. He hadn't yet been able to keep his promise to her. Try as he had, hire as many private detectives as he had, he'd yet to find her brother. Until he did he wouldn't be able to rest, knowing that somehow Mercy's brother and Mercy's accidents were connected.

God, but he was tired, though. Three days of making sure she was never alone, never without protectors—whether himself or the men he'd hired to watch her. And, he smiled ruefully, three days of viewing her fair back.

She treated him as though he did not exist. She refused to acknowledge him. He couldn't blame her. He'd taken her maidenhead and then threatened her desperate illusion that her brother was still her darling, affectionate sibling. She'd clung to that illusion, he knew. She needed it to make reparations for some long-ago guilt. Well, he knew all about guilt and he knew all about atonement.

A movement at the door of the brothel caught his attention. The man exiting looked half done,

Hart noted with disgust. He lurched as he started down the icy steps, pulling his long coat closed with one fist.

Hart left the carriage and made his way to the opposite side of the street, waiting beneath the orange glow of the gaslight until the man was within a few feet.

"Good evening, Henley. Odd quarters your constituents choose for a meeting."

Henley Wrexhall staggered to a stop and peered blearily up at him. The smell of alcohol and cigar smoke was overwhelming and Hart's nose wrinkled with disgust.

"Hart!" Henley blustered, nonplussed and weaving on his feet. "What are you doing here?"

"I might ask the same, since your wife assured me not three hours ago that you were at some civic-minded meeting."

"Damn you!" Belligerence surfaced suddenly, released by alcohol-imbued courage. "How dare you spy on me! Did Beryl put you up to this?"

"No."

Henley's lips curled in bitterness. "Should have known," he muttered in disbelief. "Has to run to the great Earl of Perth whenever she wants something. A house, a husband . . . a career for her husband."

"You're drunk."

"Yes," Henley agreed. "I am. I might not be able to choose where I live . . . hell, we even had to vacate the Actons' at your whim. At least let me choose my own vices."

The man was beyond reason, ranting. At any minute he looked as though he would topple over. Hart grasped his arm, jerking him forward.

"Come with me, Henley. We'll discuss this in the morning."

"We'll damn well discuss it now," Henley said, trying to shake him off. "I haven't had the guts to say this to you sober, but"—he took a deep breath—"I don't want your help, your aid, or your house. I want my own life back with no beholding to anyone, most of all you."

"Oh, for God's sake, Henley, if you don't like Bentwood, move," Hart said in disgust. "I couldn't care less where you live."

Henley blinked. "You don't?"

"No."

"What about the rest?" he asked.

"What rest?"

"The money. All the extra money Beryl uses for the soirées and the fund raisers and the political parties."

"Henley, you would know better than I what the estate brings in. I haven't given Beryl any extra money."

"You have," Henley insisted. "Where'd it come from if not you?"

"Who keeps the accounts for the home farms? Who manages the estate?" Hart asked.

"Beryl," Henley said. His expression grew sullen. "She says she likes it."

"Then I imagine you can thank Beryl for any

additional income. She's always been good with figures."

"She didn't tell me." Henley's brows drew together in one thick line. "But what about my career—what about your interference there?"

"I don't know what you're rambling on about."

"Bullocks! Beryl tells me. She tells me how you put the bug in the right people's ear, use your influence to see that I'm noticed by the up-and-uppers. You know. All those silent, helpful little pushes you've given my career."

"I haven't done a bloody thing for or against your career now or ever."

Without a word of warning Henley swung. Hart ducked the blow easily, feeling each moment as though the situation was taking on the more bizarre aspects of a music hall mockery. He easily caught hold of Henley's arm and twisted it behind him.

Henley squirmed wildly, flailing with his free arm. "Lemmee go! How dare you call my wife a liar!"

"Listen to me, you complete ass," Hart said through clenched teeth. "If you do not stop, Henley, I shall hit you. I hit very, very hard. It will doubtless leave a mark and then Beryl will be very, very angry with me."

His words had a magical effect. Henley slumped in his grip, his sullen expression replaced by a mournful one. "Why should she care?"

"Because she loves you, though God alone knows why."

"She don't love me," Henley said. "She doesn't think I can tie my shoe without help."

Hart released him and Henley just stood where he was, swaying and staring disconsolately at his boot tops.

"Henley," Hart said, lifting his hand and hailing the carriage, "I think it's past time you spoke with Beryl. I don't begin to suggest I understand her reasons for telling you I have been aiding your political rise, but I do know she loves you. Perhaps she wanted to make herself appear indispensable to you and used me as the vehicle to do so."

"I don't understand. Beryl *is* indispensable to me. Always has been."

The cab drew to a halt beside them and Hart opened the carriage door.

"Did you ever tell her that?"

Henley clambered inside and, once seated, stared owlishly back at Hart. "Didn't think I needed to. Thought it was obvious. Beautiful, witty, ambitious woman like Beryl . . . she could have anyone she wanted. Afraid if I didn't make a name for myself she'd regret throwing her lot in with an untitled nobody like myself."

Hart shook his head. "Tell her."

He closed the door and rapped on it, sent it off into the night. He stood for a long while gazing after it, wishing he could say to another what he'd just advised.

Chapter 27

*M*ercy entered the lobby tentatively, for the first time in memory feeling shy and uncertain. Even after . . . after that *night* she'd not felt shy. Overwhelmed, excited, and frustrated, but not shy. If Hart was in the lobby—and she fully expected he was, given he'd been there every morning since she'd taken up residence—she must talk with him. She took a deep breath and looked around.

Hart wasn't there and neither was Beryl. But there was a note waiting for her from Nathan Hillard.

He'd found Will.

She flew back to her room, donned her coat and gloves, tucked her Colt revolver into her pocket, and set out hatless for the hotel door. Nathan's note said he'd meet her outside the hotel door at nine o'clock. It was nearly that now. True to his word, Nathan was waiting outside.

"Miss Coltrane." He doffed his hat and bowed

as she hurried past him to the waiting hansom. Wordlessly, he handed her into the carriage before shouting an address up to the driver and entering himself.

"I was surprised and dismayed when Lady Acton informed me you'd left Acton Hall," he said, tucking a carriage blanket around her legs.

"Where is my brother?"

"A short ways, m'dear," he said, his smile faltering a bit. "The party ceased to hold any appeal without your sweet, lovely presence. I left there yesterday."

"Oh." She plucked at the window shade, peering outside.

"I have since put into effect every means I could think of in order to make myself of some small service to you. I have hunted and, I fear, badgered everyone I know, looking for your brother."

She shook off her preoccupation. He deserved better than a view of her profile. "I can't tell you how I appreciate your efforts."

"It is my pleasure to do anything for you that I can."

There was an ardor in his voice that she could not ignore. His brilliant eyes were riveted on her face.

"I heard hints. . . . They say an indiscretion resulted in your leaving Acton's," he said, clearly embarrassed. "Miss Coltrane, if anyone has insulted you I will—"

"No. No one has insulted me. Are we almost there now?"

"Soon." A soupçon of impatience pinched the soft timbre. "Your happiness has come to mean a great deal to me, Miss Coltrane. More than I can easily voice."

"Thank you." She didn't want to do this now. She was too distracted by the thought that soon, very soon, she would see her brother again. But Hillard had found Will. She owed him a great deal. Kindness, at the very least. "You must excuse me. Perhaps at another time I can properly attend you. That time is not now."

He flushed. "Of course. Forgive me. I was carried away by my own feelings and did not stop to consider yours."

"Please," she hastened to say, leaning forward and touching his gloved hands with her own, "don't think me ungrateful. I am very, very grateful for your help."

He nodded and averted his face. She relaxed slightly against the back cushion, relieved by his sensitivity. She was going to see Will. Anxiety and happiness jumbled together, setting her thoughts to a whirlpool of emotion. She stared out of the small window, watching as elegant facades slowly gave way to soot-blackened brownstone and wide streets became crowded alleys.

"I must warn you, m'dear," Nathan finally said, breaking the long silence. She jerked to attention at the sound of his voice. "I do not think your brother is well."

"What?"

"I believe your brother is a very sick young

man. I . . . I hesitate to have you see him like this, but . . . but from what I am told, I have had doubts whether there would be another opportunity."

"What do you mean?"

He gazed with the utmost sympathy into her eyes and took her hand in his own. "Sometimes a man can indulge his appetites more than his body can endure. There is a point where it is impossible to reverse the effects of such hedonism."

"Oh, Lord—" Hart had been right then. Will *was* an addict.

"It becomes a downward spiral," he continued in his mild, regretful voice. "I fear your brother is past the crisis point."

"No, it cannot be!"

"I pray you're right," he said.

"When he sees me—" She broke off. When he saw her what would he do? "Does he know I'm coming?"

Nathan shook his head. "I did not want anything to set him off. I only heard of his presence in this place from another, who heard from yet another. I had my man go around late last night to verify whether or not the rumor was true."

The cab rocked to a halt, the clop of the hack's hooves ringing sharply on the cobbles. Mercy emerged in front of a dank, hulking building. Its blackened windows stared down at the cramped, deserted street like sightless eyes.

"We're here," said Nathan.

"Good morning, Hart," Beryl said to him outside the entrance to Browne's. The icy wind
plucked at her sable collar and teased color high in
her narrow face.

"Beryl," Hart greeted her wearily as he handed
the cabdriver his fee. "What are you doing outside
at this time of morning?"

"I have been walking," she said. "I have had a
lot of thinking to do." A melancholy yet composed
quality had replaced the tense lines of anxiety in
her thin face.

"I see. Henley?"

"Yes."

He felt a tug of compassion when she offered
him a weak smile. Last night he'd wanted nothing
more than to bloody Henley's face for the grief
he'd caused Beryl. But he'd played a part—unsus-
pecting as it was—in that grief, and Beryl herself
was not blameless. Whatever she decided, he
would stand behind her decision.

"Where is Mercy?" he asked after a moment,
looking up at the rooms where he knew she slept.

"It's only nine-thirty, Hart. She hasn't come
down yet."

"Beg pardon," the doorman, a Mr. Phipps,
said.

"Yes?" Hart asked. "Mr. Phipps has been keeping me apprised of Mercy's activities," he answered Beryl's questioning look.

"And will lose 'is position if the manager ever gets wind of it," the doorman said uneasily, glancing around.

"He won't. Now, what is it? Has someone been asking after Miss Coltrane? The young American I told you about?"

"No, sir. Not 'im. I was goin' ter say how Miss Coltrane left the hotel with some English gent."

Hart frowned. "Who?"

"Dunno. Some toff-lookin' gent about half an hour ago."

"Hart, I'm so sorry," Beryl said in dismay. "I never expected she'd leave so—"

"It doesn't matter," Hart said impatiently, a frisson of anxiety racing along his exhausted nerves. "Do you know where she went?"

Phipps nodded. "Heard the toff tell the cabbie Fifty-four Rector."

"Rector?" Hart said. Rector was in one of the more disreputable sections of Soho . . . an area remarkable only for the easy availability of illicit pleasures. The sole reason Mercy would go there would be to find Will. Perhaps, he thought with growing urgency, Will had even sent one of his friends for her so that he could—

Hart pushed past the doorman, racing into the hotel and up the lobby staircase to his rooms. Inside, he heaved his leather grip onto the bed and snapped it open. He dug through the few clothes to the carefully wrapped oiled wool package beneath.

He dragged the bundle out, ripping open the leather thongs. The Colt .44 gleamed lethal and expectant from its oiled wool bed as Hart rummaged around the satchel for its attendant box of shells.

He spilled the brass cartridges into his palm and, grabbing the gun, shoved them into the chamber, clicking it shut as he raced back down the stairs, through the lobby, and out into the street.

"Cab!" he shouted, fear coursing like fire in his veins. If Will had her down there, he could kill her. There'd be no witnesses. No one to help her.

A hansom rolled toward the curb. Before it had stopped, he'd jerked the door open and was half-way inside. "Two sovereigns if you get me to Rector Street within the quarter hour!"

---◆-◆◆-◆---

Nathan led her around the side of the building down a narrow foot alley. Perpetually shadowed by looming buildings, the ancient brick pavers underfoot were slick with a dark, brackish mold. He motioned her toward an uneven flight of steps that ended at a scarred, heavy-looking door. He knocked thrice.

Scraping metal revealed a tiny slit in the wood. An instant later the door creaked open and a fragile-looking Oriental man, thin white wisps bobbing from gaunt cheeks, beckoned them in.

Nathan withdrew a silk handkerchief from his pocket and handed it to her. "Cover your mouth, m'dear. The stench is overwhelming."

Mutely, Mercy complied, staring in horror

about her as Nathan led the Oriental man a few feet away and began a whispered conversation.

She stood in a dim, low hallway. A few candles, set on rude shelves, waded in pools of their own wax. They gave off a vile scented smoke that stained the rouge-colored walls behind them with black halos.

From where she stood she could see myriad little rooms opening onto the hall through crouching archways. More rooms were honeycombed behind these, some alcoves curtained, some open. In each alcove was a rough bed and between the alcoves squatted octopuslike water pipes, tubes extending from their swollen brass bellies.

The hiss and bubble of water gurgled from a dozen different sources. Their soiled, silk-wrapped tubes twined like snakes beneath the heavy draperies covering untold numbers of crannies. Moans and mutters punctuated the low, incessant bubbling sound, and worse, an occasional laugh, private and cheerless.

It was a catacomb. A catacomb for the living.

And Will was here.

"Miss Coltrane, please." Nathan Hillard motioned her ahead of him and she fell into step behind the old Oriental man. Before long he stopped and pointed at an uncovered niche.

A low pallet crowded the wall, a candle sputtering erratically near its head. A figure lay on the pallet, curled on its side, facing away from her.

"He be no smoke, two day now," the Oriental man complained. "No money. No smoke. Won't go." He shook his head and turned, leaving her to stare at the figure, so alien and familiar. Nathan touched her arm.

"I'll wait over here, m'dear," he said. "Please, be quick. I don't trust the Chinee."

She nodded, grateful for his consideration, and stepped closer to the pallet.

"Will?"

No movement, not even a twitch. Nathan's warning spun through her thoughts. Dear God, he could not be dead!

"Will?" Her voice rose anxiously. The man turned over.

"Oh," she said. "Oh, Will . . ."

Her heart twisted. He was gaunt and pale and his eyes were so dark, they looked black. He blinked at her like an old man.

"Mercy?" he asked, a soft, wondering smile in the hoarse whisper. Her heart broke.

"Yes, Will. It's me, darling."

He pushed himself into a seated position and immediately groaned in pain. He wrapped his thin, shaking arms around himself and doubled over. She fell to her knees beside him, embracing him.

He shook. Little paroxysms rippled through him, his eyes rolled back in their hollow sockets, his lips twisted in a grimace. She clung to him all the tighter. Whatever agony he had felt passed and he squinted at her. He cocked his head to one side, grinning at her as though he did not remember the pain that had gripped him seconds before.

"Is that really you, Mercy?" He sounded as

happy as a child. His smile was just as ingratiating, just as infectious. The blond, guinea-gold curls were matted on one side of his face. She was going to weep.

"Yes, dear. It's all right. I'll take you home now."

The pleased recognition died on his face. *"Home?"*

"Yes," she said, stroking the dirty hair back from his damp brow. "Back to Texas."

He encircled her wrist and held it away from his face. There was surprising strength in the slender fingers. "I'm not going home. I'm staying right here."

"Darling, you're not well," she coaxed. "You need to come home. You need someone to take care of you."

"She's gone," he said with an expression of pain and loss so stark that Mercy sobbed.

"I'll take care of you. Father and I, we'll take care of you."

The sorrow passed as quickly as it had come. A humorless curve cracked his dry lips. *"Father* and you?" he said. "I don't think so, Mer. Father and I, in case you don't remember, aren't what you'd call boon companions."

"I know. But that will change." Tears fell freely down her cheeks. "It will all change. Whatever differences you two have, I'll see you work them out. I promised Mom."

He stared at her a second and then he began to laugh. He laughed until pain filtered through the horrifying, broken sound, ending it in a fit of coughing. He wiped his mouth with his shirtsleeve and shook his head as he regarded her, amused and sickly and tragic.

"Shouldn't make promises you can't keep, Mercy," he said. "Why in God's name would you think you could fix what was wrong between Father and me?"

"Because I helped make it wrong!" There. She'd said it. "Forgive me, Will, but I did. I was happy he didn't . . . didn't . . ."

"Like me?" Will supplied with more interest than shock.

Mutely, she nodded.

He groaned suddenly, slouching against the filthy wall. Desperately she searched for some way to ease his pain. "What can I do?" she asked.

His eyes were squeezed in thin lines. "Money for another pipe."

"No, Will!"

"No? Then go away."

"I won't."

He opened his eyes. "Yes. You will. Because I'm not going with you. I don't belong in Texas. You don't belong here. I do. Now go away, Mercy."

"But I promised!" she wailed.

"Like I said. You can't fix what you didn't break," he said, his mouth set as he forced the words past his lips, past the pain that was squeezing the sweat from his pores. "You take too much credit. My relationship with Father didn't have anything to do with you, no matter what you think. The only times he and I got along at all were when we all three were together, riding, shooting . . . You still a good shot, Mercy?" He turned and she could see the glimmer of tears—pain? sorrow?—shimmer in his eyes.

"Yes, I guess."

"Good. I was always kinda proud of that." The unseen demon stretched him tighter on its invisible rack. Every muscle tensed in his body, sweat dribbled from his brow. He leaned away from her, curling into a ball on his side, his hands clamped between his knees. "You sure you don't have any cash, honey? Few bucks?"

"No." She dashed the back of her hand across her damp cheeks. She wouldn't feed the animal. She'd steal Will from it.

"Oh," he answered vaguely. "I gotta rest."

"Come back with me, Will. Please."

"Not yet." His voice sounded weak, distant. "Maybe someday. You get, now, Mer. Nothin' there for me."

"But I miss you. *I* want you back." She wept. "I want my brother back." From behind the curtains other unseen petitioners added their voices to hers. The twining corridors reverberated with their chorus in a cacophony of shattered dreams.

She laid her head against Will's shoulder and sobbed. It was true. Beyond the guilt and the duty and the promise, that was finally the deepest truth. She missed her brother. She wanted him back.

He didn't respond. His breath was shallow, his gaze unfocused.

"Miss Coltrane," Nathan said in a low, urgent voice. "We have to go. It's not safe in a place like this. There are men here who'd kill you for a pair of boots, let alone the price of a pipe. It's dangerous. Very dangerous. We have to go."

She lifted her tear-streaked face. Nathan Hillard was bending over her.

"But Will . . ."

He shook his head. "He'll just fight us if we try to take him out now. We can't do anything. Not yet. We'll have to return later, with additional aid."

Beside her, as if to validate Nathan's words, Will began to thrash and groan. His eyes flew open and he looked around. Horror seeped into his dark gaze. He grabbed her arm, pulling her close, wildly looking beyond her.

"Mercy, did *he* bring you here?" He panted, his eyes glazed and staring.

"Who, dear?"

"Him," he whispered, licking at his dry lips. "That devil."

She shook her head, biting her lip to keep from sobbing. "There are no devils, Will."

He laughed, bitterness tinged with hysteria. "Oh, yes, there are. Oh, yes." He kept saying it, even after he had shut his eyes, mumbling as he fell into some semiconscious state.

Nathan took her hand and pulled her up. "Please. I don't trust that Chinee fellow. He could be rounding up a band of thugs to rob us even as we speak."

"We can't just leave him!"

"We must. I promise we'll come back later."

"As soon as we can find the authorities? In under an hour?" she demanded.

"Yes, yes," Nathan said, looking around nervously.

"One second, then," she said, pulling loose and returning to Will's side. She reached into her pocket and pulled the little revolver from within. Carefully, she tucked the firearm beneath the single twisted blanket. She pushed a few cartridges into his pocket. "Will," she whispered, "I'm leaving you my gun so you can protect yourself. I'll be back, Will. I won't abandon you. I won't be gone long."

She stood up and Nathan took her arm and led her out of the opium den and into the milky haze of the back alley.

Chapter 28

"**D**amn cabbie," Nathan muttered. "I told him to wait."

Mercy looked around the deserted brickyard. She had to get Will out of here. "Where are we?" she asked. "I have to get back to the hotel. I have to find Hart."

"Hart?"

"Hart. Lord Perth," she said, looking one way and then the other. A stack of half-rotted barrels angled away from where they stood, blocking what appeared to be the egress into a lane. In the opposite direction the small yard ended in a wall where a low archway crouched in the corner. Above it an ancient tattered handbill fluttered wearily against the smoke-stained brickwork. Mercy started toward it.

"Why would you want to find Perth?" Nathan asked. Mercy looked over her shoulder. He was not following her. He was standing in an attitude of unnatural attention.

"He'll help us," Mercy explained. "Is this the way out?"

"I can help you. I am, after all, the one who found your brother." There was a petulant quality to his tone.

"Yes," she said. "Of course."

"You know"—he came forward, a perplexed frown on his handsome face—"there was the suggestion when I left Lady Acton's that something not quite proper had occurred between yourself and Perth. I discounted it as the malicious talk of jealous people, but now I find myself asking . . . was there?" He looked up. There was nothing casual about his too-bright eyes. "Was there, Mercy?"

She stiffened, offended and subtly threatened by his aggrieved expression. "That's none of your business, sir."

"I disagree. When a gentleman plans on marrying a lady, he should be privy to her entire history."

She gasped.

"Oh!" His mouth puckered into a little circle of annoyance. He clucked his tongue in annoyance as he tugged his suede gloves off, exposing pale white hands, their trim, shiny nails gleaming in the alley's twilight. "I haven't gone about this at all well, have I?" He placed a glove on the damp ground and bent one knee atop it. "Miss Coltrane, will you marry me?"

He was watching her, his sweet smile on his

face, his brows lifted a little in self-mockery at his formality, his eyes aglow with anticipation. He actually expected her to say yes. Here. Now. He had to be mad.

She fumbled for the words. "I . . . I am cognizant of the great honor you do me, sir, but I must decline."

He stared at her as though in great puzzlement. "Is it Perth, then?" he asked.

What did he want to hear? What would stop this horrifyingly inappropriate exhibition? The truth? "Yes," she answered.

He nodded as though his suspicions had been confirmed and the revelation, while a disappointment, had come as no great surprise. He rose, brusquely swiping his knee with his glove. She sighed with relief and once more started toward the far wall.

"Too bad," he muttered. "I rather enjoyed the idea of being wedded to you rather than being saddled with that stinking derelict down there."

She stopped. His mild, disappointed tone sent gooseflesh creeping over her arms and belly.

"It was either you or him, m'dear. Can't say you didn't have a fair go."

"Go?" She turned around. He was pointing a pistol at her, smiling.

"Yes. A go." He nodded. "At living. One of you is going to have to die. Your father might be rich, but he's not that rich. At least his estate wouldn't be if it were to be divided. Not enough to satisfy my . . . requirements."

"Your requirements," she echoed, feeling her way backward with one foot. Her only chance was to run.

"Bills," Nathan Hillard said mournfully. "Bills and debts and promissories and, oh, Lord, I won't bore you with the details. Suffice it to say I was very pleased to make your dear brother's acquaintance. He was so very, very ripe for the plucking. In fact"—he grinned again—"I can honestly say I have never seen anyone embrace vice with quite the enthusiasm of your brother."

Horror chased realization. He'd brought about Will's addiction. This gentle, smiling, debonair man . . . *he* was Will's monster.

"My God. You planned this from the first!"

"Oh, no, no, no." He clucked his tongue. "Not the first." There was a hideous modesty in his voice. "At first old Will was merely someone to pick up the tab, don't you know. But his appetites grew, and so did his bills and, consequently, my bills. We encountered problems.

"I knew he came from a wealthy family. It only seemed fair that he should have what was due him, but you know how Will is." He shook his head with something like fondness. "Stubborn to a fault. He would not ask for money. He wouldn't and when he discovered you were in England, the silly boy indulged in a disgusting bout of self-recrimination. He was going to throw me over. After all I'd done for him. Me!" He lifted his hands, appealing to her for justice. She shivered.

"Couldn't let that happen. So we just introduced him to a more potent form of opium. That put an end to that nonsense, I'll have you know. Yes, Willy boy likes his vice.''

Her breath caught in her throat.

''Oh, I'm sorry. You don't like vices, I take it? Well, probably just as well we won't be getting leg-shackled then, isn't it?''

''How is killing me going to get you Father's money?'' Mercy asked, playing for time. Inch by inch her feet, concealed beneath her skirts, edged her back toward the alley. He didn't appear to notice.

''You've seen him,'' Nathan said, waving the gun barrel at the stairs. ''He's utterly and completely my creature. He has been from the moment I placed the pipe in his mouth and he suckled like a babe at his mother's breast.''

''God, you're disgusting.''

''*Tch tch*. You sound like your brother in his more lucid moments, not that there are many of those.'' He spread his fingers in a gesture of comic defeat. ''I have always been fascinated by the odd points of principle Will clings to. Do you know he wouldn't even ask your father for money? No. *I* had to write those notes. Fine forgeries, if I do say so myself.

''And when you arrived . . . that was nice. You were so forthcoming with the money. I had only to scribble a note, and it was like money in the bank. At least for a while.'' And then, well, I decided that I might as well take the whole of the fortune for myself, what with having two options open to me."

"How is that?" she asked breathlessly.

"Will or you," he said in surprise. "And I don't mind admitting that I'd just as soon you'd agreed to marry me. You are so dashed pretty." His smile was terrifyingly sane and sweet. His bright eyes dulled. "Then you decided to investigate. I wasn't ready for you to find Will quite yet. He wasn't completely malleable."

"You were responsible for my accidents."

Gravely, Nathan nodded his head. "I never meant to kill you, you understand. Why would I? I was courting you, for God's sake! Only an imbecile would try and murder the bride *before* the wedding. No. I was just trying to incapacitate you. Didn't want you to find your brother before the proper time."

It had all been planned, orchestrated from the moment she'd arrived.

"I'm afraid I'm not nearly the shot you are, m'dear," Nathan apologized. "If I were, I would have winged you right neatly and you would have sat in bed for weeks sending old Willy boy money."

"The pheasant hunt. How did you manage that?"

"Plug of dirt in the barrel. Nothing could have been simpler."

She was almost to the entrance. She could feel the cold, dank air ruffling her hair. If she spun and ran . . . Another few feet.

"I don't understand. If I had agreed to marry you—"

"I would have killed old Will boy. He would have conveniently died this very afternoon. I told you how poorly he was looking." He sighed. "Now I'll have to clean him up for the passage home. We'll take your lovely corpse back to wherever the hell it is you come from. Poor Daddy Coltrane shall doubtless succumb shortly—"

She wheeled and plunged forward. A tall black figure appeared in the alleyway, one hand brandishing a revolver, the other reaching for her.

"Hart!"

Bang!

Agony exploded in her head. She spun toward the burning impact and staggered. Her eyes widened with astonishment and . . . .

He caught her as she collapsed.

"No!" The single word erupted from him. It rose deep and hoarse, a howl of anguish and denial fashioned from his soul. The sound echoed off the slick walls and down the wind-pricked alleys.

"No!" He clamped her sagging body against him and his free hand snapped up. He fired. Hillard fell.

Not enough.

He flung his head back and roared with wounded fury and shot again. Even as Hillard's body crumbled behind the barrels, disappearing from his sight, Hart fired. Again and again and again, he jerked the trigger, emptying the chamber into the barrels, splintering and shattering the rot-

ted wood, ricocheting bullets off the filthy brick
wall, striking sparks of fire, noise thundering down
the twining dark corridors. And still he fired. Even
after there were no more cartridges, just the mechanical click of a hammer repeatedly striking an
empty chamber, he fired.

Finally he stopped, the gun drooping in his
nerveless grasp. He sank to his knees, his precious
burden limp in his arms. Blood sheeted the left side
of her face, covering her one eye and streaming
down her cheeks like crimson tears.

"Mercy."

He prayed. Without words, without volition,
he prayed. Every shudder of his fingers passing
over her blood-cauled face was a petition. Every
quiver in his body as he strained to perceive
some—any—evidence of life was a supplication.

And his prayers were answered.

She flinched, suddenly and abruptly. He
stopped breathing. She shifted in his arms, squint-
ing up at him through her unclotted eye.

"Ow."

He laughed, a hoarse, broken sound. She
peered at him. Tears ran down his face.

"I'm glad . . . you find this amusing."

"Oh, God, Mercy," he said, dabbing the blood
from her eye with his shirt cuff. A deep furrow cut
across her temple and disappeared beneath her
hair. "I thought that you . . ." He couldn't get the
words past the constriction in his throat.

She took pity on him. He looked so lost and
tragic staring at her, his expression bleak and help-

less. His eyes told her everything. They held the cursed knowledge of a man who'd tasted damnation.

"You're probably angry . . . that I was shot . . . by someone else," she whispered hoarsely. "Especially after you'd said . . . I couldn't be."

Dumbly, he nodded.

"I see." She smiled. The movement caused her to wince, but still she could not refrain from touching the stark, tormented face hovering above hers. He jerked his head around, pressing his lips into her palm and kissing it reverently. "I promise, it won't happen again," she said.

"Sorry, but I'm afraid I'll have to make a liar of you."

Convulsively, Hart's grip tightened closer around Mercy. Nathan Hillard stood beside the shattered barrels, his revolver pointed at them, smiling. Hart jerked the Colt up before he remembered. It was empty.

"You missed." Hillard laughed, a horrible sound, so human and warm and genuinely amused. "Unless you have a Gatling gun, there, Lord Perth, I'm afraid *you* are out of bullets." Nonchalantly, he aimed at Mercy.

Hart flung her beneath him, shielding her with his back as the shot rang out. He braced for the impact. Nothing. He turned his head.

Hillard was staring down at where a small red disk had appeared on his white shirtfront. He collapsed watching it spread.

A cough drew Hart's attention. There, on the

staircase leading to the opium den, Will Coltrane stood leaning against the doorjamb, the .38 still smoking in his hand.

"But I'm not," he whispered.

Chapter 29

$\mathcal{A}$ week later Hart stood in a shaft of late morning light in his suite at Browne's Hotel. Once more he scanned the letter he'd received from the South African bank. It was a short note, clear and toneless.

The gentleman known as Francis Jonathan Miller had not made a withdrawal from his account in over twenty-six months. Hart folded the sheet and tucked it back inside its envelope. There was only one assumption he could possibly make from such information. His father was dead. Hart was, indeed, the Earl of Perth.

He and his sisters could continue on as before, the threat of scandal averted. But still, there was a sense of loss, of emotions unresolved. He straightened. He'd learn to live with it. He'd learned to live with many things. There was only one thing he could not bring himself to consider living without.

Abruptly, the door to his room swung open.

She stood for an instant, warm and vivacious, the sunlit motes her entrance had stirred dancing like tiny fairy attendants about their queen. Her tallow-colored gown shimmered in the slanting light, her hair glistened in dark contrast to the white gauze banding her brow.

"Is it only my rooms over which you have this unaccountable sense of proprietorship?" he asked. He wouldn't voice other words. He was afraid, desperately afraid, that she would leave him if she knew how much he needed her.

"Oh, dear no," she said, stepping forward and shutting the door behind her. "I feel proprietary about all of you."

He didn't respond to her teasing. Later, he would think of some glib response. Now, he only wanted to look at her. Fill his eyes with the sight of her.

For a week he'd stood sentinel at her door while the physicians clucked and fretted and spoke about concussion and sight damage. He'd nearly gone mad. And when they had allowed that she would be fine, perfectly fine, except for a scar traversing her left temple, he'd gone.

And now . . . while her pallor still troubled him, her green-gold gaze was clear and brilliant, her lashes—ridiculous, overabundant lashes—fluttered flirtatiously. She was smiling.

"You have much more light in here than I have in my room," she said. "Doctors here seem to have a definite grudge against light."

Beryl had told him Mercy wasn't pregnant.

There was nothing to bind her to him now. Nothing. Mercy was not going to marry a man because of a thin, torn membrane. She would need a much more powerful incentive. She'd need to love the man she married.

But, God help him, looking at her as she meandered among his few belongings, he did not know how he would live without her.

She sauntered slowly through the room, her hips swaying, the flounced hem swinging. She plucked a shaggy bright yellow chrysanthemum from a vase, passing within arm's reach of him— foolish girl. She looked about and chose a seat on the foot of his bed.

"Have you heard anything of Will?" she asked.

Ah. He could let his breath go now. That is why she'd come.

"No, Mercy. I have tried. Believe me, I've used every resource I can think of, but I haven't had any success yet. Still, eventually, if we search long and hard enough, we will find him."

Her head bent forward and she studied her lap.

"Mercy," he said, choosing his words carefully, "Will's disappearance might be for the best."

"How can that be?" she asked, looking up. He was relieved that there was no suspicion in her eyes, just grave consideration.

"If he is found he will have to stand on murder charges."

"But he saved our lives," she protested.

"I know. But Will was in an opium den and he

killed a . . . conspicuous member of society. From behind. At least this way Will remains free." She didn't reply and he plunged on. "I swear, if we find him, I'll see that he receives the best counsel in England, but I can't swear what the outcome of his trial might be." He paused. "Mercy, what do you want me to do?"

She took a deep breath. "Stop looking."

He nodded and for a few strained moments they shared the silence. "I expect you'll be returning to America," he finally said, longing to gather her in his arms, to hold her and never let her go, knowing that was impossible.

"Oh. America. Yes, I suppose so."

"I'm sorry your stay here was so unhappy."

She stared at him, clearly startled, and he cursed himself for having made such a monstrous understatement.

"Well," she responded, the corner of her mouth quirking, her humor impossible to completely subdue, even now, "your stay in my country wasn't particularly pleasant either."

"That's true."

Once more they lapsed into silence. The mantel clock struck the quarter hour and Mercy scowled at it. She stood up, dusting off the glowing satin skirt. She was going to leave. Maybe this time forever.

He held on to his resolve, made himself stand still, like the rock they sometimes called him, though he felt as though he were being cut off at the knees and his heart's blood was streaming out of him and God knew he'd never been more aware of how painfully, cruelly alive he was or how infinitely long a lifetime could last.

"How many men did you kill in America?" she asked.

The question caught him off-guard and he answered, "Three."

"Were they fair fights?"

He didn't know what she was looking for, but as much as he wanted to do otherwise, he could only let her find the truth. "No. They weren't. They couldn't be. I was a better shot than they were. Much, much better."

The smooth skin between her dark brows puckered with displeasure and the bandage dipped over her eye. "You shot them in the back?" she asked, pulling the gauze off. A rosy jagged line threaded the pearly sheen of her temple.

"No."

"You drew first?"

"No."

"Then how was it unfair?"

He looked at her helplessly. "I never miss."

"Never?"

"Never."

"I see." She reached behind her throat and started fiddling with the clasp of the amber necklace that nestled between her breasts. It would own her skin's warmth as well as the heat of the sun.

"I see," she repeated. "You were remiss in not only failing to issue a statement regarding your abilities but neglecting to dispense the warning among the general population. And certainly you should have taken out ads in all the newspapers declaring 'I Never Miss.' "

He gave her a sardonic smile. "That might have exacerbated matters. There's always some fool who wants to test his skill."

"Aha!" She pounced on the admission, leaning forward like a barrister in front of a jury. "What could you have done to make them fair fights?"

"I could have not been there."

He heard it in his own voice, the regret, the deep welling sorrow. Not guilt. He had come too far for guilt. But regret. Yes. There was that. There would always be that.

She'd studied him for a few eternal moments. He had never felt more vulnerable, never; not in the shallow troughs of North Africa with a thousand rifles pointing at him; not in a Texas saloon, his back to the door and a gun barrel reflected in the mirror. This woman knew everything now. Every part of him.

She went back to fiddling with her necklace. "Stubborn, ornery . . . If you hadn't been there, I would have been dead." She pulled the necklace off and dropped it on the bed. With both hands she reached behind her again. The position thrust her bosom out, the sweet curves swelled over the tightening embrace of her bodice. Hart swallowed.

"What the hell are you doing?" he asked, feeling dazzled by the brilliant morning light, the smoky spiced scent of her, the lazy tick of the clock marking time.

"I'm getting undressed," she said.

The damn buttons wouldn't come free and her courage was fast eluding her. She needed to do this and she needed to do it now. Hart was standing absolutely motionless a dozen feet away. His expression was stony, impassive, remote. Only his eyes were alive, desperate and pleading.

He loved her.

There was not the slightest doubt in her mind that he loved her. Beryl's words echoed through her mind. He loved but he did not know how to be loved.

She would show him. He wouldn't have a single doubt about *her* love when he left this room.

Her fingers worked numbly over the small pearl buttons. Each second he stood watching her with his face calm and his eyes burning grew more torturous. Suddenly, with a growl of frustration, she seized the edges of her bodice and ripped them apart. Tiny buttons sprayed through the air and skittered noisily across the floor.

"There," she said calmly, pushing the sleeves down over her chemise. He still hadn't moved.

It wouldn't do. She could offer herself to him as though her body were a gift, but she knew he would accept it in just that manner. This man needed more than that. He needed to be courted.

Pushing the heavy cloth down over her hips, she squirmed out of it, dropping it to the floor. She stepped over the ring of discarded satin and unlaced the corset. She pulled it off and held it up as though for his inspection, dangling it from her fingertips. Then she dropped it too. Why the deuce didn't he say something?

"Mercy."

She barely heard him, could not tell if the single word was an invocation or a petition. She looked up.

Whatever she had expected, it wasn't this. He approached her slowly, as though afraid she'd bolt, or suddenly laugh. His beautiful eyes were dark with emotion. He stopped a hand's breadth away. His chest rose and fell in quick, shallow breaths.

"You don't have to do this," he said, his eyes searching her face.

"Have to?" she asked, her brow wrinkling in confusion. "Yes. I do have to. I want you. I don't know any other way. I want your body next to mine. I want you in me."

She cupped the hard angles of his jaw between both hands. His beard scratched her palm. How long had she wanted to touch him, to learn the texture of his strong, still features? She sighed with sensual gratification.

She moved her fingers lightly over his face. His jaw was strong and tense, the skin above the line of his beard unexpectedly smooth. He held her with no more than the expression in his eyes, rapt and questioning.

He was the most dangerous man she'd ever known. Everything about him was whipcord hard and lightning motion held in check. Lethal and tensile. And he shivered because she touched him.

She worked the first buttons of his collar open, revealing his strong throat. She ignored the impulse to kiss him there, instead unbuttoning the rest of his shirt. She glanced up and her fingers faltered in their task.

He was watching her warily, nearly fearfully; only a tightening of the skin near his temples and along his jaw were evidence that he'd been pushed to the wall and was clinging to this self-imposed immobility as a last defense.

The final buttons came loose and she parted the stiff white linen carefully, exposing his chest, muscled and sleek and smooth. She reached up to his shoulders and swept the material from his broad shoulders, tugging it off.

He trembled. She placed her hands on the broad span of his shoulders and raised herself on her toes. His gaze impaled her for an instant before his eyelids drifted shut and she kissed him. His mouth opened on a groan. His lips were full and firm and warm beneath hers. She nibbled at his lower lip, begging him to act, to kiss her back.

Still he didn't touch her. He didn't lift an arm to restrain or hold or keep her near. He stood, all of his body held by some invisible force, accepting her kiss.

It was so exquisitely gentle. Not a kiss at all, really. Her lips trailed over his jaw and hovered open over his mouth, mingling their breath before passing on. She felt the sleek inner lining of his lower lip, the warm, firm pad of his upper. She felt his quick, warm breaths fanning her cheek as she plied his face with tender kisses, his cheeks, the bridge of his nose, his eyelids, his temple . . . again and again returning to his mouth. He smelled of bleached linen and smoke and a deep, elusive yet ineffable masculine musk.

She combed her fingers through his hair—cool, crisp, and silky. He turned his cheek into her hand and rubbed his face against her palm, a deep rumbling groan like a cougar's purr coming from deep within his throat. Such incredible sweetness.

Fallen woman? The idea flickered through her sense-befuddled mind. A woman doesn't *fall*, she drowns in drugging, langorous kisses. He lifted his head and she made a sound of protest.

"I'm not going to do anything," he whispered raggedly. "Nothing but kiss you. I just want to kiss you," he said, trying to convince . . . her? himself? "Please."

"Yes," she answered. "Yes." She threaded her fingers through the thick brown hair at the nape of his neck, pulling him down.

"Kiss me, Hart," she whispered.

"Yes." He sounded winded, urgent. He covered her mouth and this time hunger surged beneath the tenderness. He slanted over her, his arm snaking about her waist. He widened his stance and hauled her hips hard against the berth his legs made.

She felt him. He was hard there, a thick swell pressed against the jointure of her thighs, and he was moving, a sharp repositioning of his lower torso rocking against her, one big hand cupping the back of her head, the other holding her buttocks. She should have been shocked; she only wanted more of it. She met his movement with her own and he growled.

His tongue wet the seam of her lips in a demanding stroke. She complied. His tongue glided deep within. She clutched him as his tongue played with hers, each thrust deeper and wetter and hotter. Her knees started to buckle. He didn't catch her. He followed her down, down onto the pile of sunlight-heated satin and lace and linen, his shoulders bowing over her.

She arched into the hard, tight body shading her, hungry for him. She wanted this. Wanted him over her and in her. He pushed himself up on his arms. The muscles of his chest and upper arms stood out in corded relief, bronzed and quivering.

"I want you, Hart," she said. He closed his eyes. His features were set in a mask of concentration. The light flowed like a molten veil over his straining body. "I want you."

"You don't know," he said savagely, his eyes still tightly shut. "I can't control this. I can't pace this."

"Then don't."

"I don't want to hurt you again," he said, his breath coursing in and out of his clenched teeth. She reached between them and touched his flat, copper colored nipple. He fell heavily forward on his forearm and with his other hand clasped her around her wrist. For a second he hesitated, but only for a second, and then he flattened her palm over his breast, splaying her hand and holding it there. "I don't want to hurt you."

"You didn't hurt me."

"Then why did you cry?" he demanded, his eyes flashing with brutal self-condemnation.

"Because you *stopped*. It stopped. Because you took me *there* and then left me!" She was ablaze with an unquenchable fire and she needed to follow it to wherever it led. Wantonly inspired, she dragged her chemise off her shoulders and lifted a breast so that her nipple grazed his. He doubled as though he'd taken a blow.

"Dear God."

She leaned forward and touched the tip of her tongue to his chest. "Please," she said, licking him as greedily as he'd once done her. He pulled her head roughly against him, holding her there.

"Please," she said again.

"Yes," he rasped, "I'll please you . . . or die trying."

He lowered her down and peeled off the rest of the fine white chemise. Sunlight bathed her naked breasts in warmth. He met her gaze, his own eyes dark and intent.

"I'll pleasure you." It was a threat and a promise. She tried to rise up on her elbows to recapture his mouth but he pushed her back down. The urgency had left him, replaced by an indolent, magnificent sexual assurance.

"I will kiss every part of you," he purred.

"Here." He ran the tip of his finger over her lower lip, tugging it open and gliding his forefinger along the moist satiny interior. She closed her mouth around the tip and sucked gently.

His eyes went black. His nostrils flared as though scenting her response, testing her fragrance for readiness. He withdrew his finger and touched her chin with the damp tip. He marked a leisurely trail down her throat, over her collarbone to her breasts.

"Here." He made lazy circles around the dark areolas, teasing them hard and pointed with torturous languor. Then he bent and suckled—so gently, so lightly—flicking each nipple with his tongue until she moaned and bowed, flexing her breast more fully into his mouth, squirming in an effort to deepen his possession of her.

He lifted his head. His breathing was harsh, his face set in tense, controlled lines. "Not yet."

"Do I beg?" she asked. The place between her thighs felt full and swollen and uncomfortable, replete with raw nerve endings, and each thing he did to her only made it worse, made her feel more frantic, greedier, needier. Only the hardness he'd held her to earlier had helped assuage the clamoring need, and he'd taken that away.

"Beg," he said. "It won't do any good. I'm going to please you. At my own pace. There are other places I need to kiss." His fingertips continued their gossamer journey, feathering a caress over her belly, sculpting the jut of her hipbones, and sweeping aside the lace-edged top of her pantaloons, exposing her.

"Here." He touched the shallow indentation of her belly button and she tensed. He smiled, a slow predatory smile, and his hand drifted down over the exquisitely sensitive flesh of her inner thigh. She shuddered, clutching his hard biceps. "Please."

"Yes," he murmured. "Pleasure." He moved his hand upward and her hips jerked in an elemental response. She was going to faint. Her heart was thundering. He parted the soft folds between her legs and, with one long, graceful finger, stroked her. He did it again, and again, finally finding the pulsing cynosure of pleasure that nestled therein. He rubbed it gently between his thumb and forefinger.

"Please, Hart. Have mercy." She panted, straining into his touch.

"Yes." He lifted his hand to his face and she watched in sensual fascination as he breathed deeply the scent of her on him and then slowly, his eyes never leaving hers, licked his fingertips, tasting her. "And there. Oh, God, yes. Particularly there."

She could not take any more. She pushed her hands between them, fumbling at his trousers. He did not stop her. He did not try. His chest rising and falling like a pumping bellows, he sat back on his thighs, his legs bracketing her hips, watching her hands on his crotch, his face glazed with the sheen of self-restraint.

She found the closure and wrenched it open,

and then she felt him, satin heat and hardness, a thin cloak of velvet smoothness encasing a rock-hard length. She took hold of him in both hands and stroked him.

Once.

All control vanished. He came over her with a growl, suiting his mouth to his hand's journey. Tasting and kissing and pulling her deeper into a maelstrom of sensation and pleasure. And after he'd pleasured her with his mouth and she shivered in the hot sunlight, drawn as tight as a violin string, suspended at the juncture of painful anticipation and exquisite sensual fulfillment, he pleasured her more, with finger and word and sigh, until her body was flushed and so sensitive, a butterfly's wing would have seemed an abrasion.

He settled his hard body over hers and cupped her buttocks and lifted her. She met his thrust greedily, countering it with her own. She wanted him in her, filling her, stretching her. He took her in one deep movement.

She smoothed her hands over his back. His smooth, clear skin rippled over hard muscle. He panted hoarsely in her ear and she bucked against him, trying for a closer contact. She cinched his hips between her thighs and clung to the hard contours of his buttocks and he groaned deep in his throat and started . . . oh yes, oh yes, the rhythm, deep thrust, retreat, hard and filling, sliding heat, masculine potency, until she was there, cresting the wave of pure raw pleasure, riding the sensations out along the thick molten spirals of sensation.

She cried out with the sheer intensity of it and then he was throwing his head back, singing a deep hoarse cry of completion that echoed her own.

———◆———

Hart touched her face, dabbing at the single tear that fell from the corner of her eye. "Did I hurt you?"

"No," she denied immediately. "It was simply . . . it was . . . it was the most profound . . . it was—" She gave up. "Oh, Hart. I love you. I love you so much."

He caught her close, but not before she'd seen the look of bedazzled incredulity. He cradled her against his chest, rocking her in his arms, his heart thundering beneath her ear.

"Say it again," he asked weakly.

"I love you."

He stroked her hair. "Sweet Jesus. To hear you . . ." and then, suddenly, fearfully, "Dear God, Mercy, you must know that I—"

"I know you love me. I haven't any doubt."

"I do love you," he said reverently. "I have since you strode into my bedchambers and black-mailed me. I didn't want to, but I couldn't help it."

"Hart—"

"Let me tell you. God, I want to tell you. Beryl asked me once if I could live without you. I said yes. It's true you, know . . . I can. I would. But for the rest of my life I would regret it. Whatever gave me joy, I would know it could have been a keener joy were you with me. Whatever caused me sorrow, it would only be a bruise because I had already endured the greatest sorrow." He watched her intently, willing her to understand. "And when I finally died, Mercy, no matter how many years had passed, how many experiences, whatever happened, you would be with me, my last thought.

"God knows I love you, Mercy. I tried not to let it show. I tried so damn hard."

She leaned upward and kissed his eyelids, his mouth, and his throat until the despair seeped from his haunted gaze. "You did a very good job too," she said finally in a gruff little voice, and won a smile. "You are so remote, so reserved. I was quite sure you loathed being in the same room with me, and later, when I suspected you might return my feelings, why, even then I might not have been absolutely certain except for one thing."

"Mercy?"

"You missed."

"Missed?" he asked.

"In the alley. You missed. You *never* miss. You said so yourself. Only a very strong emotion could make a dangerous, coldhearted man like yourself miss an easy shot like that. I'm convinced it was love."

He didn't argue. Instead he rolled her onto her back. "Coldhearted?"

"Yes," she purred, feeling his body swell against hers once more. "And dangerous."

"I would not say coldhearted," he said. "But as for dangerous, the greatest danger you face, my love, is when, or if, you'll ever get out of this room."

Epilogue

"*A*ny interesting letters?" Hart asked, dropping into the leather chair across from his wife.

Mercy flicked a finger in the direction of the correspondence she'd already read. "Beryl writes that Annabelle has finally achieved an heir for Acton," she said.

"Bully," Hart said.

"Now, Hart. She is your sister. And you do have to admit her determination to achieve her goals is . . . amazing."

Hart snorted, unconvinced. "She's amazing, all right. But at least some justice has been served. Having snared her duke, she is forced to share a

breakfast table with her mama-in-law each morning. I seriously doubt the Dowager will ever fully
relinquish her title."

"Eventually she will pass on," Mercy said.

"And give up her claim on her son? I doubt it."

Mercy laughed. "Someday we will have to visit
Annabelle. She's been asking for some time now."

Hart shrugged. He still hadn't forgiven his sister for refusing to attend his wedding to Mercy.
Mercy was working on him, but she didn't expect
any tangible results for another decade or so.

Hart had an incredibly protective streak where
she was concerned. Not, she thought, that she
minded. He looked fit and relaxed and masculine
sprawled in the chair like that, his muscular thighs
wide, his big hands resting on his knees. The nightmares he'd garnered in his youth still occasionally
plagued him, but now she was there to hold him
when he awoke. And they slept in a bed . . . most
of the time, she thought, her interest turning from
domestic matters to other things.

"Anything else?" he asked, distracting her.

"Oh," she said, grinning. "Father has written
asking when we will keep our promise and spend
another year in Texas."

"Oh, Mercy . . ."

"I know. But you did promise. Two years in
Texas, two in England. A far more reasonable arrangement than you deserve."

"Hm."

"Besides, Father sent you a present." She

tossed him a brown-paper-wrapped package. He caught it one handed. "Your latest exploits."

"What the hell . . ." Hart ripped the package open. A small yellow-covered book dropped into his lap. He turned it over and sputtered disgustedly.

"Can't we sue the publisher or something? For God's sake, that makes three in the last two years."

She smiled innocently. "I don't think so, Hart dear. After all, who could have guessed when you decided to reveal your history that society—with Beryl and Henley's invaluable aid—would embrace your past as titillatingly delicious. You yourself say that American and English society are incestuously close. It only stands to reason Americans would be eager for the latest gossip from their cousins across the seas."

"This isn't news, this is libel." He waved his hand at the book on his lap. *"The Mercenary Marquis,* for God's sake." He sputtered in disgust. "They can't even get the damned title right."

"That would be libelous," she said, noting the high color on his lean, handsome face. "Be nice. After all, you are a dangerous and fascinating character," she said, lowering her voice to a melodramatic whisper. "So cold. So controlled and so—" She started giggling when he sprang up from his seat. He strode across the room and swept her up into his arms. She caught him around the neck and nestled closer.

"I'll show you how dangerous I am," he promised meaningfully.

"Your Ladyship," a frantic voice hailed them from the hall. Hart swore but made no move to lower Mercy to the ground. A breathless young woman appeared in the doorway, her cap askew, her face flushed.

"What is it, Brenna?"

"It's the neighbor's girl."

"Viscount Sheridan's chit?" Hart asked impatiently. "What of her?"

"She's crying."

"Is she hurt?" Mercy asked in concern.

"I don't think so, M'lady. Mostly she's mad as a hornet and screaming that she's going to tell her daddy."

"Tell her daddy what, Brenna?" Hart asked, his hand moving immodestly nearer Mercy's breast.

"That young Master William shot her."

"What?" Mercy and Hart shouted in unison.

"With the slingshot what Her Ladyship made for him. He shot her straight in the bum."

"Oh," Mercy said, meeting Hart's eyes. She started to chuckle and Hart answered her amusement with his own unrestrained laughter.

"Fine fer you to laugh, but what am I to tell Lord Sheridan," Brenna asked, "about Master Will shootin' his daughter?"

"Tell him he'd best look into reserving St. George's Church," Mercy said.

"M'lady?"

"That is how all the earls of Perth begin a courtship."